IF YOU GIVE A RAKE A REASON

Pirates & Petticoats Book 2

CHLOE FLOWERS

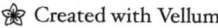 Created with Vellum

DEDICATION

Special thanks to my family and handsome husband
for overlooking the dust bunnies,
cold stove and empty pantry,
so I could follow my dream.
I love you all.

IF YOU GIVE A RAKE A REASON

HE'LL CRAVE A CARESS TO PLEASE HIM...

PIRATES & PETTICOATS SERIES BOOK TWO

CHAPTER 1
THE PERFECT CRIME

Charleston, South Carolina
June 1811

I f they were going to steal it, tonight would be the perfect time. The pirates watched.

And waited.

The moon was nothing more than a sliver in the sky, leaving the night almost as dark as pitch. A single sentry strolled along the street in front of the warehouse. He passed the main doors and continued until he reached the far corner. He yawned, stretching his arms out wide. Removing his floppy hat, he scratched his head vigorously and then jammed the hat back on. After a lazy glance up and down the street, he pulled a bottle from his pocket and took a swig before he leaned against the wall and yawned again.

A dog barked in the distance, provoking a shouted curse from one of the city's sleepy residents. The sentry sank to his haunches, tipped the bottle to his mouth and then rested his head against the bricks behind him. Once more he looked around. Finally, with a bored sigh, he sat on the ground and placed his bottle within reach before resting his arms on his knees. Within minutes, his head slumped to his forearms. The gentle sea swayed against the pilings with the easy rhythm of a rocking chair. The street was quiet except for the gently breaking waves and the soft snoring of the sentry.

Drago Viteri Gamponetti, Gampo to his men, leaned around the corner and gestured to a pair of wagons waiting behind him. A few men slipped down to lead the teams forward. A loud 'clop' on the cobblestones made everyone freeze in stunned silence.

"One of the mufflings has fallen off," whispered a driver.

"Crowe, you'd best check them all before we head on," he hissed. "And check all the wheels!"

"Aye, Cap'n Gampo, sir." Crowe muttered, as he scampered hastily about doing as he was told. All metal parts should still be wrapped in strips of dark cloth to keep them from jingling with the horses' movements. He ran his hands over the strips of oiled leather covering each wheel. As soon as everything was secure, Crowe motioned for all to move out. The caravan stopped near the warehouse doors.

With the stealth of a shadow, Gampo descended from the lead wagon. Producing a key, he placed it in the lock and turned it until it gave a dull 'click.' After a quick glance toward the end of the building and the sleeping sentry, he pulled a glass bottle from his pocket and squatted by the door hinges, then removed the cork with his teeth. After the hinges had been fully doused with the oil, he stepped back and gently pulled one of the doors open a bit and then closed it again, testing. He repeated this procedure several more times. Satisfied he'd eliminated any squeaks, he opened both doors wide.

One of the men gestured toward the snoring sentry near the corner. Gampo studied the man, noted the whiskey bottle next to him and gave a slight shake of his head. The other shrugged, stepped down and grabbed the halter of one of the horses, then led it inside. Gampo followed and pulled the doors shut.

Once inside the warehouse, the men remained motionless while Gampo struck a match to the candle wedged between the boards of the wagon seats.

"Take the blankets and cover the windows facing the street," he directed in a dry whisper. "Once they're secure, light your lanterns and get to work."

"Aye, Cap'n."

The men went about doing what he'd ordered. They all were well aware there was no room for error. Failing to execute even one small detail could get them caught. Getting caught would get them hanged. It gave the men strong impetus to do the job correctly.

An hour later the wagons were loaded with casks of brandy and whiskey, rolls of silk fabric, boxes of spices, ammunition and countless other treasures from across the sea. They snuffed out the lanterns and removed the blankets from the windows. Gampo was the last to exit. The sentry hadn't moved. He chucked to himself. The poor tar would have a great deal of explaining to do when his employer arrived in the morning. Still smiling, he reached into his pocket, pulled out the key and locked the warehouse.

That ought to give 'im something to think about.

THE SENTRY SHIFTED SLIGHTLY. Steel blue eyes glinted from under the rim of his hat as he watched the wagons pull away. After giving a slight nod to the roof of the boarding house across the street, an oil lamp flared in answer. Landon Hart rose and headed in the direction taken by the wagons seconds before.

"THEY TURNED east down the next street," Landon whispered to his friend Captain Conal O'Brien, as they followed the path of the thieves, staying near the darker shadows. "They're heading in the direction of the warehouses we scouted earlier."

Conal nodded. "Hopefully they take it to the one containing the rest of our cargo. It'll be harder to find the first half if they put this load in a different place."

It was a risky venture, but the only way to find out where their goods were taken was to leave the rest vulnerable. Conal had bragged at the pub near the docks that they had rented the most secure warehouse in the city and had complete confidence in the quality of the locks. They were so convinced, he'd boasted only one man was needed to guard the lot.

The thieves swallowed the bait, and now Landon had his hook embedded deeply.

An ugly image of Keelan in the brutal arms of one of those leering pirates nudged its way to the forefront of Landon's daydreams. He couldn't get the fiery-haired vixen out of his mind. His chest felt twice its size. The world around him settled. Keelan was *his*. He couldn't think of a better way to live out his days aboard the *Desire* than with Keelan by his side.

This was no time to be preoccupied with thoughts of a woman, but this wasn't just any woman, it was his heart, his love. It was difficult to avoid thinking about how sweet her mouth tasted or how she smelled of jasmine and sunshine...

Stop it.

An entanglement was the last thing he'd wanted when they made port in Charleston. He and Conal had suffered a major loss, Conal's Uncle Fynn at the hands of Gampo. Bloody, ruthless pirate.

Fynn planned a trade route to include a stopover in Charleston so he could meet with Commodore George Grey, who'd turned out to be Keelan's father. Fynn had been very secretive about the reasons why he wanted to meet with the commodore. So, following the run-in with Gampo, they tucked their ships in dry dock for repairs. Landon and Conal kept Fynn's mysterious meeting out of curiosity more than anything.

While visiting Twin Pines plantation, he'd met Keelan, who was masquerading as a boy and dueling with swords with her father's valet. It was only after he'd had given her a brief lesson in knife throwing he'd learned Keelan was actually a young lady. Conal found it highly amusing and had retold the story several times at The Whistling Pig Tavern, where they'd rented rooms.

What Conal hadn't seen occurred later the same morning. Landon had caught Keelan eavesdropping from the depths of the garden bushes. At the time, he didn't know she was the commodore's daughter. He saw her as a curiosity. Up close, she was more than that. She was smooth and sleek with the quickness of a cat and the curves of a woman.

Eyes wide like a startled doe and lush lips parted in surprise, she'd have bolted if her hair hadn't been severely tangled in the branches. How could any normal man possibly *resist* the opportunity to kiss her? So he did.

She froze in shock at first, of course, but after a moment her lips softened. His boyish prank soon became something over which he nearly lost control, especially when he pressed his hips against hers and instead of pushing him away, she slid her hands over his forearms and pulled him closer.

Enough! Focus on the task at hand. Retrieve the stolen cargo without getting killed.

Then, he'd locate Keelan and find out why she had not yet arrived. Less than a week ago, she'd promised to sail away with him on the *Desire*. The Blue Peter was flying above his top gallants, signaling the ship was preparing to sail. She should have already arrived.

Unless... she'd changed her mind. Life on the sea could be hazardous and hard.

It could also be invigorating and prosperous.

Running away with him was a risk for Keelan. She'd have to leave behind the shelter of what little family she had left: an uncle, aunt and cousin, as well as the possibility of marriage. Dr. Garrison had already asked for her hand. Her uncle would have her marry Pratt, a wealthy plantation owner old enough to be her father.

To accompany Landon on the *Desire*, she would have to accept that there'd be a certain degree of uncertainty with each dawning day. Danger presented itself in many forms: British warships, pirates, privateers and tempests. Had she changed her mind and decided to stay within the protective embrace of the Charleston Lowcountry? Had Garrison convinced her that she'd be better off married to him, a country doctor, rather than a merchant ship captain?

Stop.

There was work to be done.

Landon pulled a bottle from his pocket and took a mouthful of the amber liquid. He sloshed it around, then spit it into his hands and rubbed it on his face and shirt. He handed the bottle to his friend.

"Seems a shame to waste it," Conal muttered sadly, as he repeated the same procedure.

Landon grinned. "Leave it to an Irishman to mourn the loss of a mouthful of whiskey."

"Look who's talkin'."

Landon threw his arm over Conal's shoulders. "Let's go."

The two men staggered down the alley.

Conal broke into song:

Oh, my wee lass is a fine, young lass if ever a lass there be...
Her bosom's as big as a bowl of figs,
Hips broader than a wil... (burp)... low tree,
Oh my wee lass is a fine young lass I hold in high regard,
I know she loves me because her bannocks
Are shaped like me cock,

...and just as hard!

They burst into bawdy laughter and stumbled past the first warehouse with no incident. However, as they passed the entrance to the second building, a wide bulk blocked their path.

"'Hoy there, mates. Where're ye headin'?"

Landon and Conal halted, each swaying slightly.

"Why, we be headin' to Miz LeBlanc's housh, my big man," Conal slurred. "Gonna bed me a strong Irish lash wi' the biggest breasts in Charson. Char-lesson." He shook his head numbly. "Town," he finally stated firmly.

Landon jiggled the bottle enticingly. "Ha' yersef a slosh and join us, man." He thrust the bottle at the burly guard. "But we git firs' choice of the wenches, since it's our idea."

The man frowned and shook his head. "Ye couple of drunken sots can't find yer way to a wench if ye was locked in a room full of 'em. Madame LeBlanc's be two blocks west of here."

"Two more blocks, ye say? Wish way is west?" Landon scowled and squinted over the tar's shoulder. The windows were covered, but there was a sliver of light shining from the side of one, along with a bright red bolt of fabric. *His* silk, he'd wager.

Conal made an exaggerated turn toward his friend. "Did not the wench say three streets north and two streets east?" he said with arms crossed and fingers jutting into the air.

"Aye. She said two streets east and three streets south," Landon bobbed his head then staggered a couple dizzy steps sideways.

"Ha' we been goin' east or wes'?"

The warehouse guard rolled his eyes. "Listen lads," he said impatiently, pointing back up the alley. "Turn yer arses around and go two blocks that way and turn left." He waved his left arm and pointed. "Madam LeBlanc's be the white house with the red front door. Ye can't miss it."

"Two up then left ye say?" Landon repeated, blinking.

"Yes, man. LEFT. Turn LEFT," the sentry confirmed in an exasperated tone as he batted his hand to the left yet again.

Conal brightened. "Oh, well then. It's not sa far from here. We thank ye verra mush, me good man." He clapped the man on the back and nearly fell down.

Landon made a show of helping Conal regain his balance, then wrapped his arm over his friend's shoulders and spun him around. "Let's be off then. Ahead and to the lef'!"

"The left!"

Conal thumped Landon on the back and pointed up the street. "To the wenches!"

"The wenches!"

They staggered a few steps before pivoting around again to face the surly guard.

"Ye sure ye won't join us for a romp?" Conal shouted, although he was only ten feet away.

The man gave a wave and shook his head. "Nay lads, I'm workin' this night. Have a warehouse to guard." He pulled aside his vest to show the handle of a pistol sticking out of his waistband. "Ye go on."

"Suit yershelf," Landon slurred. They swung back around and shuffled away.

The guard chuckled as the drunkards staggered down the alley and paused a moment before making a right turn. Leaning against the warehouse door, he gave a dry laugh, shaking his head. "Ye'll not lay a lass this night, lads."

CHAPTER 2
PLANS TO ELOPE

Keelan Grey stood at the foot of the grave, gazing at the sharply chiseled marks on the stone without really seeing them. This afternoon, they'd buried Papa in the Circular Congregational Church cemetery on Meeting Street. The death bed confession still had her stunned. What would Landon think of it all?

She'd made a promise. Two, actually. The first, to elope with Landon Hart. The second, to find her true father.

She intended to keep both.

Aunt Sarah patted her shoulder. "Keelan, please walk with us," she prodded in a quiet voice. "Your uncle has arranged a luncheon at Rosewood's boarding house."

"I'm not hungry now, Aunt Sarah," she responded, giving her aunt a small smile. "I need a few moments alone, then I'll return home."

And gather my things and go.

The afternoon sun was obscured by a layer of gray which threatened rain. Aunt Sarah hesitated a moment. The older woman glanced around. Probably worried Captain Hart would appear from behind one of the large oaks lining the cemetery, or Dr. Garrison would show up and cause a scene.

A valid concern.

Keelan had been entangled in two terribly scandalous events, one involving Captain Landon Hart and the other involving... Captain Landon Hart.

First, there was an outing without a chaperone. Then there was a kiss in the garden the night of the ball, resulting in a broken engagement with Dr. Garrison, who'd taken the news badly, and she couldn't blame him. While that seemed like a very casual and abbreviated chain of events, it really wasn't.

Although wildly handsome and devilishly charming, Landon Hart was everything Mother had described when she spoke of 'men of the sea'... men who could seduce a woman with a look and leave her the following day, off to the next port, the next woman, the next adventure. Keelan understood this; Mother became bitter and lonely while Papa had been away sailing with the Royal Navy. She never wanted to live her mother's life, married to a man who's mistress was the sea, therefore, she'd instead reluctantly accepted a marriage proposal from Papa's physician, Dr. Everett Garrison, a few days before her cousin's ball.

Dr. Garrison was a quiet, practical man with a quiet, practical life.

Landon changed all that with three short words:

"Sail with me."

He had no intention of leaving her behind, and that changed *everything*.

They would be together aboard the *Desire*. There'd be no lonely life of waiting for a ship to bring her beloved home. The thought sent a comforting warmth swirling in her chest.

If Papa hadn't worsened that night, she'd have run away with Landon that moment he'd asked. Now, with her uncle as her guardian, things were more complicated. He'd not approve, so she couldn't reveal her plans.

Didn't dare.

Aunt Sarah fidgeted with her bonnet ribbon a moment, then said, "Don't stay too long. I'll ask Slaney and Daniel to wait for you. You shouldn't walk home alone."

"Thank you, Aunt Sarah."

Her family was always vigilant. An assassin had murdered her mother and Papa's eldest brother and his family back in England. She suspected it had to do with Papa's court-martial. He'd fired on the wrong ship; it sank, killing innocent passengers. After a huge uproar, Papa had been court-martialed, the family the main gossip topic for weeks.

After a word from her aunt, Keelan's maid, Slaney waited a few feet from the grave site. Daniel, her father's valet, joined her.

Daniel had been Papa's valet when he was home, and her tutor when Papa was at sea. He taught her not only to read, write and mathematics but also how to defend herself. She was quite proud of her skills with a blade. She had Daniel to thank for that.

After making his daily trip to the pier and back early this morning, Daniel had informed her that Landon Hart's ship, the *Desire*, was flying the blue flag signaling it was ready to depart.

It was the signal she'd been watching for. He was ready to leave port.

Fluttery ripples of anticipation spread through her stomach. Soon, she'd be away from here, away from plantation life and on toward unknown and exciting places with Landon.

Daniel held out a hand for the maid, Slaney took it, allowing him to help her rise to her feet.

"It's hard to believe he's gone." Keelan took one last look at the grave of the man she'd called "Papa" all her life.

"Yes, mistress. I know you'll miss him. As will I," Daniel said, voice cracking.

"We all will, lass," Slaney added, blotting beneath her eyes with a handkerchief.

"What will you both do now?" Keelan asked. Slaney and

Daniel had been like family to her since she was small. With Papa at sea most of the time and her mother in Chatham, England, running their shop, Daniel and Slaney had practically raised her.

"We'll fulfill our obligation to the commodore and accompany you safely back to the country cottage in England, as promised," Daniel said. "Unless you have decided to remain here, instead."

"No." She shook her head. "I have no wish to remain on the plantation. You heard what Papa said. He's left me nothing. His entire estate has gone to Uncle Jared. I no longer have Twin Pines as my dowry."

Which was fine with her, she wasn't angry or upset at this sudden turn of events. In fact, it was a relief. A small smile tugged at her mouth. She had other plans involving Captain Hart, a wedding, a ship and a life of adventure.

"By removing you from his will, the commodore thought he was forcing you to act on his request to find your real father," Daniel said gently.

Although truly, it was unnecessary; her curiosity and longing to find out who she was and where she came from would have driven her to search for the man, anyway. But Papa hadn't known that.

He hadn't known her well at all.

"I made a promise to find him, and I will," she responded. They strolled along the cobbled street, the scent of damp soil and salty air hinting a spring rain.

"Then Daniel and I will be ready to join ye," Slaney said. "Yer like a daughter to us both. We'll not leave ye unless ye wish it." She looped her arm through Keelan's and gave her a secret smile.

The words tugged her heart; she swallowed past the lump in her throat. "Thank you, Slaney. Hopefully the contents in Papa's trunk will help my cause and not hinder it."

He'd mentioned an old trunk tucked in the library of the country house near Chatham, England. Apparently it held the answers to all her questions. She looked up at the valet. "You heard what he said. My mother and that man..." Daniel had been there, the night Papa revealed his secrets.

Daniel's eyes softened."Yes, I heard. But the commodore said the man, your real father, would *want* to know about you."

She sighed, her heart and head in turmoil. It's rare a by-blow is ever welcomed into a household. The scorn of her sire's wife might be more than she could take.

Slaney stepped over a puddle, then peered at her closely. "But what about Captain Hart? Ye fancy the man. Will ye leave him behind?"

She chewed her lip. How much should she tell them? It wasn't that she didn't trust them. She did, with all her heart. But she'd never ask them to lie for her. The less they knew of her plans, the safer they'd be.

"What about Dr. Garrison?" Daniel looked back and forth between Slaney and her.

Of course the two servants had talked. What had she been thinking? She might as well tell them everything.

"I broke the engagement. I never wanted to marry Dr. Garrison. Without Twin Pines as a dowry, I'm sure the doctor's interest in me would have dropped drastically, even if I wasn't born on the other side of the blanket."

Daniel's voice carried a note of relief. "Begging your pardon, Mistress, but I've never cared much for the man. He has a dark air about him sometimes, makes me wonder if he's hiding something."

She gave him a quick glance, thinking about the doctor's uncharacteristic behavior toward her the night of the ball. It had looked as if he were about to strike her. "I have had the same concerns, especially recently. And sometimes I wonder..." A thick foreboding seeped into her thoughts, questions she'd asked, but no one seemed to be able to answer while Papa struggled with his health. Why he would have a few days of improvement, then drift back into the illness sending Dr. Garrison in search of new medication? Why were there days he would eat voraciously and days he could keep nothing down?

Daniel furrowed his brow. "I remember your mother's funeral when Dr. Garrison introduced himself. The commodore had been grieved, but robust, then." The valet jingled a couple coins in his pocket and stared pensively at his shoes while they waited for a wagonload of casks to pass before crossing the street.

The shame of Papa's court martial had always lingered about his countenance, adding to his depressed state, but Daniel was right. He hadn't been ill back then, only sad. He and Dr. Garrison became friends and spent many hours together, engaging in various activities to distract Papa from his grief, but still it consumed him. He ate less and lost weight. He slept more and became sickly.

A shudder skittered across her shoulders. She met Daniel's gaze. "I've been wondering if Dr. Garrison might have recommended the wrong medicine, or made the wrong diagnosis."

Daniel was silent for a moment. "It's possible he made a mistake."

A mistake.

Everett was young, right out of university. Perhaps he was too inexperienced.

"I've wondered the same thing..." she murmured.

Daniel straightened. "Then it's good he's out of your life."

Keelan plucked at a loose string on her cuff. "Captain Hart asked for my hand and I accepted," she finally said, unable to prevent the blush tingling her cheeks at the anticipation. "I plan to marry him and sail with him aboard the *Desire*."

A startled look flashed across the valet's face, but he recovered quickly. "Is that something which appeals to you?"

Slaney smiled. It truly was impossible to hide anything from them. Both had heard her mother's lectures and her own vows to find a husband with feet firmly planted on solid ground.

"Very much." She smiled, but a dark thought rose to the

surface. "In light of recent events, I hope his offer will still stand," she murmured. What if it didn't? What if he wouldn't want to marry a woman who'd been born out of wedlock?

Daniel became thoughtful. "Mr. Hart doesn't seem to be the type of man to let social inclinations dictate his actions. If he changes his mind, we'll simply book passage on the next passenger ship heading north, if you wish to do so."

Slaney harrumphed. "Well, a choice like that would brand him a fool, I says."

Keelan swallowed. Daniel made it seem like the decision had no real significance, but it wouldn't be so easy for her.

Sailing away with Landon had been the only thing keeping her own shadow of grief from blanketing her in darkness over the past two days. A niggling fear had shadowed the anticipation as well. Given her current requirements, would Landon assist her? What if he wanted no part in her quest to find her true father?

"I'm glad you'll both be with me. It gives me comfort knowing I'll not have to make the journey on my own should things change between me and Captain Hart."

"We wouldn't ever leave ye at a time like this, Mistress. We'll help ye find yer Da," Slaney squeezed her arm.

With fresh eyes, she took in the ocean in the distance, blending into the infinite blue of the South Carolina sky. Worrying about it would not bring the answers to her questions any sooner. "First, we must gather our things and take them to Captain Hart's ship. We don't have much time to finish packing our trunks, hire a livery and depart before Uncle Jared and Aunt Sarah return home from the luncheon." Uncle Jared would try to stop them. He expected her to marry and stay in Charleston. He certainly wouldn't approve of her eloping with Landon Hart.

Daniel nodded his agreement. "I'll arrange for transportation to the *Desire* while you and Slaney have the trunks brought down."

"It shouldna' take long," Slaney said. "I haven't unpacked much yet, seein' how we just got to town yesterday."

"Good." Keelan had a little more confidence now. A shiver of excitement shot through her chest as her uncle's townhouse came into view. She fingered the red ribbon holding the signet ring around her neck.

The coat of arms bore four lions, a knight's helm, shafts of wheat. She had no idea what it meant or stood for. What was her real surname, if not Grey?

Who was she?

CHAPTER 3
EDGE OF MADNESS

The man who murdered his family and fiancée was finally dead.

Yet Dr. Everett Garrison still waited for the thick, suffocating burden of grief to lift.

But it didn't.

A brief swell of panic surged against his chest. Once Commodore Grey was dead, things *should* have changed. The rock in his stomach should have disappeared, the sharp pain clenching his heart every time he inhaled should have subsided, and the black emptiness filling his soul should have receded.

The morning light was still dull, his feet were still heavy, the air still empty, and his hands still stained with blood. No matter how many times he washed them, it lingered.

He had committed a heinous sin.

Commodore George Grey undoubtedly deserved to die, but Everett was more familiar with saving lives, not taking them. If Rachel hadn't screamed for vengeance in his dreams every night when he closed his eyes, he would never have considered it.

Anguish clawed through his voice. "Rachel... I miss you."

Everett didn't bother to brush away the tears or dry his

cheeks. How he missed her smile and adoring gaze. Her quiet words. Why was he still so tormented?

He stared down at the letter on his desk. And now, the bank was unwilling to extend him any more credit.

This presented a problem.

In exchange for Dr. Garrison's personal medical care, the commodore and his older brother, Jared Grey, had given him money to set up a practice in Charleston. Instead, Everett had used it to fund his plan for revenge. The slow poison he carefully dosed to the commodore had been very expensive to procure in a discrete manner.

He tossed a bundle of papers on his desk. It had been worth every cent he paid for justice to be done. That idiot had given the order to sink the ship carrying his parents and brothers.

And his fiancée, Rachel.

It didn't matter that the commodore had claimed to have mistaken the passenger ship for some devious French privateer. He deserved to be punished, and Everett had complained loudly and frequently to those in charge of his court martial. But, before justice could be done, the commodore's friend, an aristocrat, had used his wealth and influence to whisk away the disgraced Navy commander and his daughter, Keelan, to Charleston, South Carolina. The man even purchased a small plantation for them. A place for them to hide... far away from the gallows in London where the commodore belonged.

Everett slammed his fist on his desk. "Did he not deserve to suffer the same pain as I?"

Last fall after murdering the commodore's nephew, the man he'd hired in England also arranged the carriage accidents killing the wives of both the commodore and his older brother. According to the assassin, the women were low-hanging fruit, easy to pluck. Everett didn't have the stomach to do it himself. He was a physician trained to do his best to preserve life, not take it. Besides, such things were best left to a professional. He had no desire to risk botching the job and getting himself hanged in the process of attaining justice.

But the loss...the agony. He tried *everything* to relieve it. Brandy and opiates wore off, left him groggy and sick, didn't solve the problem, and only delayed the execution of a solution. It was, however, during one of those binges when he came up with the brilliant idea of hiring a man to exact revenge *for* him.

Less guilt to deal with if they didn't die by his hand. A deed he could live with, so he'd thought.

Everett opened the desk drawer, cradled a pale lavender handkerchief, then pressed it to his lips and inhaled. Rachel's perfume grew fainter each time. Soon, like her, it would be gone forever.

"The commodore needed to feel the same suffering," he murmured into the scented cloth. "He had to understand that his transgressions had *consequences*." He hadn't expected he could actually go through with it. The first time he had dosed the commodore with a small amount of poison, the man complained of an upset stomach and went to his cabin. Everett had vomited over the side of the ship. His hands quaked for an hour afterward.

The assassin he'd hired in London had been thorough. He'd finally sent the announcement of the death of the commodore's eldest brother, along with a letter requesting the last and final installment owed for his services.

Everett returned the handkerchief to his drawer and then picked up the missive next to the one from the bank. He reread the letter from the assassin. His gut clenched. The words blurred. His heart thrummed in his ears, sounding like a drum of war signaling death to the enemy.

DOCTOR GARRISON,

We agreed that upon the notification of completion of the duties required of me, that payment would be available for me at your barrister's office. Unfortunately, according to the documents your barrister showed me containing your signature, it appears you withdrew the funds prior to traveling to Charleston. This is not acceptable. I request you rectify this immediately. Should I not receive your payment in a reasonable amount of time, I will consider you in breach of our contract and will contact a man in Charleston to perform the same duty for me, which I have so diligently performed for you.

Regards,
Munsford

❧⚜❧

THE PROBLEM WAS, Everett had to use some of Munsford's funds to keep up appearances here in Charleston and to handle a slight problem in the form of Captain Landon Hart.

The gaping hole Rachel's death left in his life didn't shrink with time; it grew. If he didn't find someone to fill it soon, it would continue to grow bigger and bigger. It would eventually consume him until there was nothing left but the edges of his soul.

It seemed like poetic justice to have Keelan Grey be the one to fill the void.

He'd not been prepared for the ripples Captain Hart had caused. Everett's scheme had been progressing well until the man showed up at Twin Pines. Everett sat heavily in his chair, gripped the hair on each side of his head and rested his elbows on the desk.

It had taken him *months* to court Keelan to the extent where she'd agreed to marry him. Then the captain interfered with his courtship, distracted her, and made it difficult to regain her full attention and affection.

He'd had been at the table one day when Hart explained the attack by Gampo's ship. Apparently, Hart's fleet and the pirate had some sort of ongoing feud. It only took a couple inquiries in the pubs near the wharf and a meeting with Gampo's first mate to get a message to Gampo himself.

The pirate and Hart had a history of clashes on the open sea. Gampo helped Everett develop a scheme to distract Hart. In exchange, Everett was supposed to find out if a woman named Marisa sailed with Hart's fleet. How was he supposed to obtain that information? It was almost impossible. However, he had indeed tried. One bright morning he'd walked to the pier, up the ramp, and asked the first mate. The man looked at him as if he was daft.

"Having a woman aboard is bad luck, mister. Any sailor knows that."

He couldn't very well approach Hart, his adversary, and ask him, could he? Surely Hart would lie to him. Gampo wouldn't accept that answer, however. Unfortunately, he still had no information for the pirate, and that was disconcerting.

Thankfully, the plan they managed to execute may yet generate additional funds. As soon as he found the right buyers for the cargo the pirates took from Hart, there would be enough money to pay the assassin.

Hopefully.

The bloody pirates had some sort of hard and fast rule on dividing things into "like shares."

Even after they stole the goods, Hart had seduced Keelan, and she broke her engagement to Everett. Their plan could still move forward, but now, he would have to make a few adjustments, since it appeared Keelan was not going to come to him willingly. He didn't dare ask Gampo, but he'd found two of the pirate's men who were willing to work a side job while at port.

But it was going to be costly, because getting to Keelan was going to be more difficult now.

Keelan Grey, the commodore's daughter...

Beautiful, cold, and distant, he understood she wasn't the type to enjoy country life. More than once he'd overheard her plead with her father to sell Twin Pines and move to the city of Charleston. She was not the soft, gentle woman Rachel had been. Keelan was bold and impetuous; Rachel had been quiet and reliable.

Rachel was water.

Keelan was fire.

Everett recalled that night when the commodore had spoken privately with the young woman. A glass placed against the wall in the next room allowed him to hear much of their conversation. The commodore spoke of a treasure he'd hidden for Keelan back in his country cottage.

A thought struck like a lightning bolt. Everett straightened. Why hadn't he thought of this earlier? Obviously, his grief muddied his mind. Rising, he began to pace the floor and tried to recall the commodores words.

"The contents are of great value... promise me you'll go back to Wind Briar and find my old trunk..."

There! The answer to his financial woes rested in a trunk at the Wind Briar estate. They only had to find it. Then he could leave the assassin's funds with his barrister. Everett spun on his heel and snatched his hat from the hook by the door. He had to change his strategy, which left behind a few frayed ends he'd have to clip. Soon, his sword of justice would do its duty. He'd already sacrificed significant time, money, and energy to this endeavor.

He deserved to reap the rewards from his service.

It was his due.

And Keelan would share it with him.

As his wife.

CHAPTER 4
OLD EMBERS

Landon waited in Annette Camsby's parlor, choosing to stand by the window rather than take the seat offered by the house slave. He didn't plan on being here long enough to relax in a chair. Instead, he gazed down the narrow side street in Charleston.

Frustration still had him grinding his teeth. His visit to Twin Pines had answered some questions, but raised others. He'd been informed the commodore had been buried earlier in the day, which explained Keelan's delay in meeting him. He'd not known of the commodore's death, although he'd been aware the man had been ill for some time. With the hot, humid temperatures in Charleston in June, there was not much time for long wakes. Bodies had to be buried as soon as possible. He'd stop by Jared Grey's town house and offer his condolences when he returned. Hopefully, by this evening or tomorrow morning, Keelan would be able to join him aboard the *Desire*. If not, he'd either wait, or make a quick run up the coast to Philadelphia, then return for her.

A small bag of coins clinked in his coat pocket, making him frown.

"Why, if it isn't Captain Hart!" Annette Camsby floated into the room as if transported by an invisible stream. "What an unexpected, but delightful surprise." Beautiful, rich and once again widowed, Annette captured his gaze with eyes the color of dark coffee. She sank to the deep gold velvet sofa and leaned forward just enough to provide him with an unhindered view of her cleavage as she reached for a cup. "Join me for tea?"

Landon's throat was dry, and he had to clear it before he could trust his voice. He could use a drink, but hot tea wasn't what came to mind. "Thank you for the invitation, however, I can't stay. I came to refund your fare for passage to Philadelphia. Henry should not have accepted it. We're unable to take on passengers this time." He pulled the bag of coins from his pocket and placed it on the desk.

Annette's gaze chilled. Full, ripe lips thinned to a flat line. "And why, may I ask, do you feel obligated to do that?"

He hadn't expected Annette to make this easy.

It was bad enough Conal had thrown up his hands in mock terror when he'd asked him to return the fare, leaving Landon to ride to Annette's town home to return it.

She'd been a tigress in bed once. Every trip to Charleston had been enhanced by her attentions. Normally, she'd accompany them to Philadelphia or even as far as New York and then occasionally make the return trip back to Charleston with them, keeping his bed warm and active. Now, the thought no longer held the allure it once did.

He'd have never guessed he would marry again. But Keelan was like no other woman he'd ever met—spontaneous and reckless, yes, but also clever, passionate, and witty. And luscious. He inhaled deeply and allowed himself the luxury of taking time to expel his breath. Otherwise, he feared his more primal reaction would rise to the forefront, especially when he recalled the sight of the lithe, young Keelan Grey floating naked upon the lake at Twin Pines. It would certainly be misinterpreted, fighting an erection while standing in the middle of Annette Camsby's parlor.

"Well?" Annette cocked her head to the side, her deep black ringlets dangling near her ears. She raised a brow, but her expression was accusing and wary rather than inquisitive.

Landon clenched his jaw and forced a tight smile upon his face. "I'm afraid I've cancelled the journey to Philadelphia for now. A large portion of my cargo has been stolen and until it's located, I cannot depart port." A cowardly way to put it, but he wasn't in the mood for one of Annette's tantrums.

Her eyes widened, and she placed a hand to her chest. "Oh dear! How terrible! What will you do?"

He clasped his hands behind his back to keep himself from crossing his arms in frustration. "Make every effort to find it. When we do, we'll have to reassess its condition, which might take time. If we don't locate it, then we'll have to change our trade route. Either way, I'm afraid our departure will be delayed, at the very least, and likely to be cancelled. I'm not sure at this time what our plans will entail going forward." That was mostly true. His plans going forward included spending a lot of time with Keelan on deck and in bed.

Annette rose from her seat and glided over to him, a slow sultry smile playing upon her face. She stopped an inch in front of him and then leaned in, running a bold hand up his torso, over his chest, and down his arm.

She took his hand and entwined her fingers with his. "Well, then we should make the most of your time while you're here. It would be a shame to come all the way to my home and leave... empty-handed." She placed his hand on her breast.

In the past, he'd have needed no further urging. He would have locked the parlor door, and they would have sated their lust on the large Persian rug he'd given her. However, today there was no stirring, no passion aroused to drive him into her open arms and thighs.

"I'm sorry, Annette," he said, removing his hand and dropping it to his side. "I cannot. I will not."

Her smile slipped from sultry to sad. "Such a shame. I hope you remember to send word to me when you are ready to sail." She was testing the barrier he was building. "You know how fond I am of our sojourns together." Her gaze shifted to a doleful hurt. Her lips in a full pout.

She'd guessed he had another woman of interest. *Good.*

"I'm afraid my next destination will not be one you'll be willing to travel, Annette."

"I see," she said, turning toward the window Landon had stood near earlier. "Well, if the winds shifts in my favor, do send me a word."

"They will not."

There was nothing more to say other than farewell, and he hated those. "Stay well, Annette. I wish you the best. I'll not call again." He spun on his heel and left the parlor. A house slave opened the front door, and he strode to Orion and unwrapped the reins from the post near the steps just as Dr. Garrison and Miss Doreen Grey were sending their mounts with a stable boy.

He nodded a greeting to the doctor and tipped his hat to Miss Grey. Keelan's cousin had been accompanying the doctor on his calls and assisting him with his patients. It appeared, thankfully, she had diverted the doctor's attentions away from Keelan.

He turned his horse toward Jared Grey's town home. Now, to find his betrothed.

CHAPTER 5

TIME TO GO

The early summer heat in the Charleston Lowcountry had become oppressive. As she'd quickly become accustomed, Keelan dipped her handkerchief into a basin near her bed and patted the base of her neck with it. The black garments she wore for mourning did nothing but absorb heat, and the dress itched like the devil. The now familiar trickle of sweat ran between her breasts and she pushed the damp handkerchief down her bodice to absorb the moisture.

Her stomach quivered with a thousand butterflies. The night of the ball, when Landon had taken her into his arms in the moonlit garden and asked her to sail away with him, he'd given her hope that she'd spend her life with someone of her choosing. Her uncle's choice, Pratt, was an aging plantation owner. Doctor Garrison was a colorless, bland physician. Hart had offered her an opportunity to flee from her father's and Uncle Jared's scheme to be certain she was "properly" wed and cared for before the start of the harvest season.

What Papa and Uncle Jared didn't realize was over the years while Papa was at sea, her mother spent every moment in the shop, leaving no time to develop any kind of relationship with her daughter. Keelan had learned at an early age how to take care of herself. Unlike many women, Keelan did not *need* a husband, and until Landon, she hadn't wanted one.

Early this morning, Slaney had started to pack their things. It was important for them to depart quickly, before Uncle Jared approached the topic of her future. Only Slaney and Daniel knew of her plans. The rest of the family simply assumed she and Garrison had a tiff, but were still engaged. Dr. Garrison hadn't mentioned anything either.

"I wish we didn't have to sneak away," she muttered to Slaney. "Uncle Jared and Aunt Sarah were kind to move to Twin Pines to help Papa and me. We had no knowledge of running a plantation, and Uncle Jared's management was a godsend. I would have preferred to be able say goodbye properly."

"I know, lass," Slaney replied, closing the trunk. "But yer uncle is responsible for ye now, and he promised your Da' to see ye married to Dr. Garrison. Both took a likin' to yer suggestion to rent out the plantation to Mr. Pratt and use the rents to help ye open yer shop in town. If yer uncle caught wind of your promise to go back to Wind Briar or run off with Captain Hart, he'd marry ye off this instant, instead."

Aunt Sarah would want her to stay and marry Dr. Garrison and start a safe, placid life in Charleston. But after Papa's death and her aroused suspicions of Dr. Garrison's choices, marriage to him would have been out of the question even without Landon Hart in her life. Her uncle would have been happier if she'd agreed to marry Pratt, because of his wealth and landholdings. The neighboring plantation owner not only had a penchant for overindulging in food and drink, but was heavy-handed with his slaves as well.

Keelan shuddered. She'd rather be a spinster than marry either.

"Well, after we're gone, Uncle Jared can sell the plantation to Mr. Pratt outright. I'm sure he'll be happy to be rid of the responsibility. I'm simply not comfortable with it." She closed the lid on the smaller, worn trunk, looking longingly at her dagger, sword, and waif's clothes. She normally wore them in the early hours each morning when she trained with Daniel, another activity of which her uncle disapproved. She always suspected the commodore had secretly been proud of her skills with both sword and blade.

She sighed. It was hard to stop thinking of Papa as her father and instead as a man who played the role. He was never around very often or for very long, but still, she was fond of him and he'd acted fond of her.

It would have been easy to simply ignore the promise to him and go on with her life, but Daniel had taught her a promise kept built on one's integrity. And drat it if curiosity wasn't driving her crazy, anyway. Sending Daniel and Slaney was a satisfying compromise for all of them.

The day Hart had bartered a kiss from her in exchange for untangling her hair from a briar bush had changed her.

Her heart tripped at the memory of his wet, fiery kisses, and glacial blue eyes that looked at her as if they knew every secret she'd ever possessed. She let her lids drift shut and savored the sensation of his arms around her waist, his palm capturing her breast. He had left a mark on her heart she'd never be able to erase.

She pulled out a bag of coins before lowering the trunk lid. After providing for their passage to Boston and enough for emergency supplies, little remained. How she managed beyond that would depend on Landon or the information contained in the letter her father had placed in a chest in their country home, Wind Briar.

There was also the ring and the man in the locket to consider.

She wandered to an open window, greeted by the sickly sweet scent of aging Magnolia blossoms in the dense, humid early summer air. Heat had settled over Charleston, turning the dirt to a fine dust and coating everything, muting nature's colors to various shades of red tinted gray.

Even if she found her father, there was no guarantee he would want her. According to the tale she had been told, he had a wife and other children of his own. Thinking back to the conversation a few weeks ago between her uncle and Landon, she still wasn't sure she would be able to make it back to England. With an inevitable war approaching, the crossing became even more treacherous because both countries had unleashed privateers, who were little more than pirates with permission to plunder. Landon's merchant fleet would be a prime prize. As badly as she wanted to finish her quest and find her father, she'd never ask Landon to take such a risk.

Daniel, true to his promise to the commodore, had slipped away and booked passage to Boston for himself and Slaney. She'd heard the northern colonies were more tolerant of the British, and more likely to offer safer passages to Great Britain. From there, they'd find a vessel bound for England. Both Daniel and Slaney had family there, and with the letters of recommendation she'd provided, both should easily find employment. Daniel had promised to locate the trunk and keep it safe until she could retrieve it.

A light knock sounded upon her door. At her summons, it opened, and Dr. Everett Garrison poked his head in.

The doctor glanced curiously about the chamber, noting the trunks in the middle of the floor.

"Are you going somewhere?"

Slaney exchanged a wary look with Keelan.

"Dr. Garrison, would you join me on the porch?" she asked. "We can discuss my plans in private. The heat is overwhelming in here and I could use some air. I'll be along in a moment."

He nodded and retreated.

She huffed out an agitated sigh. So much for leaving unnoticed. As much as she dreaded it, she'd have to face Everett once more. Everything was packed and ready to go. "Slaney, please have our trunks brought down to the street. The carriage should be here shortly."

The maid nodded and Keelan went downstairs and out to the veranda, pondering the best way to tell Dr. Garrison she still would not marry him. Nothing came to mind to add ease to the task, making her stomach churn.

Jared Grey's house was typical of most Charleston homes. Since they were taxed by frontage, houses were built close together. Residents also built them narrow and deep. It was as if they took their home and rotated it ninety degrees, so the side faced the street. Long covered porches, which normally embraced front doors, instead ran the side length of the house. The proximity of their neighbor added shade to the porch during most of the day. A hedge along the street front didn't do as much to muffle the city's noise, as it did to offer a bit of privacy for those enjoying a respite outside on the long side-porch.

Dr. Garrison was looking over the foliage at the activity out front. The street wasn't a particularly busy one, but there was the occasional rider or carriage passing by, as well as people bustling along the walks. Keelan sat, her back toward the road and the clop of horses hooves and the jangle of carriages. There was less chance of being overheard out here.

Dr. Garrison pulled his hands behind his thin, rigid back. He leveled a flat stare at her. "Please tell me what is going on."

"I leave for Boston in a few days," she lied. "Slaney has packed our things. We're going back to England."

He jolted as if struck. "What—why—" he sputtered a moment before he continued. "Miss Keelan, I have no objection to returning to England, but first we are to be *married*."

"Dr. Garrison, we discussed this the night of Doreen's ball. I cannot marry you. Going home to England is my decision. I am going at the request of my... at Papa's request."

His chiseled expression hardened further. Muscles rolled in his jaw. She waited for him to continue. She'd not spoken to him alone since the night in the garden, after she privately broke their engagement. That was when the doctor's darker side had surfaced. He'd become almost violent. Even now, there was something a little off in his demeanor, a cut in his gaze, a stark parlor on his face, which made her even more uneasy in his presence.

When he finally spoke, his words tumbled together in a clumsy rush. "Miss Keelan, my behavior at the ball was abhorrent, and I am here to offer my sincerest apology. I wish to mend our relationship. You were—well—the wine was..." He shrugged tightly and dug his thumb into his palm. "Perhaps you weren't quite yourself, and you said some things you did not mean, and I said some things I certainly did not mean."

Oh dear, this was going to be harder than anticipated. He'd seen her kissing Landon. It would have been best if his pride forced *him* to break the engagement, which was apparently wishful thinking on her part.

Indeed, she had been slightly tipsy at the time. Seeing Landon waltz with the stunningly beautiful Annette Camsby had affected her recollection of the amount of wine she'd sipped. It had given her the courage to tell the doctor she didn't love him, and she'd rather not marry him. Unfortunately, she'd done so rather bluntly. The doctor didn't take the news well.

"Dr. Garrison." What could she say now, without hurting or angering him further? A multitude of expressions crossed his face. They moved across at such a pace, she struggled to follow them. Shock, anger, confusion, fear.

"Please, *please* accept my apology, Miss Keelan." He approached her with his hands spread and palms open. "I don't want to break our engagement. I truly want to marry you. I've no one, *no one* but you, now. My family—" He coughed and blinked a few times. "They all perished at sea a few years ago. I've been so lonely. I... I need you with me. Believe me when I say I will take care of you. I promise." He reached forward and grasped her hands.

Her heart lurched in sympathy, stirring her guilt at distressing him further. This was going to be more difficult than she'd anticipated. She shook her head. Maybe a different tack will work better. She shook her head. "Dr. Garrison, you don't want to marry me."

His eyes widened. "I do! Yes, I do. I will marry you and take you all the way to England." He sank to one knee. "If the commodore wanted you to go back to Wind Briar, then I'll take you as soon as we're married."

How could he know about Wind Briar?

Her heart gave a hard jerk, then began to pound more closely to her skin. She'd said nothing about Wind Briar, and there was no reason he should have known about the country house.

Keelan thought back to when her mother died. She and Papa had been staying in Camden when they'd met Dr. Garrison. She shivered. An uneasy feeling, like a cold finger trailing down her spine, raised gooseflesh on her arms, although the day was already suffocatingly hot.

She swallowed, doing her best to block the tremor from her voice. "For reasons I cannot explain to you at this time, Dr. Garrison, a marriage between us is impossible." She couldn't tell him about her plans to run away with Landon. He'd tell Uncle Jared and then Uncle Jared would have an apoplectic fit and probably insist she marry the doctor today.

How did Everett know about Wind Briar?

Dr. Garrison slowly stood, a vein jerked erratically at his temple. He drew his hands down and clenched them at his sides. Although he tried hard to hide it, Keelan couldn't ignore the anger flashing across his features, like heat lightening before a storm. Her guilt at hurting his feelings added to her burden, but his response fortified her resolve. Perhaps a more financial perspective would help.

"Dr. Garrison, Papa left everything to Uncle Jared. I don't have a dowry. I can't return to Wind Briar to live. I'm not even George Grey's kin by blood."

Everett jerked as if shot. He stared at her like he was seeing her for the first time. "Not blood kin," he repeated so softly she could barely make out his words. "Not blood kin!" His eyes lit with something almost feral, and he pulled her to him, enveloping her in a stony hug, startling a frightened gasp from her throat.

His arms banded hers to her sides, preventing any opportunity to push him away. There was no delicate way to extract herself from his embrace without inciting his anger again. Thankfully, the hedges blocked the awkward embrace from view.

He swayed with her in his arms, mumbling into the hair on top of her head. "I knew you could never be like *him*. I knew it. This is perfect. You will be *perfect*. Everything will be as it once was, perhaps even better!"

That last cryptic sentence sent another chill skittering down her spine. Bells clanged in her head to the tune of *something is not right*. She shifted, hoping her movement would cause him to loosen his hold. No luck there.

Without releasing her arms, he stared into her eyes, smiling wildly. "I know of the treasure chest the commodore hid in his country house. Together we'll find it, and everything will be as it should be."

"Treasure chest?" What in the world was he talking about? Before Papa died, he'd mentioned only the trunk containing information about her real father, no treasure.

And I was alone with Papa at the time. Everett had been eavesdropping!

"Yes!" His eyes were wide. Maniacal. "I heard the commodore talking about it. He said it was extremely valuable and wanted you to have it, so it's not as if we'd be stealing. It's yours. We need only to retrieve it."

Whatever he heard the night Papa died had planted a seed in the doctor's mind that would bear no fruit. She needed to clear up this misunderstanding now. It wasn't the items inside which were valuable, it was the information, and it was valuable only to *her*.

"Dr. Garrison, you are mistaken."

"Please call me Everett, my love."

Before she could say another word, he lowered his face and kissed her. The pressure of his mouth on hers took her by surprise and she gasped. He took the opportunity of the slight opening of her lips to plunge his tongue inside.

Her stomach took a sickening dive. Locked in the harsh embrace, she couldn't move. She couldn't breathe. The more she tried to arch away from him, the harder he kissed her until she was sure her teeth would break through the skin of her lips. His thick tongue swirled in her mouth, and for a second, she thought she might gag. This helpless feeling churned up both anger and panic.

At this point, she cared not a whit if she angered him or not. She kicked him in the shin, eliciting a pained grunt. Enraged, she tried to twist away. Before she could say a word, a voice stilled every muscle in her body.

"It wasn't my intention to interrupt a tryst." The deep baritone behind her pulsed with an undercurrent of fury, like thunder from a far away, but fast advancing storm.

Garrison broke the violent kiss and sliced his head toward the voice.

Landon! *Thank God.* Her relief immediately dissipated by the realization of what he'd just witnessed. Oh no... her stomach lurched. He'd obviously misinterpreted the stolen kiss. Everett held on to her like she was anchoring him to the earth. She wiggled and jerked and when she stomped on his foot, he finally released her, stepping away, although he twisted her hand behind the small of her back. Pain sliced through her wrist and she was forced to sink into a chair.

Everett glanced at her, the warning pulsing in his eyes shocking her into temporary silence. Her mind was too slow to process the meaning behind the erratic behavior. It was too tangled up in denial. This was not the Everett she knew. *Nothing was making sense.*

Everett looked up, still clasping her hand in a painful vise. "What brings you here, Hart? I daresay, unless you have an invitation or a summons from Mr. Grey, it's my understanding you are not welcome." Acid dripped from his voice. "Isn't that so, my love?"

"You know that's not true," she hissed to Garrison, wishing she had her dagger. Her hand shook as she reached up and wiped her mouth, then glared at the doctor, speaking through her clenched jaw. "Release my hand this instant, Dr. Garrison." She wanted to slap him hard enough to make his ears ring, but was unwilling to start another brawl. The last one ended badly enough. Surprisingly, he let go. She jumped to her feet.

"Landon!" She scanned the street.

He wasn't there.

Lifting her skirts, she dashed down the porch steps and rounded the corner toward the street. Landon, already astride his horse, was trotting back toward the wharf, well out of earshot. There was no way she could hail him without luring unwanted attention, even if she could raise her voice above the din of the activity on the street. A livery carriage slowing in front of the house soon blocking him from view.

Damn that man! How could he possibly think she'd ever willingly kiss Dr. Garrison? Surely he'd noticed her predicament. She glanced over the hedge, pursed her lips at the sight of Garrison staring at her, and then understood.

Only the doctor's upper chest was visible over the hedge. Her pinned arms had been out of sight from Landon's view. When

Garrison forced her to sit, it must have looked like she was trying to hide from him.

She groaned. Landon's ire was understandable. He'd been betrayed before; his first wife died giving birth to another man's child. Landon himself had once said to her: "Marriage doesn't suit me."

That was before the ball, before the kiss that revealed her secret, before she'd admitted she loved him, before he'd asked her to marry him and sail aboard the *Desire*. Things had changed, hadn't they? He'd told her he loved her. Landon Hart had made her feel cherished, energized, strong, and weak in the knees.

She expelled an annoyed breath and resisted the urge to stomp her foot. Well, this issue could be resolved with a simple, civil conversation. As soon as Garrison was gone or occupied, she'd slip out and head straight to the *Desire* and speak with that stubborn sea captain.

She'd make him understand.

Keelan clenched her jaw and straightened her shoulders. He'd listen to her if she first had to clobber him over the head and tie him to a chair in order to say her piece.

She quickly tried to walk past the doctor. He grabbed her arm, and the glare she gave him should have frozen him solid. Pausing, Keelan dropped the temperature of her voice enough to the chill a harsh winter wind. "If you touch me again, I will chop off your hand with a hatchet."

Eyes widening, he lowered his arm and took a couple of steps back. He opened his mouth to say something, his Adam's apple jerking up and down. Rather than extend the torture of his presence, she flew down the hall and up the stairs to her room.

Slaney was closing the lid on her trunk when she entered, winded and furious.

"Did ye square things away with Dr. Garrison?"

She shook her head. "Things are worse, actually. He seems to think we are still to be married." Keelan grabbed her quill and a piece of parchment. "And Captain Hart seems to believe so too."

"What?" Slaney stepped back as if someone flung cold water in her face. "Why in the world—"

"Our course is set," Keelan answered swiftly. "The livery carriage Daniel summoned is here. We must leave *now*."

CHAPTER 6
CAUGHT

K eelan signed the letter to her uncle stating her plans, saying goodbye and left it on the dressing table. She grabbed her reticule and bonnet and slipped down the servant's staircase; the aroma of toasted pecans and raisin scones wafted up the passageway. She would miss Ruth, the soft, brown kitchen slave who loved cooking and all things spicy-hot. Under Ruth's tutelage, Keelan had learned to cook and also dress meat and fish, and prepare a good many household remedies from removing rust stains to making lard candles. Things that could come in handy, depending on her future.

They quietly exited the back door and made their way to the side street where the carriage waited. Her uncle and aunt were hopefully still at the luncheon. Thankfully, there was no sign of the doctor.

Daniel helped both women step into the carriage. As she settled herself on the seat, the sound of running feet and a shout drew her attention. To her horror, Uncle Jared was approaching the carriage. Dr. Garrison was close behind. When her uncle took in the trunks strapped to the back and the three of them, his expression darkened.

"What is the meaning of this?"

"Please, Uncle Jared. Allow me to explain—"

Her uncle's brows slammed down his face thunderous. "No need. Garrison has explained everything to me. I *forbid* you to leave on this fool's journey."

"But Uncle—"

"Have you forgotten why you and your father fled England?" His face turned a mottled purple. "Someone has a serious vendetta against our family. Your mother, aunt, cousin and uncle were all *murdered* within weeks of each other. In addition, our country is but a hair's breadth away from a full scale war and I'll not permit you to endanger your life by attempting a return to England now."

"Please her me out." She couldn't explain her reasoning about Garrison while the doctor stood there, listening. Better to explain her suspicions in private. She gave the only lame excuse to pop into her mind. "Captain Hart said a passenger ship would be able to make it safely from Boston."

Uncle Jared's expression darkened further. "I don't give a damn about what Hart said. I made a promise to your father that I would make sure you're safely married, and so I shall."

Keelan reached out and grasped her uncle's arm. "I made a promise to him, too. He made me give my word to retrieve something vitally important." This was the wrong place to have this conversation. She needed comprehension and understanding from Uncle Jared. Instead, his face showed an even more hardened resolve, making her shoulders tighten, and her stomach dive to her toes.

She lowered her voice. "It was his dying request, Uncle Jared. Please."

His expression softened slightly, and for a moment, it appeared he understood. Then he shook his head. "I'm sorry, Keelan. Such a journey can never be made safely by you or anyone in our family. I cannot let you go in good conscience. It's now my duty to see to your welfare, and so I shall."

Horrified, Keelan glared at Everett, who stood a little straighter at Jared's words, but wouldn't meet her angry gaze.

Everett stepped forward. "Sir, I am prepared to marry your niece as soon as you deem necessary."

Uncle Jared glanced at Everett and uncrossed his arms. He frowned and lowered his voice to a more soothing tone, one that had warning bells sounding in Keelan's head. "I'll consider your offer with Pratt's. We shall discuss particulars in the study."

No!

Keelan could only stare in disbelief at her uncle. A marriage to Pratt was a prison sentence. How could he even consider such a thing? She certainly would not.

"Uncle Jared, please don't do this. I will *not* marry Pratt. He is unsavory and cruel—"

He batted her words away. "Keelan, those rumors are typical of those spread by the house slaves. You'd do better not to listen to them. They carry no credence." He managed to look a little sympathetic. "He's older by more than a bit, but trust me, Keelan. You'll live quite well."

Tears burned in the back of her eyes. She couldn't let this happen. She simply couldn't. It was time to admit her plans. "Uncle Jared, I cannot marry Pratt. I... I have a confession."

Uncle Jared's brows rose. "I don't doubt it. You tried to sneak away, rather than confer with me about your plans, so obviously you knew I wouldn't approve."

She hoped if he understood her true motives, he'd let her go. "If truly your motive is for me to be happily wed, then let me go. I will be fine. I've promised Captain Hart I would marry *him*. He's waiting for me. I'm on my way to his ship. Daniel and Slaney will go to Boston and then on to England. They will secure Papa's trunk for me. He told me there is important information within it which I must secure." She moved closer to her uncle and murmured, "I believe I've discovered who is behind the assassi-nations."

"Really?" Her uncle looked at her in surprise. "How? Who?"

She stepped down from the carriage, pulled him out of the doctor's earshot, and told him her suspicions about Everett Garri-son. "The 'accidents' began after the sinking of the ship," she whispered. "Then Papa got sick and died while under his care." She tilted her head in the doctor's direction. "It makes sense, don't you see?"

Jared inhaled deeply, then let his breath out in a sympathetic whoosh. "Keelan, my dear, I understand your reasoning a little, but it doesn't quite fit with the events."

"It does, Uncle Jared, think about—"

He held up his hand and closed his eyes. "He can't be respon-sible, my dear. I received a post today from my eldest brother's barristers. Edmond was found murdered in his home. The assassin is in England. Dr. Garrison has been with us for *months*, Keelan."

Everett coughed and raised his voice, "Miss Keelan, you might consider that you have been duped by Captain Hart. On my way to retrieve your uncle, I passed by the docks and witnessed both the *Seeker* and the *Desire* departing the port for open sea. For South America, I was told by the harbormaster. I'm sorry, Miss Keelan, but perhaps you misunderstood Captain Hart's intentions?"

His words hit her like a blunt blow to the stomach. A sharp jolt pierced her chest. Her tongue was paralyzed; she could only stare. No, it had to be a lie. She did not misunderstand Landon. He wouldn't leave without her.

Would he?

"*COME AWAY WITH ME, KEELAN,*" *he had whispered. "Leave behind your secrets and schemes, and let me show you what it is like to be loved and worshipped for the goddess you are. Let me take you aboard the* Desire *and show you the world.*"

"*I'll meet you as soon as I can," she'd promised. "I will slip away to Charleston within a fortnight for certain.*"

"*I'll await you aboard my ship.*"

࿓

LANDON HAD TOLD her the *Seeker* had to deliver cargo to Harbour Town and then meet the third ship in their fleet. By the time the two returned to Charleston, the repairs to the *Desire* would be complete. He'd hoist a blue flag with a white square in the middle when they were ready to depart. All three ships would then sail north to Philadelphia. He'd told her this. He'd promised to await her aboard the *Desire*. Why did he leave her behind? How could he possibly leave without allowing her to explain?

She fingered the handle of her reticule. Had she let Landon stir her passion so strongly with his kisses that she'd been that blind?

Had she been nothing more than a diversion for him?

The bitterness in her mother's tone remained vivid in her mind:

"*There's no settling down for a man of the sea. She's his mistress and forever calls him away from the arms of those on the land. A sailor will eventually leave you alone and lonely. Mark my words, girl.*"

Jared's face smoothed and his eyes flooded with pity. "Come child, I'll have Ruth make you some tea."

A small voice in the back of her mind needled her, "*Had he not told you marriage didn't suit him? Hadn't you been afraid something like this would happen? That he might use you as nothing more than a dalliance while at port? That he'd never trust another woman to be faithful?*"

And he'd seen Garrison kissing her!

She and Landon hadn't known each other long. It would be understandable for him to question her fidelity, just as she was now questioning his promises. Numbly, she followed Jared into the house. By leaving, he'd made sure there would be no happy life for her sailing the seas with him. No exotic places to visit. It was as if a curtain had been pulled to shut out her view of the outside world. Allowing nothing to be visible, except four plain, lonely walls.

How could they live a happy life together if he couldn't trust her love for him?

Do not cry. Do not cry.

Jared's voice was soft and compassionate. "Keelan, my dear, you've had a heartbreaking week with the death of your father. I'm sorry your plans can't be put into action. I gave George my word to care for you as your guardian." He glanced at her uneasily as they walked, then cleared his throat. "I'm well aware he raised you in an unconventional manner, dear girl. Therefore, I will not give you an opportunity to run away." Jared swallowed and continued, his voice solidifying to granite. "And, as added security, you will remain locked in your chamber until the wedding."

She stumbled, felt her eyes widen in horror. "Uncle Jared," her voice came out as a dusty whisper. "Please don't do this. I was raised as your brother's daughter, I don't think he would want—"

"Stop." He was already shaking his head. "I will hear no more. I've already penned a missive to the family barrister in London to auction off all holdings owned by my two deceased brothers." He sliced his hand through the air. "There will be no journey to England. My family and I prefer life in America, and I do not wish to endanger anyone by allowing them back into that assassin's lair, or subject them to such a dangerous journey in these uncertain times."

Her uncle opened the door to the house and nodded at Simon, who dutifully held the door.

"Miss Keelan is not to leave her chamber for any reason. Do you understand?"

"Yessuh." Simon's eyes shifted from her to Uncle Jared, then to Garrison.

"You are to lock the door and keep it locked except for the normal care and cleaning of her room and delivery of meals."

"Yessuh." Simon's voice sounded very small.

Uncle Jared grasped her elbow, dragging her upstairs, despite her protests. When they reached her room, she tried to beg her uncle once more to reconsider, but he quickly shut the door. The key clicked in the lock.

Keelan took a seat near the balcony doors and stared out the window. Jared's footsteps grew faint and soon all she heard was the silence of the air, still and hovering in the room. Despair clawed at her throat, its weight crushed her heart. She expected to break down and weep, but strangely, no tears came. Landon Hart had seduced her with his kisses and caresses. She'd fallen in love with him. And he had broken her heart by leaving without demanding an explanation, without giving her a chance to even offer one.

She was a fool.

A few minutes later, the scrape of a key in the lock drew her attention back to the door.

"Miss Keelan?" Simon spoke through the door.

A tear finally broke free and crept down her cheek. She quickly brushed it away. "Come in."

Simon stepped across the threshold and paused. His voice dropped to a conspiratorial whisper, and she had to strain to hear him. "If there's anythin' I can do to help you..." He toyed with the keyring he held. "I mean *anythin'*, Miss Keelan. You saved my boy's life, and I'll never forget dat, an' you helped the others runnin' for their freedom after the storm."

At her questioning look, he whispered, "Mister Pratt never caught them, they free now." The servant leaned in. "Well, you jus' say the word, Miss Keelan." He quietly swung the door wide and stepped back, waiting.

Her heart jumped. The slave offered her freedom, but she couldn't bring herself to take it. At least, not yet. Where would she go? Until Slaney or Daniel came to see her, they couldn't devise a plan. If she left now, Simon would be whipped for sure.

"Thank you, Simon, but I will not jeopardize your position in this house."

The slave started to argue, but she silenced him with her hand. "There is one thing you can do for me. Find Daniel," she said. "If we require your assistance, he will tell you when and how."

"Yes'm. I can do dat. I'll be happy to do dat." Simon gave her a firm nod and retreated, closing the door behind him.

Less than a minute passed before the door opened again.

Keelan ground her teeth as her cousin Doreen bounced into the room.

"Daddy is sending a letter to Mr. Pratt, I hear."

Doreen's taunts and gloating observations were the last thing she wanted to hear right now. She pressed her lips into a hard line. "I have nothing to say to you, Doreen. Please leave."

Doreen's cool laugh echoed in the room. "This is no less than you deserve for trying to take Everett from me."

Keelan rolled her eyes, but held her tongue. Doreen began to saunter about the room. "Thank goodness Mr. Pratt is available to take you." Her cousin gave a dramatic shudder. "I have heard he is quite heavy-handed with his slave girls. Although, with you as his bride, they might suffer a reprieve."

Keelan's dug her fingernails into her palms to keep them from trembling. There was rage, yes, but also fear. That dark, ragged monster invading her brain, forcing her to writhe and flail under its cold, contemptuous shadow. It was something she kept pushing frantically to the far places in her mind when the topic of a marriage to Pratt arose. Only her anger at Landon Hart kept her from covering her ears, collapsing into the corner, and becoming nothing more than a limp pile of pathetic mush.

Keelan's shoulders tightened as her cousin walked up and stopped in front of her. Doreen pretended to study her intently. "This might be the last time I view your face unmarred." She whirled and skipped from the room.

Her cousin would *not* crumble her pride and throw her into hysterics. Still, it was a long time before her body stopped quaking. The uncertainty of her future mauled her mind and spirit. She desperately wanted to believe Everett lied to her about the ships leaving port. Was it so far outside the realm of possibility that hurt and anger drove Landon to make a sudden decision to just *leave?*

A ship bound for Boston currently anchored in the Charleston harbor, set to sail tomorrow at sunrise. If Landon had indeed left her behind, was still her intention, and now perhaps the sole purpose of her life, to be aboard.

CHAPTER 7

NEW PLAN

"I'll not leave without ye!" Standing in the middle of Keelan's chamber, looking like a silver whirlwind, Slaney crossed her arms.

"Neither will I," argued Daniel. He stepped away from the doorway where he and Simon were keeping watch for Jared or Doreen. "I made a promise to Lord Grey, and I don't intend to break it." He walked over to the maid. "Slaney, you *must* go."

"I will not!" Slaney countered. Her eyes flashed in defiance. "Who's going to take care of me mistress?"

Daniel sighed softly, taking Slaney's work-toughened hands in his own. "*I* will. I promise." He rubbed his thumbs over the top of her fingers. A slight blush suffused the maid's cheeks. "Slaney, if you are safely gone, then I can concentrate all my efforts on getting Keelan away. If I have to worry about the *both* of you..." He shrugged his shoulders and left the rest unsaid. "Miss Keelan and I shall meet you aboard the ship. We'll have to wait until we can slip out unnoticed, which will probably be late, hours before dawn when the house is still abed. We can move faster with only two."

Keelan's heart tugged with affection for the two people who'd

48

cared for her for the past nineteen years. To think for most of her life, she'd taken their loyalty for granted. Gratitude radiated in her chest and emotion closed her throat.

She added to Daniel's logic with her own. "Slaney, I'm grateful for your concern, but if something prevents me from boarding to the ship in time, *someone* has get to Wind Briar and retrieve the chest. I need those papers inside if I am going to find my real father."

Keelan took a breath and willed the thought of failure away. She *would* make it. "If Uncle Jared's instructions to auction everything are carried out before we can get to it, I might never get a chance to read them." She pressed an envelope into Slaney's hand. "Here are letters of recommendation to help you find employment and give you permission to stay with your sister at Wind Briar."

Slaney's shoulders slumped. "All right then, I'll go on," she muttered. She shook a finger at Daniel. "Ye best bring her safely home and yerself too, or ye'll be answerin' to me." She sniffed and rubbed her nose.

Keelan held out a small purse. "Your passage has been paid. The receipt is inside, along with enough coin to get you to Wind Briar. Go *now*. Daniel told Simon to gather your trunks and wait for you in the stables. I want you away before Jared finds a reason to detain you."

With a soft sniffle, Slaney circled her arms around her in a warm hug. Keelan held her tightly and kissed her cheek.

"Everything will be fine. You'll see. Don't worry." Her own words sounded thin, meager, even to her.

With forced bravado, Slaney heaved in a deep breath. "I'll go then."

"God speed, Slaney," Daniel said, squeezing her arm.

Slaney let out a choked sob and then threw her arms around Daniel's neck. He stood stiff and shocked for a second then slowly wrapped his arms around her, hugged her fiercely then kissed her forehead. "We'll see you soon." He released her and stepped to the door.

Slaney opened her arms and perhaps for the last time, Keelan walked into the safety and solace of the familiar embrace. Warmth curled in her chest and her throat tightened. She prayed she'd made the right decision, and she wasn't sending Slaney into danger. The uncertainty of the future, the ease of the journey, even the weather all weighed heavily upon Keelan's conscience.

Slaney pulled away and wiped her eyes with the corner of her apron. "Well, then. I'm away." With a last wave, she slipped from the room.

Keelan prayed she would see her again.

CHAPTER 8
EVERETT RETURNS

A loud commotion broke the post-dawn silence downstairs and Simon slipped up to whisper through the door that Doreen had run off with Doctor Garrison, and Master Jared was in a rage. Sarah was still in a state of shock and Ruth was on her way to the herb garden to make her a special tea.

This was an unexpected surprise. Hopefully Uncle Jared would be so consumed with locating his daughter, that he'd postpone corresponding with Pratt long enough for Keelan to make an escape. Still, she nervously paced in her chamber. The afternoon sun had begun to warm her room, and still no sign of her uncle, or Daniel.

She waited out the day in solitude. No matter how hard she tried to drive thoughts and visions of Landon from her head, they persisted. Broad, masculine shoulders, clear blue eyes, strong, corded arms, and full, urgent lips.

Damn her naïveté and her weak, weak heart.

And damn Landon Hart's stubborn Irish temper.

How could he believe she would choose Everett Garrison over him? Was he not convinced of her affections? She had told him she wanted to be with him. She had agreed to elope with him. A single thought rose to the surface of her mind.

She'd never admitted to him that she loved him.

Admitted. As if it were a crime. What was *wrong* with her? Was her pride so powerful that she could only confess to herself the effect Landon had on her?

A key clicked in the lock and drew her away from her musings. The door opened to reveal Uncle Jared and Simon. Her uncle entered the room with short, agitated steps. Simon shifted from foot to foot in the hall, looking worried.

"Your maid has disappeared." Uncle Jared snapped, pacing the floor. "Your father's valet has refused to tell us her whereabouts. He claims he doesn't know where she went." He whirled back to face her, his eyes thunderous and his scowl making Keelan's belly twitch with fear for Daniel. "I expect he's lying. Where has she gone?"

Keelan's mind jumped quickly to various explanations which might keep Daniel out of trouble. Slaney went to the apothecary, for... what? Slaney was delivering a letter... to whom? About what? None would keep him safe enough. It was simpler to tell the truth.

"I sent Slaney back to England to secure the documents which I promised Papa I would retrieve."

Her uncle paused, his face reddened. "Keelan, we discussed this."

There was no reason to keep her secret any longer. Perhaps, if Uncle Jared understood that she wasn't actually a blood relative, he'd relinquish his guardianship.

If he believed her.

"He said they'd explain the identity of my true sire." The words seemed to stick in her throat and she paused a moment to clear it before continuing, "You see, Uncle Jared, Papa confessed to me that I'm the illegitimate child of my mother and another man. I'm not even his kin."

A small vein pulsed in his temple and he sliced the air with his hand. "Nonsense!" He stepped forward and clenched his hands into fists before grasping her fingers. He expelled a thick sigh and closed his eyes, the obvious battle for calm raging behind his lids. "Keelan, my dear, you must understand, your father was not in his right mind at the time of his death." He finally met her confused stare. "He'd been babbling the night he died even before Sarah came to get you, of revenge and a stolen love." He gently squeezed her hands. "Of *course* you are his daughter. I have a document signed by him stating I am *his daughter, Keelan Elizabeth Grey's* legal guardian in the event of his death. He also left a will in his desk stating Twin Pines goes to you as your dowry."

What?

That was so far from what she'd heard from Papa himself, she couldn't reconcile it being any sort of misunderstanding. Keelan drew her brows together in confusion. "Before he died, he told me he left everything to you. He instructed me to return to England and find my father."

Jared's composure softened a little more. "Don't take the ramblings of a dying man as any more than what they actually were: simple ramblings."

The night Papa had died, he *did* seem to have trouble staying in the present, but she had the signet ring he'd given her weeks earlier, and the tiny portrait of the man in the locket who bore such a striking resemblance to her. Those were tangible things that fortified his claims. Why would he possess those items if the tale was false?

They couldn't be explained away. If she showed Jared the ring and the locket, he'd probably believe her story. But what if he took them from her? She'd have no way to prove who she was to her real father when she found him, if he even existed. No, she must not give up hope. Everything had all become too confusing.

Jared must have taken her silence as acquiescence to his way of thinking. He let her hands go, leaned in, and gave her a cool kiss on the cheek. "Your father cared about you, Keelan. He wanted you to have a secure future."

Secure future. That meant marriage to money. "I cannot, I *will not* marry Pratt," she whispered. Her heart belonged to another. Even if the stubborn oaf had left without her.

Jared expelled a loud sigh. "I'll not force you. Although I pray, please take the time to contemplate the security of a life with him against the alternatives. You may, of course, stay with us as long as you wish. We can sell Twin Pines to Pratt outright, then do what we can with the funds to see to your comfort, or continue with the plan to lease it. Let's discuss this when I return. I should like you to assist me with the draft of the purchase proposal before I take it to my barrister, should we decide to sell."

"Thank you, Uncle Jared." He'd understood. Hopefully, he'll leave quickly and she and Daniel could still escape to the wharf and find Slaney's ship.

He turned toward the door. "I must find my daughter first. Once I locate Doreen and that rascal, Garrison, I will deal with Pratt and Twin Pines." He paused, then addressed Simon. "Keep her here until I return." He spoke to her, although he didn't dare make eye contact. "I'm sorry, Keelan, but I have to assure that you'll be here when I return, and not make some impetuous decision that will endanger your life."

He knew her too well.

"Uncle Jared, I beg of you—"

He left, locking the door behind him.

She stared at it, not quite believing what had just occurred. For a moment, she'd thought she'd convinced him to allow her the freedom she desired. Now it would be harder to accomplish her goal, but not impossible. The worst thing that could happen would be if she and Daniel missed the ship.

"I'm sorry, Miss Keelan," Simon said through the door.

"I'll be fine, Simon." She hoped. "Will you please tell Daniel I need to speak with him?" All was not lost.

"Yes, Miss Keelan."

۞

Soon, Daniel entered carrying a bucket of water. After Simon retreated into the hall, the valet leaned forward and whispered in her ear, "Simon has agreed to leave the key out for us." The valet continued, "We'll go in the predawn hours. I've rented a room tonight at a pub called, The Whistling Pig."

She raised a brow. "Rented a room? Why?"

Daniel's mouth pressed into a straight line. "The ship to Boston departed at high tide today. We missed it."

"Slaney—"

"She boarded just in time."

This made things harder. Not impossible, but definitely harder.

He straightened his jacket and plucked a piece of grass off his sleeve. "The tavern is near the docks. We can hide there and wait until we can board the next vessel sailing north... if you still wish to do so." He fidgeted with the bucket handle before clearing his throat.

Still wish to do so? Why wouldn't she? She narrowed her eyes. "What is it, Daniel?" Even a blind man could tell the valet had more to say.

"The *Desire* and the *Seeker* are still anchored out in the harbor, Mistress. Both are flying Blue Peters."

The Blue Peter signaled for the crew to return to the ship. Her hand flew to her mouth. "He lied. Everett *lied*!" A surge of relief hit her so hard she sank to a chair. Landon had not left her. He was still here. Would he let her explain? Even now, was he waiting for her to come to him? A more terrifying thought invaded her mind. What if this delay made him think she'd changed her mind? She flew to the desk and took out a piece of stationary, then grabbed the quill.

"Daniel, would you please deliver this note to Captain Hart?" She wrote furiously.

"Of course, Mistress." He paused and cleared his throat. "I must warn you, the accommodations at The Whistling Pig might be a bit rough, but I fear we might be easily found by your uncle if we stayed at a better boarding house."

She nodded, quickly sanding and sealing the letter. "You made a wise choice. Please don't worry about me, I'll be fine. I hope to confer with Captain Hart at his earliest convenience."

Daniel caught her gaze and held it. "I'll come for you tonight. Be ready to flee. Wear your shirt and breeches, we'll move quicker and draw less attention." He hefted her smaller trunk. "I'm sorry to say you'll have to leave the bulk of your things behind, unless by some miracle Mister Grey allows me to return and take procession for you."

She didn't care. If given a choice between all the riches in the world or the opportunity to set things to rights with Landon Hart, she'd take the latter in a blink. She was almost giddy with relief. Surely, he'd at least allow her to explain. A thought hit her like a ringing slap. What if Everett had lied to Landon as he'd lied to her? Suddenly, the sun couldn't set fast enough.

When it was nearly dark, she doffed her dress, glad to free her body from the sweaty, prickly mourning gown. Keelan dipped her hands in a bowl of tepid water and splashed it over her face.

If only she could change into her waif's clothes, she'd be better prepared when Daniel returned. However, if Uncle Jared made an unexpected visit after supper, she would be hard pressed to explain her wardrobe. It was best to wait. She slipped on a clean chemise and dressing gown, then sat at the small table and nibbled on the cold supper Simon had delivered earlier.

Her tray held chicken, bannocks with brandied peaches, a glass of wine, and some of Jared's prized boiled potatoes. No doubt, Simon gleaned more than a small bit of pleasure, giving Jared's favorite dish to Keelan. She ate every last morsel.

She had a few short hours to get some much-needed sleep. She climbed into bed, only to stare at the ceiling. Nothing seemed right. Her mattress was too hard. The tree frogs sang too loudly. She tossed and turned before her lids became heavy enough to resist her twitching and worrying.

She must have finally dozed off, because she was awakened by the prickle of hair rising on the back of her neck. It took a moment while she waited for her vision to adjust to the darkness. Had Daniel signaled her from the yard below?

She rose quietly, turned up the oil lamp at her bedside, and slipped on her dressing gown. Pulling the curtain aside, she scanned the ground below. No signs of Daniel. Yet something had disturbed her sleep.

A barely audible click behind her made her whirl to face the door. It eased open inch by inch.

"Daniel?" she breathed, afraid to speak any louder.

The tall, lean shadow of a man moved into her room. The figure was too tall to be the loyal valet. Her heart began to hammer in her chest. A scream caught in her throat, and without thinking, she snatched the heavy pitcher next to the washbasin and held it high, ready to bring it crashing down on the intruder's head.

"Keelan," the man whispered hesitantly. "It's me... Everett. I have come to take you from here. I cannot let you be married to that brute, Pratt!"

Relief washed over her like a clear, cool rain. "Good Lord, you gave me such a start!" she clutched the neckline of her dressing gown as she sat weakly on the chair, still holding the pitcher.

He hastened across the room before dropping down to one knee and peering at her. His voice was low and urgent, his frame slightly illuminated by the low wick of the lantern. "Please, Miss Keelan, you must get dressed so we can depart immediately."

Perplexed, she peered at him closely. "Uncle Jared said you'd run off with Doreen. I am quite shocked to see you here. Surely you must realize Jared is determined to seek you and his daughter out."

Everett gave a derisive snort, "Mr. Grey will not find her, of that, you can be certain."

Something beyond Everett's words unnerved Keelan. He sounded almost emotionless. The detached, dead tone of his voice was wrong, like a string out of tune. He spoke with an unusual iciness. As she stared at him, her throat dried, and the air seemed to leave the room.

Something was wrong. She could sense it.

"Dr. Garrison..." she said. "What are you saying? Did you not take Doreen away to marry her?"

He snorted. "No, although she seems to wish it. She is hiding... for a little while longer, anyway." He paced the room, grinding his fist into his palm. "I'm still angry with the way she acted the night of the ball. I worry for your reputation, my dear. If we are to be married soon, I want to make certain you have the respect and admiration you deserve." A slow, thin smile creased his gaunt face. "She thinks I'll return to marry her, but in truth, I want her out of our way for a while. It distracts her father."

Icy fingers of trepidation slid across Keelan's throat. The faint glow of the lamp cast dark, quick shadows, making Everett's face appear contorted and hard.

"Wh—what..." she stammered, "What exactly have you done to her?"

He gave a harsh laugh. "She's staying with Mrs. Camsby." Everett walked to the window and peered out, casually clasping his hands behind his back. He turned to face Keelan again. "When we arrived, Captain Hart was just leaving. And Mrs. Camsby seemed a bit disheveled. Did you know they were lovers?"

She froze, then fought to keep her expression blank. Dr. Garrison had lied to her earlier. This time she wouldn't be so gullible. She'd finally made the decision to trust Landon, and she would continue to do so.

He moved to the small table and lit the candle, casting the room in a faint, yellow glow and sending shadows clamoring up the walls. "Your cousin needs a respite." He lowered his voice to a more soothing tone, one he used when addressing his patients. "She's upset with herself for giving your father too much pain medicine. It likely killed him, you know. Seems she misunderstood my dosing instructions."

Doreen? Could that be true? She clutched the arms of her chair while mind twitched from thought to thought. If she fled from the room, what then? He would catch her. She'd be faster in her sparring clothes. Somehow, she needed to get him to leave her alone in the room to change. "Dr. Garrison, did you explain any of this to Uncle Jared? He's frantically looking for her."

He stepped forward and knelt before her again. "Of course he is. That was my plan. He is too distracted to worry about *you*. We shall leave tonight." He reached over to take her hands in his. The skin over his knuckles was thin and icy white. "I am doing this for you. My dear, you deserve a better life. I'm going to take you away and marry you." His eyes glittered in the dim light, voice lethally soft. "Think of our future. The two of us will live the lives we were meant to live, happy and prosperous. We'll have the children we always talked about. Please Rachel, leave with me, now."

Rachel? She stood and backed away. "Dr. Garrison, you just called me Rachel," she whispered, horrified at what she was hearing. It was as if he was having a conversation with someone else... not her.

Everett paled. "I... I...." He stood and reached for her hands again. His white lips seemed to just stretch over his teeth. A grim smile. "A silly slip. Come, we have to go."

His manipulations of Doreen and Uncle Jared seemed so uncharacteristic of him on the surface. Yet, when she thought back through the events over the past weeks, his demeanor had slowly shifted from charming and docile to unpredictable and angry. She should have noticed. She shook her head and tried to keep the panic from her voice, "Uncle Jared and Aunt Sarah—"

"Will not be a concern," Everett finished. "There will be no one to displace our claim to Twin Pines or any of your father's other properties. You and I will live out our lives surrounded by wealth. We can even live at Wind Briar, if you'd like."

"Wealth?" He went from calling her 'Rachel' to *this*? And he'd never been to Wind Briar. "Papa left nothing—"

He pressed his fingers over her lips. "Shhhh. Enough, my love. We must go *now*. There will be time enough to discuss our plans later when we are safely away. I have everything perfectly planned." He pulled her from the chair and toward the door.

"Stop."

It was as if he hadn't even heard her. Not one word. In his mind, she was acquiescent and willing. That mind was no longer functioning as it once did. Her heart thrashed in her chest like a small fish jerked out of the water. Something was terribly wrong with him.

She had to dissuade him. Keelan furiously worked through her options. She could go, and hope to make an escape later, or refuse and then alert the household which would likely make it impossible for her and Daniel to slip away tonight. Uncle Jared would probably not even believe her. She'd already accused Garrison of being an assassin. Her uncle would probably think she was being melodramatic or—

"I cannot go with you." The words fell out of her mouth before she could stop them.

He froze. "What... *what* did you say?"

Her knees were trembling, and she hoped her voice wouldn't tremble too. Perhaps if she simply refused him, he'd leave.

She spoke again, slower this time. "I can't go with you," she repeated. "My life travels along a different path now. I cannot do it. I will not do it." Cautious and tense, she stated it in a tone that was both firm and confident even though she was not in the least.

Everett stared at her. His breathing was quick and shallow, as if his lungs merely quivered instead of expanded and emptied his breath. He stood quietly for a long time, studying her before he responded.

"The events of the past few days have put a tremendous strain upon your ability to think clearly. Don't fret, it's normal for a woman's mind to become a bit maladjusted when dealing with a tragedy and loss." He reached out and gripped her shoulders, his fingers like talons. "I'll help you through this. We love each other, my dear. You will be well-cared for, as your father wanted. We'll be happy, as we've always wanted. We'll have the children you've always wanted."

She almost laughed at the irony of Dr. Garrison diagnosing her with a maladjusted mind while his own was fracturing to the point of changing his entire personality. He stepped closer and traced his fingers along her jaw, and she barely suppressed a shudder.

His next words sent icy tremors down her spine. "I will not let you make a decision that is detrimental to your future. You must think about what I've said. When you do, you'll understand it as I do. I think you only need time to let my words sink in. Time and rest." He caught her hand and raised it to his lips. "Get dressed. I shall return soon."

He slipped out the door.

Weak-kneed, she sank back to the chair. It was a moment before her breathing slowed to a normal pace and her brain kicked into action. The door! She jumped up and tried the handle, but it wouldn't budge. Drat. She needed to change into her boy's clothes and search for Daniel. First, she would pen a letter to Uncle Jared, explaining where Garrison took Doreen. Pulling the quill and parchment from her desk, she sat down and scribbled another note.

After completing it, she knelt on the floor and opened her trunk to change. Keelan paused at a small scratching sound outside the door. Just as she stood, it swung open.

Two cloaked figures swiftly entered her room and headed toward the bed. Finding it empty, it was only a second before they noticed her. She opened her mouth to scream, but could only clutch her throat in terror, desperately willing her voice to work.

It was then she noticed the ropes.

With a frightened squeak, she darted toward the open door. The shorter man reached out and grabbed for her wrist. She ducked and dashed under his arm, sending an elbow into his kidney as she passed. Releasing his breath in a loud grunt, he stumbled forward. The tall one was quicker and grabbed her hair as she sped by. She spun and kicked at his shins with her bare feet.

"Dammit! Grab her, Orvis!"

She let her legs buckle and fell away backwards. Her head slammed into Orvis's nose, causing him to let out a howl.

"Quiet, idiot! You'll have the whole house upon us!" The taller assailant still had his hand in her hair, and he jerked her head painfully forward. Keelan swung her forearm up in an arc and struck him in the throat, eliciting a strained hiss of breath. His hand loosened slightly. She opened her mouth to scream as a wide fist made contact with her chin. Little white dots exploded in front of her eyes, then vanished into utter darkness.

CHAPTER 9
IN THE PIRATES' LAIR

Keelan woke to a dull throbbing pain in her jaw and moaned. The sound came out raspy and choked. Her mouth tasted like she'd chewed on a horseshoe and gargled with sawdust. She opened her eyes to inky darkness. In a panic, she squeezed them shut before carefully opening them again.

Was she *blind*? She was in a heap on a hard floor. Rough planks pressed ridges into her cheeks. She wrinkled her nose at the stench. It smelled like a barn. The faint *chink* of metal links when she moved quickly brought her to the realization that she was chained. Panic swallowed her breath, and she sat up quickly. A blunt rush of dizziness crashed into her, and she braced her hands on the floor to keep from collapsing. Her head was throbbing.

Where was she?

Slower this time, she straightened. Flexing her fingers and rotating her wrists, she winced. The manacles were heavy and roughly made. She tugged at the shackles, which was futile. It might be possible to wriggle her wrists out, if she could collapse her knuckles enough, but the links were securely fastened to the wall about knee height from the floor. Twisting her hands only managed to make her skin chafe and burn.

A sound disturbed her work, and she stopped moving to listen. The lumbering shuffle of heavy footsteps grew louder. They stopped, and the door creaked open, swinging on under-used, rusty hinges. A faint light from a low lantern fanned into the room. At the sight of dozens of empty shackles hanging from the surrounding walls, a renewed wave of panic crashed through her chest. She glanced frantically around, trying to get her bearings, and find for something to use as a weapon.

There was nothing.

Aside from the manacles on the walls, the room had two doors. One was nestled in a far corner. The other was obscured by the form of a short, round man carrying the lantern. He moved forward to the center of the room and held the light high.

"Yer awake, finally. Feared I might've hit ye too hard." He eyed her smugly before placing a bottle of ale and a small bundle wrapped in a bit of cloth within her reach, then warily stepped back.

"Who are you?" she demanded sharply. Her voice was almost commanding. Almost steady. "Why have I been chained?"

The man cocked his flabby head to study her, then chuckled. "None o' yer business who I be. You're locked in 'ere for safe keeping until yer new master comes to fetch you."

"New master?" A sharp jolt of panic tightened the skin across her cheeks.

Keelan struggled to her feet, tried to ignore the wobbly dizziness, and leaned against the wall. She held her pounding head until the spinning subsided enough to focus on the hulking form in front of her.

Fear twisted in her stomach and the only way to keep it from totally taking over her body was to funnel it into anger and indignation. Otherwise, the hysterical scream churning in her chest would surely burst out.

"Release me at once!" She fought to keep the terror from shaking her voice, but failed.

He shrugged his broad shoulders in indifference. "I do the bidding of me employer. He'll deal wi' ye."

Her voice shook with barely contained fury. "What's his name? I demand to see him." Her words echoed in the chamber, thin and weak.

"Gampo will see you when he's good an' ready."

Gampo. That was a familiar name. Conal O'Brien and Landon Hart had told a story about the man during breakfast several weeks ago. Gampo was a *pirate*, with whom they had an ongoing feud. He was the one responsible for killing Conal's uncle, Fynn. The trouble she might have thought herself in a minute ago had just increased a thousand fold.

He pointed at the bundle he'd put on the floor. "I brought you somethin' to eat. You'd best get at it before the rats take it."

"I demand you release me!" She raised her voice, but it sounded more like a warble than a shout.

Instead of responding, he backed quickly to the door.

Keelan reached down, grabbed the knotted piece of cloth, and angrily threw it at him. He flung his pudgy arms up to protect his face and ducked. The bundle opened and a piece of bread and two chunks of molded cheese rained down. The cloth floated crazily to the floor at his feet.

Realizing the worst was over, he straightened and pointed at the scraps. "Them is all the rations you get, woman!" He stepped nearer, careful to stay just out of reach. "You're lucky I brought you anything at all after you cracked me bloody nose!"

She studied his face. Both of his eyelids were purple and the man's nose was indeed slightly askew. The sight was grimly satisfying. "What kind of reception do you expect when you enter a lady's chamber in the middle of the night and attack her?"

He touched his nose gingerly. "Well, it hurts like the devil."

"Good."

Added irritation darkened his features. Growling, he opened the door, pausing first to slam the lantern on a large iron hook on the wall. He scowled at her over his shoulder then stomped out, pulling the door behind him, and muttering words that were probably best she couldn't clearly hear.

A spinning head forced her to sink back to the floor and close her eyes, unable to fight off the wave of fatigue that descended. She must have managed to doze off for a short while because she was awakened by the low rumble of hunger from her stomach. She stared longingly at the cloth still crumpled in a small heap.

The bread and cheese had disappeared.

The ale still sat nearby, and she quenched her thirst gratefully, then placed the bottle close to her blanket and hugged her knees to her chest. An overwhelming waterfall of despair unfurled within her heart. She choked back a desolate sob; she shouldn't allow herself to cry. If she started, she might never stop.

CHAPTER 10
STOLEN CARGO FOUND

It was nightfall when Landon and Conal met Commodore Hall and Sheriff Pinkerton outside a pub near the waterfront. The air was still thick with humidity, even though the sun had set over an hour ago. They walked along the pier rather than meet inside. Spies were everywhere, and extra cautions had to be taken to avoid being overheard. A small sliver of a moon occasionally darted from between quick-moving clouds. The wind had picked up and was caressing the land below with gentle gusts hinting of rain.

Sheriff Pinkerton's voice was steady. Confident. "We have a total of sixty able seamen and deputies between the four of us, Commodore Hall." He checked the priming of his pistol. "If Captain Hart is correct about the men in the warehouse, we'll have them outnumbered. Let's hope they're smart enough to surrender without a fight."

Landon wouldn't bet they'd be *that* smart. "We'll meet there in an hour's time with our men," he said. "With only the night watch up and about, we should be able to catch them off guard."

"I like the odds." Commodore Hall clasped his hands behind

his back. "In an hour then." The three men walked along together for a short distance, then the Commodore parted company.

Landon and Conal walked for several moments in silence.

His musings drifted to Keelan Grey.

Again.

He'd tried to banish the woman from his consciousness, but the memory of their time together in the abandoned cabin cellar during a fierce storm last month haunted him in both sleep and wakefulness. Keelan's soft curves and passionate kisses left him hungry. Many nights he lay awake wondering what it would be like to make love to that fiery tigress.

When they'd reached the plantation after the storm, her father and uncle were understandably furious that he and Keelan had been together without a chaperone.

He'd offered to marry her that day, to appease her father and do the honorable thing.

Certainly for no other purpose than that.

On the surface, he supposed it looked as if he did so to save her reputation. Truth was, he spoke without contemplating the consequences of his words. It was as if his reasonable, mortal mind shrugged off its duties and allowed his blind, foolish heart to take the helm. He'd vowed to *never* tie himself to another woman in marriage, but the idea of waking every morning to Keelan's soft warm flesh pressed against him had pushed out any trepidations he would normally have had with regard to the bonds of matrimony. Something about her drew him like a parched man to water. She was impetuous and reminded him a bit of Conal, who acted first and asked questions second. She was compassionate. She'd not hesitated to rescue Simon's boy from a rabid dog, even at her own peril. She was daring. Training to fence in boy's clothes, swimming in a cool lake with none...

In the end, she'd saved him by choosing the physician, Garrison.

Or so he'd told himself over and over and over.

And over again.

He was bound only to the sea. The freedom of the open ocean and the thrill of finding exotic treasures to trade and sell along the shores of the Americas had nourished him as well as any plate of food. Perhaps even better. He was sated. Content. Happy.

Lonely.

Which is why he'd tried to gain Keelan's favor while in Charleston.

Never would he permanently weigh anchor and retire to a landlocked life. Keelan seemed to sense that from their first meeting. She'd made it very clear his "type" would never make her happy, and she'd not marry a man who would sail off for months at a time, leaving her behind, lonely and alone.

He knew too well what lonely women did when their husband's left them alone for too long.

Her decision to accept Garrison's proposal had been a relief. Certainly.

His freedom had been preserved.

As soon as they recovered the cargo and brought to justice, the band of thieves who took it, he'd set sail north along the coast to trade the rest of his goods, make a tidy profit, and enjoy his riches.

Alone.

However, after a month had passed, the desire to be with Keelan again had nearly driven him mad. Her decision grated against his peace of mind. She came to him in his dreams, floating naked on the water, sparkling drops of sunlight dancing all around her, light pink nipples flowering on her supple, round breasts and her hair flaming like rays of a burnished sun. He could still feel the velvety warmth of her lips on his neck, and the touch of her slender fingers twined in his hair.

He had indeed goaded her into a final kiss the night of the ball. He'd found her in the garden, away from the dancing and the guests. She didn't... *couldn't* love Garrison, and he'd intended to prove it to her. A person doesn't agree to kiss one person when they are in love with another. If they do kiss someone else, especially someone they find undesirable, they couldn't possibly do so with passion and heat.

But *that* kiss... even the memory of it made his pulse quicken.

No woman could have kissed him with that kind of fire and been in love with another. It wasn't possible.

Her lips, soft and eager, stirred a heady passion from deep inside, leaving him hungrier rather than sated. It was at that moment, he couldn't imagine sailing for the open sea without her.

He'd asked her to join him and his heart had flung itself at the walls of his chest when she'd accepted, promising to come to him by today. Yet she'd not arrived, nor had she sent word to him.

So, of course he'd sought her out.

Landon clenched his fists. The image of Keelan and Garrison locked in a long, passionate kiss burned in his gut. *Why* had she changed her mind? How had he been so wrong about her? His chest tightened and his heart railed and thrashed. He tried to divert his thoughts elsewhere, but his mind wouldn't obey.

Originally, Keelan had revealed her desire to live in town and open her own shop. Perhaps she'd changed her mind about life on the sea with him? Did her desire to be a woman of substance and independence outweigh her desire for him?

But why choose *Garrison*? That bastard had been violent when he confronted her in Twin Pines' garden. How could Keelan go back to him knowing the kind of man he was?

Only one answer made sense.

She wouldn't.

Unless he was more wrong about her than anything or anyone he'd ever been wrong about in his life, she would *never* bind herself to Garrison willingly.

It would be a mighty blow to his pride if he was mistaken, but he'd speak to her one last time before he left port. He wanted to hear the reasoning from her own lips. The ones he wanted to devour.

On the morrow, he would call on her and wouldn't leave port until they spoke, and he heard a worthy explanation. She might tear his heart open further, but he had know if she ever wanted him, or if she had been using him all this time to spur Garrison into marriage.

"I wish I coulda rounded up more men," Conal said, interrupting his thoughts.

Landon struggled to force the images of the fiery-haired beauty from his mind. "I'll not take a drunk man into battle," he said firmly. "Only those with clear eyes and a steady hand can help us." He clapped Conal on the shoulder. "We'll do fine with what we have. The good Commodore Hall has offered his assistance. The odds weigh heavily in our favor."

"Aye," Conal agreed. "Let's go gather the men." He fingered his pistol. "Been too long since the last brawl. I'm ready for a fight."

Landon grunted in agreement. So was he.

CHAPTER 11
NEVER DEFY A PIRATE

A large rat sat in the middle of the floor, sizing up Keelan with a cocky, jaundiced stare. She grabbed the empty ale bottle and cracked the bottom against the brick wall. It shattered, leaving a long shard protruding from the bottle's neck. Ha! She had a handy blade now.

"Come any closer, you bloody rat, and I'll have *you* for *my* supper." She picked up a piece of glass and threw it at the filthy creature, causing it to scurry into the shadows of the far wall.

Scuffing footsteps outside the cell door broke the quiet, and she tossed the blanket over her new weapon.

"Slow down, Orvis. It's dark on these steps."

Orvis was back, and he had brought a friend. She wrinkled her nose. By the stench, neither had bathed in quite a while and at least one, if not both, had been drinking. They confirmed her suspicions when they staggered into view.

"She's awake now, Crowe." Orvis gestured at her with the bottle in his hand. "Little Miss 'igh an' Mighty." He managed two steps toward her, but the third strayed to the right.

Her skin gripped her flesh as Crowe stared at her, a lusty sheen in his eyes. She returned his stare with a frosty one of her own. As she sat up, the filmy white dressing gown slipped over her right shoulder, baring her pale skin.

Crowe's lewd grin revealed several brown, broken teeth. Keelan glanced down. The curve of her breast peeked enticingly from the silk chemise. Firm nipples stood erect against the thin fabric in the cell's chill. With bravado she did not feel, Keelan put every bit of malice she could rouse into her glare as she slowly and deliberately reached up and pulled the dressing gown over her shoulder and clenched it in her fist, links clinking softly with the movement. Her heart gave a terrified jolt, its beat turning erratic with fear as she eyed the two. If they came closer, she'd make sure they'd regret it.

Crowe swallowed, his Adam's apple jerking as he licked his lips. "God, what I wouldn't give ter have a taste of that." He strode forward and Keelan scrambled to her feet.

"Are you Gampo?" Though she tried to sound authoritative and stern, she failed mightily, and she barely kept her shaking limbs from crumbling beneath her. He looked about as scared of her as he'd be of a church mouse.

Crowe gave her an extravagant bow. "Crowe at yer service milady, I be his brother in arms. His first mate."

"I want to speak with Gampo," she retorted, inching backwards until the wall pressed against her shoulders.

He grinned. "Soon enough."

Orvis leaned against the far wall and gulped a mouthful from his bottle. Keelan sliced her gaze between the two men. Her heart was now racing, her palms damp with sweat. Frigid fingers of fear threatened to paralyze her.

It was obvious their intentions were dark and ugly.

As Crowe continued to swagger toward her, he removed his belt and began to unfasten his breeches. "Methinks 'tis you who will do the service."

Orvis spoke up from the far wall. "The Cap'n said—"

"I heard what the Cap'n said," Crowe snapped, cutting him

off. "I thinks she needs ter learn different ways ter please her new husband." He reached down and pulled his hard erection from his breeches.

Keelan felt the blood flee from her face and she recoiled in horror, a scream frozen in her throat.

He grinned, reeking of sour ale. "This here is Beauregard. He wants a li'l kiss."

She gave a warbled shriek and swung a fist which he easily blocked. Grabbing her fingers in his meaty fist, he bent them back until she sank to her knees.

Biting her lip against the pain, Keelan lanced him with a deadly scowl. "Hurt me and I will kill you."

Crowe stared at her a moment, then tipped his head back and roared with glee. "A wench with spirit!" He leaned nearer, smirking. "It will be a fun to break you like a li'l pony."

Orvis Pike snorted, then touched his nose, wincing. "Give her a li'l lesson, Crowe."

The barrel-chested man released her fingers, but before she could move, he grabbed her hair with both hands and twisted his fingers into her curls. His eyes glowed with a cold, cruel light.

"I said he wants a kiss," Crowe sneered hoarsely. "Be sweet and gentle now. If ye be stupid enough to bite me, I will break yer neck."

Panic seized her. What she wouldn't give for a nice sharp rapier or even a dirk right now. Remembering the bottle, she groped madly for the blanket. Her palm closed around the cool, smooth glass neck. Gripping it tightly, she thrust it upward with all her might. He would learn that she was not some dainty, weak little woman. Until she ran out of strength to lift her hands against him, she would fight like a hellcat.

The sudden, high-pitched shriek emanating from Crowe could have shattered a sherry glass. His face darkened with fury; he shoved her backward into the wall. The bottle flew from her grasp and shattered. A thick, red stream of blood oozed from a deep gash on the inside of his upper thigh, less than an inch from where Beauregard dangled, suddenly limp.

"Where the hell'd she get *that*?" he cried, his voice racked with disbelief and pain. "The bitch nearly gelded me!" He staggered back, tore off his shirt and quickly wrapped it around his bleeding leg. He snarled, "I'll teach ye what happens to them that defies me."

Fear scraped the inside of her ribs. She was defenseless now. Keelan's mouth went dry when he limped over to his fallen belt and wrapped the end in his fist. The metal buckle dangled menacingly, inches from the floor.

"Orvis, hike her up!" Crowe spat.

The rotund man lumbered over and grabbed one of the chains. Her insides churned with a thick, dark dread. She gritted her teeth and tried to pull the chain from his grasp. Unprepared for such a reaction, Orvis crashed into the wall. He reeled away, cursing with his hand pressed hard against his left eyebrow.

"Firs' me nose, now me eye. Dammit, woman!"

He brought his hand away, his brow now sporting a rather large knot, which was quickly deepening in color. Unfortunately for her, the drink apparently dulled the superficial pain, as Orvis was not swayed from his mission. He snatched the chain and hooked the right link over a spike in the wall, grabbed her shoulders, spun her face first into the boards and crushed her body into the hard planks with his own, while he fastened the left chain on a similar spike.

Her heart pounded frantically as the sound of Crowe's footsteps neared. There was a hard yank on the collar of her dressing gown. The delicate fabric was no match for his strength and rent down to her waist. Every instinct screamed at her to fight. She pulled frantically at the cuffs, but they held fast. A renewed sense of panic seized her, and she tried to twist her hands out of the manacles. Pain shrieked through her wrists as the malicious metal bit into her skin.

"Ye shouldn't have fought me," Crowe growled in her ear as he squeezed her buttock hard and then caressed it roughly.

Keelan tried to swallow, but her throat froze and would not obey. She squeezed her eyes shut and silently began to pray.

Crowe swung the belt.

CHAPTER 12
FINDING KEELAN

"On my mark, we'll charge." The lanky sheriff checked the priming of his pistol. "Hopefully we'll surprise them and avoid bloodshed, but don't hesitate to defend yourselves."

Landon turned to the waiting men and growled low. "Ready your weapons."

Swords and sabers were drawn, pistols held at the ready.

A muffled scream pierced the night from deep within the warehouse. The men froze at the unexpected sound.

"That's a woman's scream!" Conal hissed to Landon in surprise.

Landon clenched his jaw, fury building in his chest. Gampo had gone too far this time. Their past skirmishes had consisted only of shots across the bow on open sea until Fynn was killed by falling spars. Everything had elevated since then; severely wounding young Billy and now abusing women. It stopped here and now.

"Now!" Sheriff Pinkerton roared.

The men crashed through the doors. A warning shout from the sentry inside was cut short by the heavy fist of one of

Commodore Hall's sailors. The guard sank into a limp heap as the men swarmed into the building.

Shouts of surprise and panic arose from a small group of warehouse occupants who had been playing cards on a barrel near the door. The disturbance drew an additional dozen or more thieves from the rear of the building, their roars of alarm mingling with the hoots and yells of Hart's sailors and Pinkerton's deputies. A stray pistol shot shattered a glass oil lamp. It exploded into flames, scattering a shower of blazing oil on several rolls of silk. Thin fingers of fire licked hungrily at the lamp oil dripping down the table legs and over the floor.

Landon shouted over his shoulder, "Henry! You and Marcel contain those flames before they spread. Save that silk!"

Henry's eyes widened as Landon motioned to several crates a few paces from the fire. "Captain, those are sittin' next to munitions crates!"

Landon paused and glared at Henry. "Then you had best be *quick*!"

Henry grabbed Marcel by the arm and together they knocked the bolts of silk to the ground, stomping madly at the ravishing flames. Thick black smoke began to spread through the warehouse.

That silk had cost him a small fortune, dammit. Would his luck never change? Half of Fynn's cargo was ruined during their confrontation with Gampo last month, then Landon's cargo had been stolen from under his nose. Although he'd found it, some of the most expensive items were now on fire. How many more setbacks would he be able to take before he was back to where he started seven years ago?

Conal pointed through the smoky haze to the second floor, and an open loft currently stuffed with part of their stolen wares. "The screams might have come from up there."

He glanced up at the thick timber door, which stood ajar above them. The faint glow of a lantern, somewhere within, illuminated the end of the passageway. He bounded up four steps before a dark form blocked his way. He barely raised his own weapon in time to deflect the first blow from the tar's saber.

Landon blocked the second strike and returned a parry of his own, neatly disarming his attacker. The man jumped the railing to the floor below but stopped short to avoid the tip of Commodore Hall's sword. Since the thief was in good hands, Landon continued up the stairs. He'd made it halfway before a bellowing war cry made him turn.

Conal stood on the first step, his back to Landon, holding a sword with one hand and a dirk with the other as a large man carrying a broadsword and a pistol ran directly at him. Conal roared and raised his blade.

While normally, he'd leave his friend to his own very capable defense, in this case Conal was holding a dagger instead of the pistol he needed for a balanced fight.

Landon fired. A bright red blotch seeped through the ruffian's shirt. The man cried out in pain and his weapon clattered to the floor. Conal brought the point of his sword up to his assailant's throat. Things seemed to be in order; time to check out the upper level.

He spun around, but his forward progress was halted by the cold gray barrel of a pistol inches from his chest. The twisted face of a scarred, balding man with a toothless grin met his gaze.

He'd fired his last shot to save Conal. This one was too close to fight off with his sword. Perhaps, if he was quick, he could strike out at the gun, and hope to dislodge it before the bullet discharged into his chest. It was a stupid plan, but it was the only one he could come up with at the moment.

A whisper of sound, slight as a fawn's breath, skimmed past Landon's ear. The man's snarl was replaced by an odd bewildered look, the hilt of Conal's dirk protruding from his chest.

Now *that* was a much better plan. There was no better man to have his back than Conal O'Brien. They'd fought shoulder to shoulder since before they sprouted their first whisker.

Landon stepped aside as the cutthroat tumbled forward down the steps. Exhaling with relief, Landon tossed his friend a grateful nod then bounded up the remaining steps, two at a time.

⚜

"THERE'S a commotion of some sort goin' on below," Orvis slurred.

"Probably another fight over cards," Crowe said. "Kinda figured we'd have trouble after we opened another bumpkin of that wine." He gave Keelan a swift lash with his belt.

Pain seared across her back and sank its talons into the deeper depths of her consciousness. She gritted her teeth against another scream as the buckle bit into her shoulder. A fine, warm trickle of blood crept down over her ribs, backside, and inside of her leg. The steely bite of the iron cuffs temporarily drew her attention from the sting of her back as she twisted her wrists within the bindings. Staying focused was her priority now. She couldn't fight if she was unconscious.

Focus on getting out of the manacles. Leave no room to acknowledge pain. Get at least one hand free.

With the rest of the crew downstairs drunk, she might have a chance to escape during the confusion.

⚜

CROWE DREW THE BELT BACK, ready to deliver another blow. This little diversion made his gut clench with lust, the sting in his thigh almost forgotten. Half a dozen welts crossed the haughty bitch's back and shoulders. Four of them, he noted smugly, had opened her flesh. He swung the strap again, but to his surprise the buckle cracked harmlessly against the wall. Where her bloody back had been, a manacle dangled empty against the planks.

After managing to slip one hand from its iron cuff, she worked furiously to get the second chain off the spike. The links fell to the floor with a metallic "clink." Her left hand remained shackled to the wall, but now she could dodge the lashes with better success.

The wench faced him with a glare containing such hatred and contempt, he was taken aback. He'd expected pain and fear. Submission. Instead, the small victory of freeing one of her hands had bolstered her courage; she appeared even more defiant.

He shook his head at her, chastising. "You still haven't learned the lesson yet, dearie."

He drew back for another blow, but the forward momentum of his arm was abruptly halted. When he glanced over his shoulder to determine what had impeded the progress, he screamed. Standing behind him was a man dark and sinuous as a panther.

And death glinted in his eyes.

LANDON LET out a feral snarl and with a vicious jerk, pulled the leather belt with his left hand, and crashed his right squarely into the pirate's jaw using the pommel of his sword.

The woman's tormentor crashed to the floor, motionless.

Landon stepped over the prone form and looked at the lady crouched in the shadows, backed against the wall. Pale legs, fiery hair... His heart lurched in shock, then contracted with a sharp spasm, squeezing all the air from his lungs.

He barely choked out her name. "Keelan?"

What was she doing here? He wanted to go to her and gather her up into his arms, but instinct made him pause. Her stare was wide and wild, like a caged animal with a fevered gaze. Her breath seemed to come and go in short hollow gasps, as if it was afraid to stay in her lungs.

Sounds from the battle downstairs had ebbed. Sensing the danger had passed, he gently placed his sword on the floor and held open his palms, anguish seizing his breath. As badly as he wanted to crush her to him, he stayed still, calm. She'd not recognized him yet. He kept his voice soft and even, despite the thudding of his heart that jarred his entire body. "Keelan? It's me, Landon."

Her jittery gaze jumped around the room and landed on the prone figure on the floor. Widened. Her throat convulsed.

"Keelan. Look at me, love."

Please recognize me.

She finally lifted her head and wild, wide, green eyes locked on to his face. A shudder shook her shoulders like a violent quake. Landon's heart wrenched tighter in his chest at the sight of her tear-stained cheeks and pale lips. He stepped closer, until he was an arm's length away, careful not to make any sudden movements.

"Keelan, I can take you out of here. Will you let me?"

At last, relief washed over her features and with a choking sob, she threw herself into his arms. He closed his eyes and inhaled.

Jasmine and spring rain.

Keelan.

He held her like a starving man clutched a loaf of bread. When he crushed her closer, she let out a pained gasp, and he quickly released her. His arms were blotted with blood.

With an enraged oath, he stared over her shoulder at the lash marks running across her shoulders and back. Fury boiled through his veins. "That bloody bastard!" At least four gashes were oozing blood. Raw anger roiled in his chest, and he tossed a murderous look at the still form sprawled on the floor. "I should have killed that maggot-ridden piece of filth."

More gently this time, he pulled her into his arms. A terrible ache gripped his chest. She'd chosen Garrison, and the bastard didn't protect her. He shouldn't have allowed it. He damn well shouldn't have let anger and jealousy drive him away from her. Part of him wanted to toss her over his shoulder and carry her back to his ship like a savage. He took a strangled gasp of air, and tried to speak, but his words came out strained. "He hurt you. Keelan, love, I'm so sorry." She buried her face in his neck, hot tears dampening his skin. "I won't let anyone hurt you ever again. I'm here. I'll always be here. You're safe with me. I have you. I have you."

CHAPTER 13
RETURN OF GAMPO

W hen the haze of pain and terror finally thinned, Landon's handsome, chiseled face came into focus. The lack of food and sleep was probably causing her to hallucinate. His hands slid up her arms, leaving trickles of heat in their wake. She reached out and pressed her palms against his warm, hard chest. Except he was solid. He really was here.

"Landon?" This would be a cruel trick for her body to play on her mind. She moved her hand, her fingers bumping along the ridged muscle across his chest. *Please God, let this be real.*

He sucked in a ragged breath, going still. His skin quivered beneath her fingers. "Aye, love, it's me." Relief washed over her like a cool rain. He was here. He was really here.

Landon tenderly stroked her cheek, then ran his thumb gently along her jaw, frowning at the angry purple bruise near her chin. "How did you come to be here?"

Despite fighting for calm, her voice trembled as she told him about the two strangers who had kidnapped her from Jared's home. "At first, I suspected it was Dr. Garrison. He visited my chambers earlier in the evening and asked me to elope with him, but I refused." She still suspected Garrison. Her stomach clenched, both anger and shock weaving a tight knot at the thought of what the doctor had revealed.

He eyed her cautiously. "So, you refused Garrison?"

Of course. He was thinking about that stupid kiss.

Foolish man.

How could he think she would ever choose any other man over him? A spark ignited the latent anger and frustration inside her, and shoved past the trauma-laced panic. She poked him in the chest and glared through her tears. "If you think I would ever *willingly* kiss that awful man, then Landon Hart, you are a bigger fool than he was for attempting it."

Landon's brows jumped up. There was a slight relaxing of his face, the corners of his mouth lifted, but only a little. She threaded her fingers in his. "If I had eloped with him, I'd not have been in my room when those men came for me." She understood his reluctance to nurture another relationship of the heart. He needed to trust her. Trust her love.

They needed to trust each other, which wouldn't be easy for either of them.

"What you saw today, was Dr. Garrison kissing *me*, even though I did not desire it."

He studied their entwined fingers and released a tightly coiled breath. "I would not have left without you, unless you wished it," he closed his eyes briefly. "I had planned to return to speak with you about your decision." His voice caught, then dropped to a rasp. "I shouldn't have left you behind at all." He trapped her with those sapphire eyes, making her breath catch and her stomach tingle. "All I can think about is having you with me."

He dipped his head and kissed her lightly. Her lips burned with the impression, slight as it was, against her own. Her body curved into his, relishing his heat and strength. She wanted to cling to him and tell him she was already his. But would he still want her after she told him about her heritage? Unwilling to destroy the moment, she hesitated.

Landon gestured to Orvis and Crowe. "Do you have any idea who these men are?"

"That one is Crowe," she pointed, hatred crawling hot and acidic up her throat. "The other is Orvis." There was something else they said that was familiar. What was it? Her mind was still fuzzy. Her head ached. A name they mentioned...one she'd heard before.

Gampo.

"They work for the pirate whom you spoke about, Gampo."

Landon froze, eyebrows slamming down. "Why would he come after *you*?" A muscle ticked in his cheek. Tension radiated from him like heat from red coals. "How would he know to come after you, to get to me?"

Something about that admission made her chest warm. It was strangely pleasing. "I'm not sure," she said, bringing her hands to her pounding temples. None of this was making much sense.

"It's too big a risk for them." His frown deepened.

She shook her head. "Perhaps he's here for the same reason you are. His ship needs supplies or repairs."

Landon shrugged, unconvinced. "It's possible..." Landon smoothed a rebellious strand of hair from her face, before slipping his hands around her waist, carefully avoiding her wounds this time. A tingling warmth raced under her skin.

"You're here, that's all that matters now." She pressed her cheek against his chest, where his heart thudded solidly. She inhaled him, her tremors easing, filling her with the scent of leather and sandalwood and sunshine.

His voice rumbled in her ear. "I was following our stolen property. This is one of Jared's warehouses." His thumb rubbed tiny circles on her hips. Soothing and at the same time terribly distracting. "A different portion of my cargo was stolen from another one of Jared's properties. It's too big a coincidence. Especially now, with Gampo involved."

Gampo and Jared? She tilted her head up. "Do you suspect

Jared had me kidnapped?" Somehow, that didn't seem probable. He'd always acted in a way he believed to be in her best interests, even if, as far as she was concerned, it often was *not*.

Landon's face darkened dangerously. "Either it was him or someone who had knowledge of his business or access to his warehouses." With a grim set to his jaw, he murmured, "I wouldn't eliminate Garrison as suspect yet."

Neither would she. In fact, she was convinced he was at the center of *everything*, even if Jared didn't believe it.

Landon gently released her and grasped her hands, eyes flashing blue fire at the sight of her raw, bloody wrists. After a quick search through Crowe's pockets did not produce a key, he turned his attention on the bolt securing the chain to the wall. "I'm afraid the best I can do for now is to separate the tether from its moorings." He grabbed the links, put his foot against the wooden planks and pulled. Muscles bunched, cords in his neck and arms stood out in hard lines under the strain. The fabric of his shirt stretched across strong, broad shoulders. Just when she thought they were going to have to think of another solution, there was a mournful creak followed by a loud crack; the wood splintered apart around the bolt, leaving her with four feet of chain. It was infinitely better than four feet of chain *and* a wall.

"I'm afraid, this is the best I can do for now." Landon said, a rueful slant to his lips.

"It's enough. Thank you." A tremor ran up her spine, reminding her how badly her night dress was torn. She shuddered, unable to control the shiver clamping around her neck, then winced as fire zipped across her shoulders. Landon removed his coat, picked up the end of her chain, and dropped it down the left sleeve before helping her shrug into the garment.

The warmth was welcome, but the rasp of fabric against her tender wounds sent flames of pain skittering across her back. Landon cupped her chin, turned her face up to his, and studied her intently, heated blue eyes catching hers. Her heart jerked in her chest as his touch warmed her skin from the inside out.

Suddenly she had to know.

"I need to tell you something I learned, the night Papa died," she blurted. For some reason, getting this out and over with took precedence over everything else. Taking a deep, shaky breath, she plunged on before her courage failed. "On his deathbed, he told me I'm illegitimate—not of his blood." She almost kept her voice firm. As shameful as her position was, she was determined to keep her pride from crumbling away entirely. She wouldn't hide the truth, but neither would she live out the rest of her days in shame. Still, she couldn't look at him, fearing she'd see scorn in his eyes.

She inhaled a swift, fragile breath, and picked grit from her fingernail with her thumb. "He made me promise to find documents, which will tell me the identity of my true father." She let her arms drop to her sides and set her jaw. "Papa left enough money for me to journey back to Wind Briar to retrieve them. Twin Pines is now Jared's, although Jared seems to still believe Papa left the plantation to me. I don't want it." She couldn't meet his gaze. The wooden thump of rejection beat in her chest.

He didn't respond. Keelan's heart ripped and fresh tears burned the backs of her eyes. She swallowed the sob clawing its way up her throat.

A warm finger gently touched her chin, tilting her head up. "Keelan." The way he said her name was like a husky, velvet caress.

Hope nearly stopped her heart. Tremulously, she focused on his face. Glittering azure eyes, solid, shadowed chin, full, slightly open lips. Inky hair brushing his shoulders. Beautiful smile.

Wait—Landon was smiling. *Smiling*.

"I don't care," he said softly, then chuckled. "Now, *breathe*."

She inhaled, unaware she'd been holding her breath. "You don't?" Relief blew through her like a spring wind.

He shook his head. "I don't. That isn't important to me. *You* are. I said I wanted you with me. I meant it." His crystal eyes bore into hers. He took her hands in his. "Keelan Grey, for the first time in my life, I wished I was a titled lord or wealthy landowner instead of a merchant mariner, so I could court you and be deemed more worthy of your hand."

"If I cared about wealth and land, I would be married to that old goat, Pratt," she said flatly.

Landon's mouth twitched, and he kissed her fingers, one by one. Reaching up, he gently placed his palm on her cheek; his gaze held hers imprisoned, captured by those mesmerizing sapphire-hued eyes. Blue magnets.

"At the ball, you agreed to sail away with me," Landon said. "Will you still?"

Her heart gave an elated thump. He still wanted her! Regardless of her station, he still wanted her with him.

But...what about tomorrow?

Next week?

Next month?

Did it matter?

Unbidden, the image of Landon and Annette Camsby dancing at Doreen's ball surfaced in her mind.

How could she possibly trust her heart to him?

How could she possibly avoid *losing* it to him?

Landon pulled her closer, and she gasped at the hard heat of his body against her lightly clad chest. He lowered his head and ensnared her trembling lips with his. Her body thrilled at the unexpected kiss, but the soft plying of his lips calmed her. His tongue delved deep, soft, and warm in the cavity of her mouth. A heady sensation enveloped Keelan, almost as if Landon was a dark, sweet wine, and she had sipped too much of him. Her free hand involuntarily slipped up to his waist and clutched his shirt.

A soft moan rumbled in his chest. His lips moved from her mouth to her throat. His words, husky with emotion, stole her breath. "Speak a lie and tell me you do not want to be with me, Keelan."

"I cannot," she breathed. " I want to be with you. I want *you*." Not Garrison or anyone else. She closed her eyes and let her skin memorize the strong, protective circle of his arms. She focused on his scent, his touch, his warmth, and willed the memory to burn itself into her mind and soul.

Lifting her chin, he brushed his knuckles gently against her face, wiping away the new tears streaming down her cheeks. "You will still come away with me?"

A floorboard creaked loudly, and from the direction of the far doorway a voice rasped, "I'm afraid she has a previous obligation."

CHAPTER 14
CROSSING SWORDS

Keelan's breath hitched at the voice and with a startled growl, Landon immediately twisted her behind him. "Keelan, run!"

The small door in the far corner was open. Standing on the threshold was a tall man dressed in a black hat and cloak. In his hand, a saber, honed and lethal, glinted in the low flickering light.

That voice.

Fear crept up her throat as Landon pushed her into the dark shadows of the wall, toward the far door. "He sounds like one of the men who took me from my bedroom." Daniel had taught her how to defend herself with a dagger and a sword, but he hadn't been able to teach her how to defend herself against the terror freezing her limbs and numbing her mind.

Think. What would Daniel tell her to do? *Use what you have on you and near you. Defend and distract.*

"Seems I've lost my newly acquired warehouse full of goods," the strange man croaked.

"They weren't yours to begin with," Landon snarled, slipping a dagger from his waist with a leathery whisper. His sword was several feet away on the floor, where he'd dropped it earlier.

The man shifted his stance, and Keelan could now tell he had a dark cloth covering his face. His eyes glittered through jagged holes cut in the fabric.

The man tilted his head. "Regardless, I plan to take this small investment with me, as compensation of sorts for part of my losses." He flicked his saber at Keelan, a flash of dangerous metal. "You'll be coming with me, little chick."

"I'll send you to hell first." Landon eased a step forward. There was steel in his voice.

Keelan lifted her chin, grasped the end of the links dangling from her wrist, and tried to appear as if she wasn't terrified, but the shiver quaking through her body had nothing to do with the temperature in the room. She could do this. She would fight with everything she had.

Starting with the chain around her wrist.

The thin edge of the kidnapper's saber gleamed wickedly in the sallow glow of the lantern. He flicked it at the inert form on the floor. "Did you kill him?"

Landon's eyes hardened. "Not yet."

The man lifted the tip of his sword toward Landon. "Stand aside, man. Ye be at a fatal disadvantage."

Undaunted, Landon stepped forward and over Crowe's body, stopping inches short of the deadly saber's reach. His own sword now lay only a few feet to his right. He spread his arms wide and tossed his dagger from left hand to right hand. "Then we have different assessments of the situation," he responded, his steady, flat voice revealing nothing.

Keelan disagreed. A dagger against the long, sharp, deadly saber seemed to be quite a big disadvantage as far as she was concerned.

"Landon, be careful," she whispered in terror.

The man's head snapped up. "Landon? As in Landon Hart? Captain Landon Hart?"

Landon's shoulders tensed, like a panther ready to spring. "Yes, and *you* are?"

"My Christian name ain't well bandied about, but I'm Gampo to my men. And you owe me a ship." He lunged at Landon.

Landon beat the tip to the side and jumped back. "I owe you nothing!" he snarled. "Except a knife to your heart for killing my friend, Fynn Ahern."

Gampo straightened a little. "So it's true, then. Ahern's dead. A pity." He began to circle Landon. "My intention was to run that turncoat through with my saber at close range, so I could watch his life fade for what he did to my sister."

Keelan frantically scanned the room for anything else she could use as a weapon. A lantern hung from a spike in the wall; the shackles chinked with the movement as she eased it from the hook.

Never taking his eyes from Gampo, Landon flipped his dagger in the air and drew his hand back as if to throw it. Gampo ducked and jabbed his saber wildly at Landon's head.

Keelan screamed and swung the lantern. Momentarily distracted by the lamp, the man flung his arm up to deflect an attack. Taking advantage of Keelan's diversion, Landon dove toward his sword, tumbled neatly into a somersault, and finished upon his feet, sword in his right hand and knife in his left.

"Keelan, stay back!" Landon shouted. "Get out of here! Go!"

If Gampo was surprised at the new turn of events, he didn't show it. His only response was to grip the handle of his saber tighter, and coil like a snake, ready to strike. "Are ye aware how much a beautiful virgin is worth to a Persian trader?" the tall man sneered. "Fynn knew, I'd wager."

"Fynn wasn't a slave trader." Landon's eyes flashed, and he swung his sword.

Gampo parried and nodded toward Keelan. "Perhaps I'll find out how much the buzzards pay for this beautiful woman, soiled or not."

A low, dangerous growl from Landon breached the space

between the two men. "Whatever amount it is, you'll be in no condition to collect it."

Gampo's harsh laugh cut through the thick air. He chanced a brief glance at Keelan. "Watch closely, little lamb, while I cut him into half penny pieces."

They circled each other again. Landon's gaze flicked uneasily to Keelan. To place his body in a position to regain his sword, Landon had to move away from her. Their tormentor soon placed himself between them.

Landon lunged, bellowing for her to run.

Run? She'd just got him back, and she wasn't about to leave him now. Not ever. Gampo blocked and parried. Their blades hissed and clashed repeatedly while they circled and lunged, their grunts and curses muffled within the closed room.

She was helpless at this distance. Every time she tried to sneak closer, Landon would yell at her to run.

Suddenly, to her horror, the large bulk of Crowe staggered upright directly in front of her. And worse, Landon appeared oblivious to the revival. A tangle of fear knotted in her chest, tightening as Crowe pulled a long ugly blade from his boot and began to creep silently toward Landon's back. There was no more time for contemplating her options. She had to act now.

The chain.

Keelan grabbed the end, lunged forward and flung a loop around Crowe's neck. Startled, the man dropped the knife and clawed at the chain. If she could just pull him off his feet, it would distract the pirate from Landon. Keelan hauled back with all her might. Her stomach flipped in panic when her bare feet slid out from beneath her. Crowe followed her descent and crashed to the floor. She did it! She stopped him.

Keelan rolled away, taking the chain with her, then crawled as fast as she could to Crowe's dagger. She grabbed it and drew her arm back, ready to defend herself. She could easily hit her mark at this distance, even from her knees.

Except Crowe wasn't moving.

She scrambled to her feet, her stomach lurching at the sight of his head, which was cocked at an odd angle from his body.

Gampo glanced over at Crowe, who was motionless on the floor.

"No!" he roared. He lunged toward her and swung his saber in fury and rage. Landon jumped in front of her and blocked the attack.

Gampo lunged at Landon again, his face a mask of fury and vengeance.

Instinctively, Landon brought his dirk down, but he could only partially deflect the blade, the saber slashing across the side of his ribcage. He twisted with a grunt and crashed the butt of his handle on Gampo's wrist, dislodging the saber. It skidded across the floorboards and disappeared into the shadows. Roaring, Gampo put his head down and plowed into Landon's wounded side. Both men crashed into the wall with a sickening thud.

Keelan's breath froze in her throat.

Disarm or distract.

She dashed to the saber, even as Gampo struggled to his feet and pulled a dagger from his belt. The saber's hilt was in her grasp before the pirate noticed she'd moved. Swinging the weapon up, she spun and lunged.

The clinking chains gave her away, and he yelped in surprise, slapping away her blade with his dagger. Fingers of pain clawed her back as she whirled again and sent the sword slicing toward his midsection. He stumbled backward, narrowly avoiding the sting of the blade once more.

Gampo's face twisted. "Think you're strong enough to scuttle me? My first mate was taken by surprise, but I'll not be," he sneered. "Let's see how ye fair against the bite of my sword, you daughter of a one-eyed whore!" He grabbed Landon's fallen blade and lunged.

Dear God, what had she done? Whatever Fynn's actions had

been involving Gampo's sister had driven the pirate into a feud with him lasting for years. Would her fate be the same for killing the pirate's first mate?

She lifted her weapon, even as the agony from movement made little black dots drift across her vision. Her arms shook under the weight of both sword and heavy iron chain. She wouldn't last long under the strain.

"Landon!" He had to get up. She wouldn't be able to handle the pain and the weight much longer.

The next parry from her weapon was slow. She brought her sword up across Gampo's body, forcing him to jump back. The weight of the weapon threw her around, and she hissed at the burn of his blade against her shoulder as he spun past. His next blow jolted the saber from her grip, and it clattered to the floor.

She cried out, curling her throbbing hand into her chest.

He nodded toward the small door in the corner. "'Tis time for us to go. I hear footfalls in the hall and don't wish to engage in another skirmish," his voice was as cold as a London winter rain.

"You will not have me willing as long as I have the strength to resist," she snapped.

"I will have you, *claw-cat*, any way I deem fit."

Keelan chanced a quick glance at Landon. He stirred, thankfully. He was alive, but wounded. And unarmed.

Distract.

She glanced toward the rear door. Well, if Gampo wanted her, he'd have to work harder to get her. She took a deep breath, looped the chain around her arm and took off at a sprint. The pirate lunged for her and managed to grab the tail of Landon's coat, dropping his sword in the process. She stumbled against the doorframe.

So close! She squirmed, gasping for breath.

When the pirate tried to pull her to him and snake his arm around her neck, she ducked and plunged an elbow into his ribs. He grunted with pain, but still clamped his other hand over her mouth as he pulled her against him. Frustration and anger threaded through his voice.

"Be quiet, wench! If you scream again, devil take me to the fire, 'twill be the last sound you make! I still haven't reckoned whether I should kill ye now or later."

Keelan twisted her head, and his fingers slipped over her lips. She opened her mouth and bit down hard until she tasted blood.

Cursing, he jerked his hand away. She pivoted, giving her an opportunity to spin away, except she was nearly jerked off her feet.

"Oh no," he growled while holding her chain. "Ye can't go unaccompanied. Ain't safe fer a ewe white lamb like you."

She glared at the tall man holding her iron tether. "I will die before I allow you to sell me, you soulless bastard!"

He yanked hard and snarled, "Ye'll die if ye run, and ye can lay to that, says I."

Keelan's fingers silently groped in the jacket pocket for Crowe's knife. Instinct told her to lunge for the brigand's midsection; he yanked on the chain again and she stumbled. The knife bound for his belly sank into his thigh, instead.

His yelp pierced the still air of the cell. Dropping the chain, he clutched the hilt, and with a pained hiss, he jerked the blade free. Blood seeped through his trousers in a growing blotch.

A low scrabbling caught her attention and from the corner of her eye, she caught Landon crawling toward the saber, his shirt soaked with blood. Thank God, he was alive and moving.

Gampo shifted his attention to her and raised the bloodied knife. His lip curled back in a grimace of hot hatred and agony.

"You've run out of blades, dearie." He motioned to his wounded leg. "Do you really think this little nick will hinder me too much to collect ye?"

Probably not, but a lady could hope it would slow him down more than a little. Landon was almost upright, so she continued to draw Gampo further from him. It wasn't lost on her that for all his posturing and wicked threats, he hadn't dealt her a debilitating blow, even when he had the chance. Perhaps his plans were less nefarious. Unease slithered in her gut. Or perhaps he was simply keeping her in good enough condition to sell to one of those Persian princes he mentioned earlier.

Keelan backed through the far doorway, groping behind her for support. Chancing a furtive glance over her shoulder, she noted the rickety stairway leading down to a damp alley below. It wasn't the safest route, but it was certainly the most convenient. With one last prayer for Landon's safety, she turned and jumped down several steps to the landing, hitting hard enough to crumble to her knees. Rough wood scrapped the skin, and doing her best to ignore the sting, she scrambled to her feet.

Gampo roared for her to stop, as if she might actually heed his command. He clattered after her, limping down the brittle wooden stair. She'd done it! She'd drawn him away from Landon. Pausing long enough to gather up the iron links, she fled down the next flight to the street below. Several shadowed shapes poured out of a broken window and fled down the ally. Gampo's men? She hesitated. They appeared more concerned with running away than taking note of her presence, so she continued until her feet hit the dirt, then took off at a dead run.

His voice hailed her with hoarse fury, "You'll not escape me, Keelan Grey! I will find ye or may I be damned blood, eyes, and liver! Mark this—I *will* hunt ye down! You *and* that yellow-eyed bastard who bought ye! You'll pay dearly fer killing my first!"

A sickening shiver twisted in her stomach.

He knew her *name*.

She wasn't going to stay and find out what else he knew. Desperately hoping Landon had got himself to safety, she slowed enough to confirm Gampo still limped down the steps. He was almost to the alley, still bellowing like a madman.

CHAPTER 15
THE ESCAPE

Daniel. He'd know what to do.

Keelan hesitated. Talons of indecision clawed at her mind. If Daniel believed she ran away, then he would wait for her at The Whistling Pig.

Still, she couldn't go there dressed like this.

She groaned. The only place she could obtain clothing at this hour was Jared's townhouse. She almost laughed at the irony. With any luck, she'd be able to sneak in, dress and sneak out. Hopefully, Simon would aid her, so she didn't end up locked in her room again.

Gampo was hindered by a wounded leg, and she by several pounds of chain. She picked up her pace, praying her head start and speed would win out.

Zigzagging through the streets of Charleston, she was careful to stay in the shadows. Before long, her chest burned, and her legs screamed with fatigue. Tendrils of pain licked across the open wounds on her back. Cobblestones bruised her heels. Twice she slipped and fell.

She shifted the chain to her other arm. While Landon's black coat offered a small amount of camouflage in the dark night, it chafed painfully against her flayed back. She wanted badly to remove it, but her pale skin and white chemise would glow like a firefly at midnight. She gritted her teeth.

She was strong. And determined.

She would make it.

Except she wasn't sure exactly where she was.

Jared and Sarah had welcomed her and Papa to their Charleston house for the first month after they arrived. She'd visited the market by the waterfront quite a few times with her aunt. They had also shopped for supplies, such as copperas for disinfecting, and indigo, gypsum, sugar loaves for the kitchen, and dozens of other items, which led them to all corners of town. Surely, she'd notice something familiar soon.

Although it was difficult in the dark, she finally passed the apothecary where Aunt Sarah purchased needed herbs and remedies. She allowed herself a sigh of relief and a brief moment to catch her breath. Not much farther to go.

More confident now, she wove her way through the streets, backtracking only once until she found the house. A hastily roused house servant spoke through the door, "What you want at dis late hour?" he demanded, an irritated edge to his tone.

She struggled to regain her breath. "It's me... Keelan Grey. Please let me in."

The door flung open. The slave peered closer. "Miss Keelan? Dat really you?"

Simon! Thank goodness! Tears burned behind her eyes, her relief overwhelming. She wasn't sure what she'd have done if Uncle Jared had answered the door.

"Yes, Simon, it's really me," she panted. "Please... let me in."

He swung the door wide. "What's happened to you, Miss Keelan? Come in! Mr. Grey is here. Want me to hustle up to wake him, or should I fetch Ruth?"

"No!" Keelan answered quickly. Jared would lock her up again, and she'd be no better off than before. She hastily added. "I-I prefer Jared not see me."

The slave nodded in understanding. "Of course, Miss Keelan. I'll get Ruth to help you."

"Thank you, but I desperately need to get word to Daniel."

"He ain't in da house. Don' know what he done wrong dis time, but Mastah Grey locked him up in the barn."

Keelan frowned. Likely Jared's attempt to get Daniel to tell him her whereabouts. Information Daniel didn't have. Recalling the house slave's offer of assistance before, she decided to call in a favor. "Simon, I need your help."

"Yes, Miss Keelan, I can see dat. Stay here." The servant moved quickly down the hallway.

She waited a moment, not sure what Simon had in mind. Surely he wouldn't rouse Jared? Her stomach dropped, and her heart began to pound harder. She put her hand on the door handle and gave it a turn just as Simon reappeared.

"Here, Miss Keelan," he whispered. "Just leave it in the tack room door, and I'll put it back."

He pressed a key into her hand. A swell of relief softened her shoulders. She gave him a quick nod. "Thank you, Simon. I won't forget this."

"Stay safe, Miss Keelan." He reached around her and pulled the door open.

She slipped outside and darted to the darkened barn.

࿐

"DANIEL?" she whispered. "Daniel?"

"Mistress! Is that you?" he responded in a muffled whisper. The barn was dusty and dark. The night offered only the slightest sliver of moonlight.

"Where are you?" She peered into the shadows.

His voice became a little louder. "In the tack room."

She followed the sound of his voice. Keelan couldn't help glancing over her shoulder., expecting Gampo to emerge from every nook and every corner. "Why did he lock you in?" She worked the key in the door, but the lock didn't turn.

"Because you went missing. Jared got up and checked your room and found you gone. I've been so worried about you. Where have *you* been?"

Stubborn lock. Did Simon give her the wrong key? "I don't have time to explain," she answered. "We have to get away from here *now*. I'm being followed, I'm sure of it." The lock clicked, and she jerked open the door.

"Finally," she said.

"Who?" Daniel stepped out. "Who's following—Good Lord!" Catching sight of her standing in a tattered dressing gown and a man's overcoat, he paused and stared at Keelan in alarm. His eyes widened further when the links clinked against her leg.

She pinned him with a firm stare. This was not the time to revisit the past few hours. A shudder skittered down her spine. Those were memories she'd rather forget. "Daniel, we must go *now*!" How long would it be until Gampo and his men sought her out here?

Daniel whirled and ran to the rear of the barn. A moment later, he returned with a bulging feed sack slung over his shoulder. In his free hand, he clutched a new pair of boots and her waif's clothes.

"I purchased the boots for you after I delivered Slaney to her ship this morning," he said, handing them to her. Gesturing to the sack, he added, "I also hid some necessities in the barn in case we had to flee quickly. I wanted to be prepared in case any part of our plan went awry. Now I'm glad I took the precaution."

"Thank God you did," Keelan breathed. She couldn't be more grateful for the protection for her sorely abused feet. She quickly changed in the tack room, stuffed her torn clothes into Daniels sack, and together, they crept out to the street.

The night air remained still and thick. With the boots covering her feet, she was able to move more efficiently. By the time they reached the docks, Keelan had informed Daniel of the kidnapping, the suspicious involvement of Jared's warehouses, Gampo, and the rescue by Hart.

Daniel shook his head grimly. "I can't believe Jared would do such a thing,"

"Landon said much the same," Keelan whispered. "Yet, it seems too big a coincidence."

"Who was the tall man you spoke about?"

"He introduced himself as Gampo, the pirate with whom Captain Hart has been feuding. He kept his face covered and wore a long, dark cloak, and a large hat. For a moment, I thought it could be Everett, except this man was quick and skilled with a saber." Keelan recalled Everett's lack of grace in the ballroom. "He spoke only once, but after I struck his throat, he was only able to whisper."

Hopefully, the damage was permanent.

They heard the distant clop of hooves. The valet reversed direction and ushered her into a narrow alley, as a small cluster of men trotted past. The two fugitives pressed against the alley wall and held their breath.

Several more sets of footfalls approached from the opposite direction.

"Seen anything yet?" a low voice questioned.

"Nay, not a hair of either of 'em."

"We'll get the devil's pay if we don't find the lass fer the cap'n."

"Aye. I dinna want to be the one to tell 'im we couldn't find 'er."

"Best keep searchin'. He said she was probably headin' northeast, back to 'er Uncle's place off Queen Street. Remus, you head right there, and set up a look out for 'er. We'll work our way there."

"Aye."

The man who must have been Remus reined his horse around and took off at a gallop. After a few moments of discussion, the others decided to split up into three groups. Before long, they were on their way.

"You were right." Daniel glanced at her. "He's searching for you." He motioned for her to sit. "The Whistling Pig is nearby."

"Daniel, how will we pay..." She dropped to her knees, exhausted. What was left of her purse was back in Jared's town house.

The valet bent down and peered closely at her face. "I am not without coin, Mistress. Commodore Grey paid me well. And I made a vow to him that I would take you safely home, or wherever you wish to go." He nodded toward the harbor. "We *will* find our way." He knelt and took her hand, grimacing as the chains chinked in response.

"Miss Keelan. I love you as if you were my own daughter. I give you my oath, I will protect you until my death. You have always had my allegiance, and you always will. Never forget it."

She blinked away the tears setting fire to the backs of her eyes. She shook her head numbly. She didn't deserve such loyalty. "Daniel—"

He silenced her as he had done since she was a child, by holding his index finger in front of her nose.

"Please, Mistress, no more talk. You need rest and care."

Keelan leaned her head back against the bricks until the world stopped tilting. Her body throbbed with every beat of her heart. She became sharply aware of her burning legs and bruised feet and could no longer block out the flames of pain searing her shoulders and back. The muscles in her legs shook as she struggled to her feet. Sparks of fire fluttered across her shoulders. The sparks exploded in front of her eyes. Her vision narrowed until there was only one tiny little spark left.

And then even it went dark.

CHAPTER 16
NEVER BETRAY A PIRATE

Everett's chest burned as if the fires of hell were already beginning to consume him.

His plan had failed. *Failed!*

Instead of slipping into the upper room of the warehouse and retrieving Keelan as he'd planned, he'd had to turn and bolt back to his office. Something had gone wrong, and the warehouse had been overtaken. Gampo lurched down the iron steps outside the warehouse and bellowed curses at Keelan as she ran the other way down the side alley.

His words echoed in his head....

"Mark this—I will hunt ye down! You and that yellow-eyed bastard who bought ye! You'll pay dearly fer killing my first!"

Something had gone wrong, and now the pirate was enraged with both Keelan *and* him. His hands shook as he pulled a key from his pocket and shoved it toward the keyhole. It clattered to the cobblestones at his feet. Cursing, he picked it up and tried again. After several long seconds, he managed to unlock the door, slip inside and swiftly lock it again.

He had to get out of Charleston. His mind churned with useless options. He didn't own a horse, so escape by land was unavailable to him at this hour. There were three ships at the docks. It didn't matter where they were going, he needed to get aboard one of them.

Lurching to his desk, he yanked the chair out of the way then dropped to his knees. Not daring to light a lamp, he skimmed his fingers in the dark over the rough planks for the slight gap in the floorboard. Once located, he pulled it up and reached beneath the floor for the leather pouch of gold coins he'd hidden there. They clinked softly as he brought them up and tucked them into the inside pocket of his waistcoat. It was all that was left.

A fist hit the front door, sounding like a shot from a pistol.

"Open up ye spawn of a split-tongued, spindle-shanked scug," a voice growled from the other side.

Gampo!

Everett's blood congealed in his veins. He spun in panic. The fist hit the door again. Catching sight of the back stair in the shadows, he darted up the first flight, not even sure of what he would do when he reached the top, legs burning with the effort. The sound of breaking glass echoed up the stairwell, and he practically flew up the second flight.

"Where are ye, ye scabrous jellyfish! I'll have yer heart for breakfast, I will!"

Everett glanced down the stairwell to check if a figure moved toward him in the darkness. The sound of a flint followed instead, and a dull glow seeped up the stair.

The pirate had found the lantern. "Thought ye'd just be able to buy her, did ye? Corrupted my first with yer gold coins and promises of an easy mark. Know ye the penalty of turning my crew against my orders? Of runnin' with the slave traders? 'Tis death. Death!"

The pirate's bellow thundered up the stairwell, pounded through Everetts chest, slamming his heart against his ribs in terror.

Death.

Everett jolted and spun toward the window. He'd only wanted Keelan. He'd offered payment to Gampo if he kidnapped her for him. The man had *refused*. A pirate refused easy coin. It had bewildered Everett. But Gampo's first mate had been more enterprising.

He wasn't a slave trader, only a buyer. A buyer! Keelan would have been put on the block in the secret back halls of the black market underground, but he had arranged it so that his bid would win her. He'd be her savior. She'd have to marry him then. She'd be in his debt. He'd save her when Hart could not. She'd see that Everett was the only man who could take care of her.

Gampo's enraged voice continued, "'The cargo is easy pickins',' says he. 'No one will find it,' says he, the addle-brained bilge rat." The cracking of breaking wood and toppled bookshelves filtered up the stairwell.

Everett glanced around at his surroundings. Perhaps he could hide up here and wait until the pirate left, then he'd head over to the livery first thing in the morning and catch a coach north. Pirates didn't travel much to the north, did they? By land?

Highwaymen and Indian savages tormented travelers by land.

Everett's mind continued to churn. Gampo had remained in Charleston; perhaps his vessel was not yet seaworthy. An ocean passage might be both quicker and safer. He'd leave Charleston and go as far from the pirate as he could manage.

The light from the lantern began to grow and move. Was Gampo coming up the steps? The glow was still swelling, but its brightness was now muffled by a haze of smoke.

Fire!

Everett dashed to the staircase and glanced over the railing. Already the flames were beginning to lick at the bottom steps. He crept down and tried to peer through the smoke. Flames roared from his office. A surge of panic clutched his chest. His path out was blocked by the fire. Things were happening too fast. He couldn't keep his thoughts in order. What should he do?

Was there another way out? He gulped and took a deep breath. He was sweating. Knees shaking, he wrestled the window open, then leaned out and strained to make out details in the darkness. Another building stood across the narrow gap of the alley and it had a second-story balcony. Could he make the jump?

A shout echoed from the front of the building, sounding the alarm. Would Gampo be waiting in the shadows for him to flee the burning structure? If he was willing to burn down a building, the pirate would have no trouble waiting in an alley to sink a blade into his belly. Spurred by this new terrifying possibility, Everett placed a foot on the sill and heaved himself up until he was crouched in the window opening. Sweat dripped from his upper lip as he eyed the other balcony again.

More shouts rang out as nearby residents were awakened by the commotion and the smell of smoke. His breath was coming in quick, dry gasps.

Either jump or burn.

Jump or burn.

He jumped, then crashed into the wrought-iron railing before he managed to fling his arms over the top before his momentum changed from horizontal to vertical. He gripped two balusters and chanced a glance down. The ground appeared to be about ten feet or so away. His hands were sweating and even now his grip was beginning to fail. He had no choice. Letting go, he dropped to the ground, and bit back a cry at the stinging pain shooting through his ankle.

The alley was as unyielding as the railing and much filthier. It took him a moment to take account of his condition before he dared move. A sprained ankle and a bruised hip. He rolled over and pushed himself to his feet.

Move. Get away.

He limped away from the main road, through the back alleys and behind buildings until he came to the livery stable. The place was dark and vacant, except for a scraggly cat crouched in a

IF YOU GIVE A RAKE A REASON

corner perusing him with a wary gaze. Horses shuffled in their stalls, but otherwise, the place was quiet. Everett crept inside and climbed a ladder up to the loft. He collapsed on the hay and wept with both relief and terror.

Tomorrow he would take the first vessel out of the Charleston port. He didn't care where it was going.

CHAPTER 17
CHASING GAMPO

"Ye shouldn't have fought me,"

The voice echoed grotesquely in Keelan's ears as a hot pain flickered across her shoulder. Dry, sweltering darkness swooped down and surrounded her body. She cried out and thrashed until her fist made contact with something hard and warm. A shoulder?

Then, a soft baritone murmured in her ear, and she surfaced, her throat raw and burning from screaming.

"'Tis all right, lass. You are safe now. Hush, Keelan, you're safe, my sweet."

The heat suddenly left, replaced by a strange coolness. She groped for it in the darkness. Long, gentle fingers grasped her hand. A soft kiss fluttered like a butterfly against her palm. Strong arms cradled her head and shoulders. Long fingers stroked her hair. She floated into the comforting arms of Morpheus and dreamed no more.

KEELAN STIRRED, moaning softly. She rested on her stomach. The first attempt to open her lids brought forth a blinding light, forcing her to squeeze her eyes shut again. She brought her hand up as a shield and tried to open them once more. A blurry figure rose and moved to the window to pull the shutters closed.

Much better. She tried to focus on the form. "Daniel?" she mumbled, unsure.

"Nay, Keelan, it's me."

The voice was familiar, but her brain was still too fuzzy to be reliable. She was on a straw pallet covered by thick fabric. A soft quilt was drawn up to her shoulders. The bloodstained boy's shirt was gone, and in its place was a long linen one.

The figure dragged a squat, wooden stool to her bedside, then sat. It creaked as he leaned closer.

Landon.

Landon!

He was alive! Thank God.

He reached over and brushed a strand of hair away from her face. "You're in a boarding room above a tavern called The Whistling Pig. How do you feel?"

Her brain behaved as if it were coated with mud. Brief flashes of memory flickered in and out, as she fought to remember the events which brought her here. She struggled to sit up straighter. Bright bolts of fire shot across her shoulders. She sucked in her breath and eased back down to the pallet. The sting forced her memory to return quicker.

"How did you find me?"

"I didn't," he said wryly. "Although I tried. My men searched the streets for you until daybreak. We even kept watch over your uncle's house but never caught sight of you. It was Daniel who came here and found *me*."

He clasped his hands in front of him. A chair sat near the door, Daniel's sack resting against the front legs.

"Where is he now?" she asked.

"I sent him down to get some supper. I thought you might be hungry when you awoke."

As if it heard, her belly let out a loud growl. She gently rolled to her side, facing him. The heat of a blush traveled up her neck and over her cheeks at the sight of his bare chest. Apparently it was a state he found himself in quite often, because his skin had become a dark bronze from the rays of the sun. Ebony hair curled loose around his shoulders and framed his head like a great black mane. A strip of linen was wrapped around his ribs. Dried blood stained a six-inch patch on his side. His stomach was flat and firm, and the tan breeches he wore seemed to fit his body like a second skin.

Keelan snapped her eyes shut. After a second, she glanced furtively at his face and he met her gaze with an amused stare.

The fire in her cheeks was almost more humiliating than getting caught staring. A dark blue waistcoat hung on a hook near the door.

"Are you too warm, Captain Hart? Or is it difficult for you to conform to accepted modes of dress after spending so many months at sea?" She stared at the wall beside his head. It was hard, but she found a small crack in the plaster and so she focused on it. Unfortunately, he was still very visible.

Drat. She should have found a crack further away.

He grinned wider. "I found a more suitable use for my shirt today, Miss Grey," he said, imitating her formal address.

"Oh?" She raised a disbelieving brow. "What could be more suitable than using it to cover yourself in a woman's presence?" Should Daniel return and find the two of them alone in the room with Landon half dressed... well, what would he think?

Landon shrugged, still grinning, "I found someone in greater need than I. That's all. However, if I am offending you, I shall eagerly request it be returned to me, post haste."

She sighed at the guilt his words conjured. He had given his shirt to another in need and she had berated him for it. Her cheeks flamed hotter at his mockery of her stilted admonishment.

She studied her hands and shook her head, ashamed. Her nails were still covered in grime from the warehouse. She pushed up her sleeve to inspect her sore wrists. A bit of bruising and chafing, a couple places where she'd rubbed the top layer of skin off, but no more damage than that.

In the silence, he waited for her response. She finally met his gaze. He was still grinning like a... Well, she didn't know what, but he seemed to find something quite amusing, like a joke he was still waiting for her to comprehend.

She struggled to remember his last question. Something to do with his shirt, yes?

"Nay. I'm sorry. I am just unaccustomed—" She stopped herself. He would think her a child if she admitted she'd never seen a shirtless man before. She reached up, grasped her cuff, and pulled it back down over her arm. It extended well beyond her hand. She stared at it more closely. It wasn't a shift or a nightdress. The realization brought with it another bout of heat across her cheeks and probably her neck as well. Blast it all.

She was wearing a man's shirt.

And if she were given a hundred chances to guess *which* man's shirt, it wouldn't matter. She'd only need one. She fingered the fabric and then instinctively brought the collar to her nose.

And if she'd placed a bet on the name, she'd be right. It was faint, the musky scent of him and the sea and the sun.

She cleared her throat. "I guess what I should say is, I'm unaccustomed to taking the shirt off a man's back."

His dimples deepened. "I insist you keep it. It's much happier on you than it has ever been on me."

That provoked a small smile from her. "How could a shirt possibly show emotion for a person? How does a happy shirt look?"

His expression warmed, and his eyes softened to a darker blue.

"I can, for certain, tell this particular shirt loves you. See how it clings to your skin? Like a milk-sopped kitten? It's fallen hopelessly in love with you and yet has only known you a few short hours."

"If that's how you can tell, then most clothes must love their owners because most of them cling in some fashion or another." She tried not to look at his breeches again.

"Oh, not true, young maiden," Landon responded. "I can name several garments who are in extreme discord with their owners. Several of them belong to you, actually." He glanced left and right before whispering, "Renegades, all."

Keelan laughed. She couldn't help it. It was apparent Landon was diverting her attention from more serious matters by setting off on this verbal excursion into frivolity. She shouldn't encourage him, but she couldn't resist either.

"My wardrobe has always been extremely loyal, Captain Hart. Surely, I would know if there were rumors of such a discord."

He brought his hand to his chin, a finger resting across his mouth as if latching his lips shut. He sat up a bit straighter and spoke through his fingers. "Well, I for one have witnessed a few attempted escapes. Your green riding bonnet, for example, used those hideous peacock feathers sewn into the band to take flight from your head not once but twice. If you recall, I returned it to you the first time."

Her lips twitched, and she tried harder to restrain another laugh, because in all honesty, the picture was still vivid in her mind: Landon sitting on his horse, a leg thrown over the saddle horn, appearing as if he was perched on a woman's side saddle, with her bonnet sitting at a jaunty angle on his head. It made her giggle every time she thought of it. This time was no exception.

"And as *I* recall, when it was perched on your head it seemed quite at home."

"Of course it did. It knows a solid equestrian when it encounters one. I imagine it felt safer on my top than yours."

She narrowed her eyes in mock anger. "Then, good riddance to the treasonous article. To abandon a lady in her time of need—how lecherous. And deceitful."

Landon cocked his head as if searching his memory. "I do recall a jacket also left without bidding you a 'good day,' as well."

"I had tied it to my saddle. I thought quite securely," she said dryly.

"Ah, yet it departed, nonetheless. Along with a skirt, and a blouse..." His voice lowered a level. "And a shift, and a chemise, until there were... none."

The lighthearted banter they had been sharing shifted down a deeper, sultry path. The warmth of the day intruded into the room through an open window, and a thin film of perspiration covered her chest and arms.

He'd caught her bathing in a lake a few weeks ago and seemed unwilling to forget it, much to her embarrassment. It had been a foolish, impetuous decision on her part on a stiflingly hot, humid day. She'd had no idea he followed her.

"If I recall correctly, you intruded, *uninvited*, upon a lady bathing." Disrupting a perfectly tranquil moment at the lake where she had floated, peaceful and relaxed, leading to a brief second of shock, then to an intense surge of panic, which then lead to her to floundering for air, taking her deeper into the lake at which time she merely sunk.

And he'd taken his time helping her.

Dimples deepened, making her heart do that stupid flip. "It's a good thing, too. Had I not been there, the lake would have swallowed you whole," he said.

She tossed him a wry frown. "I was sinking, yet you took the time to remove your boots and stockings," she accused. "Although, I understand, taking off one's own boots can be a tedious task," she said. "And could take quite a long time, depending on the fit."

"Aye, but they are handsome boots. Made specifically for my

foot by a talented Baracoan cobbler." Landon leaned back on the stool and propped his booted feet across the corner of her bed. The tall black boots were, of course, polished to an ebony shine. "The water would have ruined them."

"So you felt the need to save the boots before the maiden in distress," she countered, unable to still the twitch of her lips. "It makes me wonder where I might rank in the scheme of things in your life."

He took her hand and kissed her fingers. "The angels must tilt their head up to find your spot in my heart, sweet Keelan."

Warmth spread through her chest, down to swirl in her belly. He still wanted her. Did he love her? He'd never said so, but she desperately wished he did. Her heart, she feared, was already hopelessly lost to him, although she wasn't sure how, or if, she could yet admit it to him.

"Your side..." She gestured to the bloodied bandage, desperate to change the subject.

"It's not deep." He glanced at the wrap. "Mrs. Schoen dressed it for me."

The memory of all that blood streaming from his side made her shudder. "Thank you for helping me escape that awful place." A shiver clenched her spine, and she closed her eyes, took a deep breath and pushed away the terrible images from her dream. "You saved my life, of that I'm sure."

"And you saved mine at least once, if not twice," he countered softly. "I am forever in *your* debt, my sweet."

Seizing on the opportunity to take advantage of his silver-tongue, she arched a brow. "If I recall your teachings correctly, in some cultures, you would now owe me a life debt and would have to stay with me until a situation arose where you could save my life in return," she quipped.

A slow grin crept across his face. Azure eyes deepened to a molten navy, swirling with something heated and sensual. "Then I would make sure you were never in danger, so I'd have to stay with you forever."

Her breath hitched. She pressed her palms against her stomach, in a vain effort to keep the darn thing from hatching the thousand butterflies housed there. Why did the man have to be so incredibly handsome? She suddenly realized that she'd protect him with her life if the occasion ever surfaced again.

The vision of Crowe stalking toward Landon's back, blade raised high, invaded her mind. She shuddered.

"Crowe, is he—?"

"Dead? Yes." Landon sobered. Concern lingered in his gaze.

Keelan closed her eyes, sickened. She had killed Gampo's first mate. Her stomach lurched as the bile rose in her throat. A clean chamber pot seemed to appear from thin air as she heaved.

Several wretchedly embarrassing moments later, Landon eased her back to her pillow. From the stool beside her pallet, he studied her, without mockery or disgust. For that, she was grateful and a little less humiliated by losing what small bit had been in her stomach.

"It's understandable, Keelan," he consoled in a low stay voice. "You defended yourself, and me, for that matter. You cannot be blamed for what you did, under the circumstances. It is obvious you are not of the ilk to kill without cause."

"I have never killed a man," she whispered hoarsely. A new fear twisted inside her. "And he wasn't just any man, Landon. He was Gampo's first mate."

Landon's eyes widened for a brief second before they hardened. The muscles in his jaw clenched. "Gampo. He's never pursued us ashore before. He's always tried to intercept us along our trade routes. He's taken this animosity to an elevated level, although I don't understand the cause." Landon rubbed the heels of his hands over his closed eyes. For a moment, he appeared incredibly weary. He leaned his forearms on his knees.

Landon's reaction baffled her. Unless... "Have you seen Gampo before?" she asked.

He shook his head. Again, the vivid azure gaze locked on hers.

Fynn. What had Gampo said about Fynn? Something about a sister?

"It sounded as if Gampo had a personal vendetta against Fynn. What did Fynn do to his sister?"

Landon gave a shrug and shook his head again. "I don't know who his sister is, or was. I don't even know if she's alive or dead. Fynn never mentioned anything about Gampo, other than he was a pig-headed privateer who'd turned into an outright pirate over the years."

"But whatever it was, it's made Gampo your enemy, too." She stilled at the other thoughts pounding a warning inside her head. "Now, I'm his enemy as well."

Landon's eyes clouded as he nodded. "This development changes things. You aren't safe here. I must get you out of Charleston as soon as possible." There was something else hiding in the depths of those dark blue irises. A flicker of anger? Fear? Distrust?

Landon rubbed his forehead and closed his eyes. After a moment, he added, "Gampo overheard our conversation, Keelan. He's connected you to me now."

When she'd escaped down the warehouse steps, he'd called out to her.

"You will not escape me, Keelan Grey!"

Landon picked up her hand and rubbed little circles over her knuckles, sending little zips of lightning up her arms. "He will seek me out to find *you*."

Keelan's brow furrowed. "So what do we do?"

Landon took a deep breath, expelled it, and stared down at his hands. "We must separate. The sooner you are safely away from Charleston, the better. I'll arrange for you to travel with a friend of mine. Although he doesn't normally take passengers, he will take you and Daniel to safety. His ship is scheduled to depart tomorrow for Philadelphia. When you arrive, leave a message as to your location with the harbormaster, he's a friend. I'll find you."

A pang of disappointment pressed into her heart. She wanted to stay with him. Gampo would seek them out, but it didn't matter. Landon was her haven. She felt safer with him than without him. Besides, who would watch his back?

His voice still echoed earnest and warm in her ears: *"Sail away with me, Keelan. Let me show you the world..."*

His jaw clenched, and he paused before he captured her gaze again. "This war with Gampo has to end. I'm unwilling to put your life at risk or constantly worry about your safety. Once Conal and I hunt down Gampo and end this, I'll sail to Philadelphia. I have friends there who will take care of you until I return."

A painful stretching sensation gripped her heart. She didn't want to leave him. If the pirate fled Charleston, how far would Landon have to chase Gampo? To the Caribbean? South America? How long would she wait and worry in Philadelphia, not knowing if he was alive or dead?

This was no longer solely his battle. It was hers now, too.

"No," her voice was low but firm. "I won't run away and hide while you put your life in danger for me. I'm not a coward."

"Keelan, love—" he began.

"No." She cut him off before he could ply his honeyed words and infuriating logic. She wasn't going to give him a chance to try to change her mind. "I won't go anywhere except with you."

He sighed and tried again. "My ship hasn't been fully repaired and restored yet. You can't stay in Charleston. The longer you stay, the greater the chance Gampo's men will find you. I'm not able to accommodate you as efficiently. Besides, you'll be safer if you *aren't* with me. Gampo would be a fool to engage the *USS Glory*. You'll be protected."

She pressed her lips into a thin line.

Stubborn man.

Well, she could be just as determined. "You don't understand what I'm saying, Landon. I don't want to be protected and safe unless I'm with you. Besides, I'm not helpless."

He rolled his eyes in exasperation. "While I admire your courage and skill with blades and swords, battles at sea are nothing like training exercises in a forest meadow with a man old enough to be your father."

Anger flared. "What are you saying? My skills aren't good enough to prevent me from being a burden rather than a self-sufficient member of your crew?" How dare he. She lifted her chin and lowered her brows.

He shifted on the stool and scratched the back of his head before answering, "I wouldn't have said it in those words, but, yes. You'd distract me. I'd worry I wouldn't be able to take care of you."

"I can take care of myself!" she snapped, indignant. Annoyed now. Why was he being so obstinate? "I have an idea," she continued hotly. "*You* travel on the *USS Glory* and *I'll* go after Gampo. I'll come fetch you when the battle is ended. You can stay with your friends and wait for me."

Landon flung his arms out wide. "That's preposterous!"

"How so?" she asked. "It's your plan."

"My plan is to keep you safe! I'd never leave you to battle Gampo alone," he snapped back.

"Exactly!"

"You—what? You agreed with me," he said warily.

He was so infuriating, she could scream. She jabbed her finger in his direction. "I can't let you leave me behind to battle Gampo alone. It's would be as hard for me as it would be for you, if we changed places."

He shook his head in bewilderment. "Keelan, it's completely different."

"It is *not*."

"It is *too*." His expression had darkened and when a knock sounded at the door, he barked, "Who's there?"

"'Tis Mrs. Schoen, sir."

He rose from his seat, then scowling, pointed at her. "This discussion is not over."

"Damn right, it's not!" she retorted back.

He paused for a moment and stared at her with lowered brows, but she met his stare with a determined intensity. He reached the door and jerked it open.

A plump, cheery-faced woman waddled in, tray on her hip and a pitcher in her hand. "Och! Goot. Yur awake. I haf something for yu to eat, my dear." Her smile was wide and warm. She shifted her attention to Landon. "Herr Hart, der iss a man waiting for yu downstairs. He says it iss urgent." She nodded toward Keelan. "I vould like to tend to der young woman's wounds, if is ok?"

"Of course, Frau Schoen." He yanked his jacket from the hook, and Keelan caught the slight grimace as he shrugged it on. He bent down and spoke quietly in Mrs. Shoen's ear.

She nodded her head vigorously.

He inclined his head, *"Danke."*

Wait! Don't go!

Keelan bit her lower lip to keep herself from blurting out those words. Contrary to what Landon believed, she felt safer with him than she did without him. She'd worry less about him, certainly.

Landon paused and glanced back over his shoulder at her. "I will speak with Daniel regarding the details of your departure once I have secured them. God speed, Keelan."

He left.

Blast that stubborn man! If he thought she was going to sit idly by and do his will like a reticent little girl, then he was most surely mistaken.

CHAPTER 18

A GIFT

By the next morning, the pain in Keelan's back and feet had eased a small amount. She sat up in bed enjoying an omelet flavored with small pieces of shallots and parsley, several mutton sausages, hot tea and bannocks made from Indian corn meal. She smoothed the front of Landon's long shirt she still wore. She really wanted the trunk and clothes she'd left at Jared's, although it was doubtful there was a safe way to get to them now.

A thump sounded outside her door. She heard a dull scraping sound as if something heavy was being pushed over the wooden plank floor. Following a light rap, the door opened a crack.

Mrs. Schoen poked her head in and grinned. "Goot morgen child. You are enjoying der food? I vill return to dress your wounds shortly, ya?"

Keelan smiled. "Thank you, Mrs. Schoen. Everything is delicious."

The woman grinned again. "Der is some ting here for you." She nudged the door wide and pushed a new standard trunk into the room.

Keelan eyed it curiously as she enjoyed her scone. Gesturing to the trunk, she said, "I am afraid you are mistaken, Mrs. Schoen. That's not mine."

The gleaming brass rivets and hinges contrasted starkly with the blunt walls, lumpy pallet, and rickety wooden chairs.

"It vas delivered this morgen. The man said to give you dis note." She handed over a small calling card.

It was Landon Hart's. He had written a message on the back, which she read quickly.

❧❧

JARED AND EVERETT at all costs. Do not return or send for your property. There are men looking for you both in town and in the country. My friend Commodore Hall will take you to Philadelphia tomorrow aboard the USS Glory. *Daniel is in agreement and will accompany you. I've known the Schoen's a long time. You can trust them to keep your secrets. Any communications to me should be sent through them. I hope the contents of the trunk suit you well.*

Your Servant,

Landon

❧❧

HA. Did he think Daniel's acquiescence to his arrangements would sway her mind? Although her anger and frustration had subsided since his departure, her convictions had not. Let him try to keep her from going with him.

Curious though, she climbed out of the bed and accepted the key from Mrs. Schoen and knelt to unlock the trunk. As she lifted the lid, she heard the Innkeeper's wife draw in a slow breath.

"Ooooh!" Mrs. Schoen said from over her shoulder. "Dat iss yust vat you need, ya? Iss goot."

She touched the soft silk chemise and stockings. "Oh, yes," she answered softly. "It's very, *very* good." Sliding several undergarments aside revealed two beautiful gowns. One was a soft gray, the other a deep green. A velvet cloak of the same dark green lay folded beneath the gowns. She also found two pair of slippers tucked neatly into the bottom, along with a bonnet identical to the one she lost during the storm without the feathers. She smiled.

"Would you please bring up some writing supplies? I must write a note of thanks to Captain Hart."

Mrs. Schoen nodded knowingly and grinned. "I will bring up to you."

In her note, she thanked Landon for the clothes. She also told him she appreciated his efforts to get her and Daniel safely to Philadelphia.

She didn't say, however, she would actually go.

❧

THE NEXT DAY Keelan was able to move about the room with relative ease. Her back would be sore for days, but Mrs. Schoen's constant tending had kept infection at bay and sped the healing process. There were few places on her body that weren't sore or tender, and after spending the last two days prone, her joints were creaky and weak. To get her legs limber again, she limped about the room. She had donned the new chemise and stockings, but with a defined shudder had omitted the corset. Her attempt at putting on the gown was met with partial success as she stepped into the skirt and pulled the bodice up over her shoulders. The fit was amazingly accurate. Either Landon was fairly talented at estimating a lady's size or extremely lucky.

Eager to be on her way, she packed Landon's now clean and dry coat into the trunk he had sent yesterday, along with his shirt. Pausing, she ran her hand over the fabric. He'd provided a way to contact him through the Schoens, and it gave her a calmer sense of strength and faith. A knock on the door jarred her from her musings. "Come in," she beckoned.

Daniel stepped into the room. His concerned gaze searched her face beseechingly. "I have been so worried. Mrs. Schoen kept assuring me you were healing well, but I finally had to see for myself."

She smiled. "I'm glad you're here. I am much better, as you can see." She moved toward the open door. "I have a strong need for some air and a short walk. Would you stroll with me a bit?" she asked.

Daniel fidgeted. "I am afraid I have some bad news."

Her first thought was of Slaney. "Bad news?" The maid's ship had sailed a few days ago. "What is it?"

"At Captain Hart's suggestion, I have been spending the last two days down at the docks. He hopes to find out who had you kidnapped. He seems to think Gampo wouldn't have gone to this length, putting his crew in peril, unless he had an advantage of some sort. An informant or man in Charleston who could give him access to important information."

"That seems to be a lot to accomplish."

Daniel shrugged and added, "The captain believes they are connected and one man is responsible."

"Connected?" This was confusing. "I don't understand how I could be connected with the events surrounding Captain Hart's cargo theft."

Giving her a thoughtful look, he suggested, "Jared Grey owned *both* warehouses involved in the theft. The one originally storing the goods, and also the one used to hide them."

The connection was easy to identify. Keelan sucked in her breath. "Captain Hart mentioned that. I had forgotten. He thinks Jared might be involved?" She was convinced now Dr. Garrison was behind the series of tragic events surrounding her family and her, but she couldn't fathom why he'd involve Captain Hart.

"It's possible that he's a common link." Daniel acknowledged.

"However, that doesn't mean that he's responsible. It could be someone who works for him, someone who would have access to the keys. There's no solid proof yet. The few pirates they captured the night he found you have refused to talk. Sheriff Pinkerton hopes their tongues will loosen when they are paraded past the gallows."

Everett could be involved, although the sudden transformation from a bumbling, yet well-meaning physician to a deranged kidnapper was hard to believe. A cold sensation skittered up her spine. It may not be that far a leap from a deranged jilted beau to a deranged kidnapper.

"What is your bad news then?" she asked.

"Mr. Schoen told me Gampo's men are searching for you."

"I know, Captain Hart mentioned it in his note."

"There is a reward for your capture, now." Daniel hesitated before continuing and eyed her carefully, "You are wanted for the murder of a man named Crowe."

Keelan gaped at Daniel. It was a moment before she could speak. "Murder! But—he—I did not mean to—he was about to stab Captain Hart!" She inhaled deeply and drew herself taller. "Take me to the sheriff this moment. I am sure once he hears all the details—"

"No, Mistress." Daniel shook his head. "Captain Hart fears if your location is known, your life would be in danger. You must understand, Keelan, it is not the law who wants you. It's *Gampo*. Descriptions of you have been given to most of the dockworkers and any ship's crew still in port, along with the promise of quite a large reward for finding you."

A sudden frigid blade of dread sliced through her, as the meaning of Daniel's message sank in. Keelan's hand crept shakily to her throat, where she could feel the erratic pulse of her heart, and she sat down with an unladylike thump.

The manservant sighed heavily. "I'm sorry. You simply cannot be seen in this city as Keelan Grey, without risk of capture by thugs employed by Gampo, or those eager for his coin."

"No wonder Landon's note said to avoid sending for my property or going back to the town house." Keelan swallowed and met the valet's determined stare.

"There's more, Miss Keelan." He took a note from his pocket. "The harbormaster gave this to me. Commodore Hall received an urgent request to set sail to Philadelphia posthaste to fend off a British blockade. They left yesterday at dawn."

"Oh. Well, good." She almost smiled. Landon's plan had failed of its own accord. He'd have no choice now but to let her go with him to find Gampo.

"Good?" Daniel looked at her curiously.

She glanced out the window, a bit embarrassed. "Captain Hart and I had a small disagreement with regard to the trip to Philadelphia on the *USS Glory*."

Daniels lips twitched. "Ah, then."

At her raised brows, he clarified, "It explains the state of irritation he was in when he and I spoke yesterday."

"He was being unreasonable," she mumbled.

Daniel cocked his head and grinned, unable to remain stoic any longer. "He said as much about you."

She might be stubborn, but she'd come out the victor this time. The walls of the small rustic room heaved in even closer. She wasn't sure she had the fortitude to hide out in the attic of The Whistling Pig for too much longer. Already, the heat and the cramped space made her long for fresh air and a brisk walk. "We should get word to Captain Hart straight away."

Daniel ran his bony fingers through his hair and shook his head. "I tried, but the *Desire* loaded her cargo yesterday evening and set sail down the coast early this morning, just prior to the *USS Glory*."

A small thunderstorm blossomed in Keelan's chest.

He left her behind! Landon weighed anchor to draw Gampo

and his men away from Charleston and her. He was probably in the midst of a sea battle right now. Stubborn, unreasonable man!

How could he depart when he told her only yesterday the repairs weren't yet complete? Unless... unless he'd been *lying* yesterday.

An even more horrible thought floated to the top of her mind. Was he trying to get *rid* of her?

Putting her on Commodore Hall's frigate and also saying the *Desire* was not ready to sail was easier than telling her he'd changed his mind. He sailed *south*. In the opposite direction she was to go. Was he *fleeing* from her?

A loud rush of noise filled her ears, and the skin on her face prickled as if a thistle had been tossed at it. Maybe he didn't believe her when she'd told him Garrison's kiss was unwanted and undesired. He may have decided he couldn't trust her. Perhaps he'd come to the conclusion that having a woman in his life was simply too much trouble. Maybe seeing Garrison kiss her had brought back too many painful memories. A thousand thoughts and fears bombarded her head.

Slaney had warned her. Mother had warned her. She had warned herself.

A man of the sea always returns to the sea.

She recalled all her fears about falling in love with Landon Hart, all the reasons why she shouldn't have allowed herself to fall for his charms, all the warnings... But she had wanted to believe him, wanted to hope they could be happy together but those things had betrayed her, blinded her.

It had been foolish to ignore the warnings.

She would never be able to take the place of his first love, a life of adventure upon the sea.

A horrible empty chasm opened in her chest and sucked in every moment of happiness, every second of bliss, every shard of hope into darkness. leaving nothing but raw desolation in its wake.

He was gone.

Tears burned in her eyes. She'd hoped a fool's hope. So much had transpired over the past day. Landon's love for his ship and the prosperity of his business remained the most important parts of his life. A trip north would endanger him and his crew. Gampo's sole purpose now was finding and punishing *her*. Even worse, Landon and his fleet were not the targets of Gampo's revenge, *she* was. He could be simply taking advantage of the distraction she provided so he could flee unnoticed. But that was a coward's route and she may not have known Landon Hart very long, but she did know enough about him to understand that he was no coward.

She wanted so desperately to believe Landon cared about her and was trying to protect her. Still, she'd known him only a few weeks. Was he capable of such deceit and treachery? Was she so blinded by her attraction to him? It's possible his true nature hid behind his handsome features and charm, like Garrison's had hidden behind his gentle demeanor and kindness.

Daniel waited patiently for her to regain her attention. She'd known him her entire life and could tell he had more to divulge. She immediately read the expression on his face. "You already have a plan," she stated.

Daniel bit back a smile. "Yes, I do."

She took a breath and released it. "And I can tell I'm not going to like it much."

The corners of Daniels mouth twitched before he grinned. "No, Mistress, you are not going to like it at all."

CHAPTER 19

THE DISGUISE

"I've managed to gain some interesting information," Daniel said, "Mr. and Mrs. Schoen seem to have a network of informants in the area. They might be able to help us." Daniel plucked his sack from the hook by the door and started looking through it. "I suspect the couple either harbors runaway slaves or provides information to assist them."

"I wondered about that," Keelan murmured. There'd been something about Landon's familiarity with the couple and a comment he'd made about gleaning information from them that had her curious, but there hadn't been an opportunity to ask for elaboration.

"Mrs. Schoen told me she'd heard Gampo wasn't the man in charge of Hart's cargo theft or the kidnapping," Daniel said. "Gampo has a silent employer, but no one seemed to know his name."

Keelan paced the floor. "As hard as it is to believe, I strongly suspect Dr. Garrison is involved somehow." His behavior these past few weeks changed. Drastically.

"He could have let the kidnappers into the house," Daniel mused, nodding.

She paused as her mind began to make other connections. "He had access to the warehouse keys." Daniel stopped rummaging and gave her his full attention.

The more she thought about it, the more sense it made. "It would have been easy for Garrison to borrow any of Jared's warehouse keys," she said. "Uncle Jared kept a spare set in his desk at Twin Pines." The full realization of what she was saying was overwhelming. She abruptly sat on the stool by her bed. Dread settled on her shoulders as a darker thought seeped into her mind. It was horrible. Ludicrous. Yet—made sense, somehow. "He's too smart to get personally involved, which could explain why no one captured at the warehouse knows the name of their employer.

"But why?" Daniel asked, shocked. "Why would he do such a thing?"

The doctor had been pleased that she was of no blood kin to the commodore. That fact had been important to him. "The passenger ship Papa accidentally destroyed," she thought aloud. "The assassin began targeting Papa's family shortly after the court martial." She clasped her hands together until her fingers ached, not wanting to accept what her mind was nudging her toward.

Daniel nodded. "Your mother's carriage accident was first. The commodore's brother's family was killed shortly after. Then the commodore became ill."

"Dr. Garrison mentioned something about losing loved ones at sea," she said, certain now that she was correct. Daniel's eyes widened, and he finished her thought for her. "This is all about revenge, isn't it?"

"If he had loved ones on the ship, he has reason to be angry."

Now she understood. *Rachel.*

More than once, he had called Keelan by that name. He carried a tattered letter from Rachel in his coat pocket, expressing her happy anticipation of their wedding day. Keelan's throat went dry.

Good Lord.

"It has to be Dr. Garrison," she breathed, glad she was seated.

"But what about the commodore's older brother?" Daniel asked. "Garrison was here when he was killed."

One didn't have to be present to be involved, did they? "He had Gampo's help here," she said. "He could have had another man's help in England."

"True." Daniel paced the small room. "When I spoke to Captain Hart, he said he suspected his ship was being watched. The other piers had spies as well, along with Mr. Grey's house in Charleston." He paused and looked at her, concerned. "That means that *both* Gampo and Garrison are searching for you."

"I'll wear my sparring clothes and boots and disguise myself as a boy." She had fooled Landon Hart and Conal O'Brien the day she met them, hadn't she? And at close proximity.

Daniel's gaze lingered on her long auburn tresses. "You'll have to cut it, you know."

She sighed and waved her hand. "It's hair. It will grow back."

A quick knock broke into their conversation. Daniel stepped over to the door and opened it. Mrs. Schoen bustled in, bringing with her a strong odor of burned ham and carrying a bucket and several rags. She sat it on the small table. Straightening, she put her hands on her hips. "You haf' to leave. Der is no time to wait for anudder ship to come going north to Philadelphia. You must leave now. I vill help."

"What? Why?" The sudden turn of events was a surprise. She glanced at Daniel. The grim set of his mouth told her he wasn't as shocked as she.

"Gampo's men are downstairs," Mrs. Schoen said in a hushed voice. "They asked to inspect the rooms for rent and I suspect if we deny them, they will make tings difficult."

Keelan pressed a hand over her thundering heart. Would the pirates insist on searching the attic? Either way, she wasn't ready to find out.

Mrs. Schoen put the rags in the bucket and continued, "A ship leaves at sunrise in der morgen. My husband has arranged for yu employment. I vill work to hide you better, so you can leave here safely."

"I have a set of boy's clothes and boots," Keelan said, glancing at Daniel, hoping he was right and the Schoen's could be trusted.

Mrs. Schoen lifted a strand of Keelan's hair and shook her head. "Is not enough to change your clothing. Your hair is like a beacon. We must extinguish it or you vill be discovered."

"Extinguish it, how?" What solution was the woman about to offer? Cutting her hair was fine, but she wasn't about to shave her head.

"It's too risky for her to try to travel as a woman," Daniel said. "We could simply cut her hair and wrap it in a scarf or hide it under a hat."

"Und if der wind took der hat? Her hair got out of der scarf? She would be spotted immediately, and turned over to Gampo," Mrs. Schoen said. She pointed to the bucket. "I've made a dye. It vill stain your skin for several days. You vill not be noticed."

Keelan sat in silent surrender as Daniel trimmed her auburn mane up to her shoulders.

Mrs. Schoen merrily scooped up the fallen tresses. "Der local toy maker vill be so happy to have dis beautiful hair for his dolls."

She hoped he would pay Mrs. Schoen well for delivering the long red curls. It was the least she could do for the woman who had taken such good care of her and Daniel.

The next step was applying the dark brown stain to their skin. Made out of boiled black oak bark, black walnut hulls, a small amount of molasses and soot from a burned hog carcass, it was pungent but effective. Daniel left to pack his things, giving Keelan and Mrs. Schoen some privacy to apply the dye.

Several times, Mrs. Schoen soaked a rag in the mixture and rubbed it over Keelan's arms, legs, face and neck. She carefully dabbed the dye around the wounds on her shoulders and back, then for good measure ran it through her hair.

"A little less like a flame, eh?" she had asked, grinning.

A little more like a tiger.

She had to admit, it did mute the auburn tones quite a bit. She picked up the rag and rubbed it through the rest of her hair.

When it was all said and done, Keelan could pass for any one of several nationality types. And she smelled very much like a charred ham.

Mrs. Schoen bade her a cheerful farewell and left to deliver the bucket of dye to Daniel.

Keelan almost didn't recognize him when he returned. "Well?" he said as he turned before her.

"You look like a Spaniard I once met," she replied, grinning.

"We are Persian," he corrected. "I am Kahlil, a horse trainer, and you are my son, Mahdi."

Mrs. Schoen appeared at the door. "It is time to go. My husband has served Gampo's men a sample of his new bier." She grinned. "He is walking among them asking dem how dey like it. Dey are not noticing der back door now."

Keelan and Daniel moved as quietly as they could along the upstairs hallway, but it wasn't easy carrying her new trunk. She looked at the narrow stairwell warily. Not only was it narrow, the steps were steep. Unfortunately, not only was it the only passage to the first floor, it also ended at the back of the common room.

Mrs. Schoen went ahead of Daniel and waited at the bottom, holding open the kitchen door. Daniel heaved the end of the chest up and led the way, taking most of the weight. However, she, stooped over and panting from the strain, still struggled with the back end. Each step down was precarious and stretched the tender wounds on her back.

Daniel reached the lower landing and turned toward the kitchen door. They'd made it. She let out an audible sigh of relief when her foot touched the last step.

Except...it wasn't the last step.

Her miscalculation threw her off balance and slammed her

into the wall, jarring the trunk from her grasp. It fell to the floor with a loud bang.

She froze. The room became deathly silent. Scowling and scarred faces turned their way. Her heart hit the walls of her chest; she was too terrified to breathe.

Mrs. Schoen's eyes widened.

Oh no. What had she done?

Mrs. Schoen recovered first and stomped her foot, releasing her hold on the door. "Vat are you doing?" She reached over and slapped the side of Keelan's head. "You clumsy boy! I told you to be careful! Now pick up dat trunk and pay attention or I'll take my husband's belt to yur hide!" She jerked open the door to the kitchen. "Git going! And have a care, dis time."

The men's attention shifted back to their drinks and conversation resumed. Daniel gave Keelan a relieved nod. She grasped the handle and followed him into the kitchen. Mrs. Schoen held open the far back door leading to the back alley. Once they made it outside, they lowered the trunk to the ground for a moment's rest.

Mrs. Schoen cast a furtive glance up and down the alley. "I tink you vill be goot from here." She gave Keelan an apologetic smile. "I hope I didn't swat your noggin too hard."

"I'm fine." She threw her arms around the woman's neck. "Thank you for helping us."

Mrs. Schoen patted the back of her head and kissed her cheek. "Yur velcome, child. God bless, and goot luck. Yu vill always be welcome here."

CHAPTER 20
NEW HANDS

K eelan and Daniel could have been any light brown-skinned man and his son as they shuffled along the street. Both held tightly to opposite handles of the trunk. Daniel's soiled gray sack was perched on the lid and tied with a short piece of rope.

It was a bright, sunny spring afternoon in Charleston. King Street was a flurry of activity as hawkers scurried about setting up their carts with wares of every sort, vegetables, jams, wine, fruits, baskets, brightly colored yarns, meat pies, smoked hams, candles, livestock and a plethora of other necessities both big and small. Women tried to save the hems of their skirts by jumping over the slimy stream of malodorous run-off oozing along the curb, then stepping lightly across the slippery cobblestones, careful to avoid the piles of waste deposited by the various beasts of burden traveling the streets.

Daniel stopped at the base of a ramp leading up to a large ship. It had three tall masts and a variety of canoes and longboats attached to the sides.

"Must have been a whaling ship at one time." Daniel tilted his head up and examined vessel.

Keelan caught her breath as she read the name painted on the side. The *Seeker*. Captain Conal O' Brien's ship, part of the same merchant fleet as Landon's ship, the *Desire*.

Captain O'Brien probably planned to follow the *Desire* south to Harbour Town, so their fleet of three could reunite and sail together. She'd almost balked when she learned they'd have to travel on the *Seeker*. If Landon didn't want her with him, why accept passage on a ship guaranteed to travel with him? He'd think she was chasing him like a loose duck, feeding his arrogance. Except, she *would* have chased him like a loose duck, anyway. She wasn't about to let him go south without her, or without telling her the truth about how he felt about her.

It didn't matter, the *Seeker* was not just their best choice, it was their only choice.

A stout, grizzled sailor sat on a small wooden crate near the ramp. He raised a shaggy brow as they lowered the trunk, and Daniel straightened to full height. He withdrew a tattered handkerchief from his sleeve to mop his face. He replaced the cloth and approached the sailor.

"I beg your pardon, sir. We have come at the suggestion of Mr. Schoen to inquire about employment. Does this vessel require additional hands?"

Keelan rounded her shoulders and did her best to look inconsequential?

The sailor scratched his chin thoughtfully as he eyed both of them.

Her fingers twitched nervously, and she studied the sailor's countenance. He was likely wondering if their claim to have been sent by Mr. Schoen was true. If he decided it was false, he'd reject them; they'd have to travel by land, which would be much more dangerous. They'd be mistaken for runaways, for sure.

She glanced at Daniel. They had dressed carefully. Their clothes were well-worn but clean. Both wore sturdy leather boots. Daniel's graying hair was pulled back and tied with a short yellow ribbon. Her now shoulder-length brown hair was secured in a similar manner. Mrs. Schoen had given her a worn straw hat. It flopped lazily on her head and she was glad for the protection from the sun, as well as from prying eyes.

"Aye, Schoen mentioned ye. We'll take ye." He held out his hand. "Name's Henry."

"I'm Khalil." Daniel shook it, then gave the sailor a brief bow. "This is my son, Mahdi."

"What skills bring ye to this ship?" Henry asked.

Daniel placed his hand on her shoulder. "This lad can cipher well. He can also cook and is knowledgeable in the use of healing herbs. I can also cipher and care for livestock. We can both handle arms of almost any kind." He drew himself up straight and raised his chin. "We are hard workers and have strong backs. While we have never worked aboard such a fine ship as this, we are quick learners."

Henry continued to study the two before him. Was Daniel's refined speech was confusing him?

"Are ye wanted for any crimes in the colonies or against the Crown?"

Daniel shook his head. "Nay, sir."

The sailor nodded, satisfied. "We lost our cook's helper a few weeks back, so the lad..." he nodded toward Keelan, "might be of use." He squinted at the older man. "How well do ye handle horses?"

"I ran a stable for my employer in England. Until his recent death, I also served as his personal servant."

The sailor nodded again. "That explains the way ye speak. The hold contains four horses, which are quite valuable. We needs a horse master with skills for care and healing. One of the mares thrashed about as we loaded her and has a nasty gash in her foreleg along with a couple of other scrapes."

Daniel felt that posing as Persians should help them avoid too much speculation from slave traders regarding their cultural orientation. Daniel had good instincts.

"Ship sails tomorrow. First light." Henry jerked his head in the direction of the ship. "Go on up and talk to Remus. Mention Schoen sent ye."

Daniel inclined his head in gratitude. "We thank you, sir."

Keelan reached down, grasped the handle, and helped Daniel heave the trunk up the plank. So far, Daniel's plan was working, thank the Lord.

The man named Remus sat on a barrel near the mainmast, a large leather-bound book perched on his knees. Mousy, brown hair hung straight down to his jaw. He was thick and muscled, making the book seem tiny in his hands. Daniel reiterated his conversation with Henry.

Remus tucked the front strands behind his ears neatly as he spoke. "Wages are one pound sixteen shillings a month total fer the two of ye. Ye'll start earning today, and at first landfall, ye can request half of what ye have earned be paid to ye. Ye'll git the rest of yer pay after the month. Ye should know we must first sail south to Harbour Town before we can deliver ye to Philadelphia."

Harbour Town. They were indeed following the *Desire* south instead of traveling north.

She stepped back. Why did Remus say "before we can deliver ye to Philadelphia" rather than saying "Before we can make sail for Philadelphia?" Did his assumption have anything to do with their association with the Schoens? Did Landon leave the Schoens with explicit instructions to get her north?

If Landon had changed his mind about wanting her with him, then the next best plan for her would be to travel back to England from Philadelphia. Her mind worked furiously. Yet, he had originally told her to stay there with his friends until he'd taken care of Gampo, hadn't he?

What if he hadn't changed his mind about wanting her and instead had lured Gampo away from her? She huffed a frustrated sigh. Too many questions. Not enough answers.

Go back to what I know.

Landon had made sure she couldn't defy his will, and put herself at risk by securing her passage via the *USS Glory*. If he didn't want her with him, then he'd not care where she went. Instead, he made sure everyone involved in her transport (including the Schoens) would take her north to Philadelphia. He'd expected her to be on the *USS Glory*, though, so the *Seeker* could set her course to trail Landon. If he left before the *Glory* departed, he'd have no way of knowing she'd been unable to board the warship.

While he went south to engage Gampo.

Was the captain of the *Seeker* aware Landon was taking on the pirate alone? She set her jaw. As soon as they were aboard, she'd seek out Captain O'Brien and inform him of her suspicions. Surely, he would know what was going on.

Daniel glanced at Keelan, oblivious to her thoughts. "It might put us behind Jared's letter to the London barristers, but we have no choice," he murmured for her ears only. "Hopefully, Slaney will get to the trunk before the estate auction takes place. Either way, we must leave Charleston now and get as far away from Gampo as possible."

As hot as the desire burned in her heart to find her sire, the trunk and its contents, it all meant nothing compared to Landon's life and safety.

She'd go south.

THE SAILOR NAMED Remus eyed Keelan and Daniel. "Any man who leaves the ship before the cargo is off, will forgo the second half his wages. They will be split into equal shares and given to those who stayed and finished the work. Do ye understand these terms?"

Both nodded vigorously.

"Then sign yer name or make yer mark here." He pointed to

the column next to the one where he had printed their names and salary. Daniel stepped forward and dipped the ragged feather quill into the inkwell. He brushed the first drop on the rim, then signed his name and gave the quill to her.

She picked up the quill and dipped it into the ink, a slight tremor in her hand.

"First time at sea, lad?" Remus asked, a friendly tone to his voice.

For a moment, Keelan wasn't sure what to say. How should a boy named Mahdi speak? Henry didn't seem to think it odd when Daniel spoke in his clipped British accent. It would be easier if she didn't have to stray too far from her real self. It was hard enough to walk like a boy. She took a chance and simply lowered her voice a little. If Daniel could get away with speaking in his natural dialect, then so could she.

Daniel gently nudged her with his elbow, making her jump.

"Oh! Uhh. N—no. No, sir. I've been on a ship before, once—last year," she spoke so softly Remus had to lean closer to hear.

"Well, then. You should get along just fine." He reached over and clapped her on the shoulder, but almost fell off his barrel at the pained shriek he got in response.

"Don't!" she reacted on impulse, pulling away from the sailor and then stumbling to her knees, blinded by the pain. He'd inadvertently struck the deepest gash across her shoulder blade.

Remus froze, uncertain what to do or say next.

Daniel's face paled.

Her lips trembled as she spoke in a tortured whisper, "I'm sorry."

Remus scowled at her, obviously offended at her disrespectful manner. Daniel jumped forward to extend a hand. Grimacing, she grasped it and allowed herself to be pulled upright. Dear God, what had she done? She'd just ruined everything. Remus surely just realized she was a female by her screech of pain, unless he thought she was a young lad who's voice had not yet changed.

She prayed it was the latter.

Reaching up, she jammed the hat lower over her brow then slid behind Daniel, fists clenched at her sides as she tried to behave in a more humble manner. She could only breathe in ragged jerks. A sick dizziness threatened to pitch her to the deck. Tears burned in the back of her eyes and she fought hard to prevent them from spilling. How could she pass for a boy if she cried like a girl? Dread seeped through her veins. Had she ruined everything? She stared at the deck, awaiting the consequences of her actions.

Daniel attempted to regain his composure as he bent close to Remus's ear and whispered confidingly, "I left him for a few days with Mrs. Schoen while I sought work. I fear he's been a bit abused by one of the tavern patrons. Please do not take offense to the lad. I'm sure he won't be quite as sensitive to touch once the lashes on his back heal."

Remus' eyebrows shot up, then his features smoothed with understanding. "Right then. Follow me and I'll show you the crew's quarters." With one last wary glance at her, he hopped off his barrel.

Keelan forced herself to steady her breathing. To distract her mind from the pain, she took note of the vessel they toured. The ship was long and broad with a lot of men moving about the deck getting the ship sea-ready. Barrels were lashed to the bases of two masts; the third had livestock fencing around it. Remus proceeded toward the main hatch, then down the steps to the lower deck.

So far, their plan was working, but neither one would let out a sigh of relief or let down their guard until they were free of Gampo, or on the grounds of WindBriar, whichever worked out for the best. She'd hear it from Landon's mouth before she made any more assumptions about whether or not he truly wanted her.

This plan had to work.

She clenched her teeth together in determination. Their plan *would* work; she'd make sure of it. Fingering the ring strung on the chain around her neck, her resolve grew.

They followed Remus down into the galley. He nodded to a slender, pale man pouring over a leather-bound book. "This is Marcel," he stated.

Marcel placed a short frayed ribbon on the page to mark his place, then slapped it shut.

"*Oui*? And who have we here?" he questioned in a thick accent.

Remus urged his charge forward. "This is Mahdi. He's your new cook's boy. He knows a bit about kitchens and healing herbs. He's taking young Billy's place," Remus said.

The Frenchman sighed and cast a skeptical perusal over Keelan. "And what would a boy like you know about working in zee galley?"

She squared her shoulders and took a deep breath, then lowered her voice as best she could, "I can make scones, bread and tea cakes. I can dress a chicken and smoke a ham. I can whip eggs and heavy cream fast enough, too."

Marcel cocked his head in surprise and then laughed. "We don't serve high tea to His Majesty here, but if you can make those things, you can learn to make hard tack. Come zen. We must first make a list for zee last of zee supplies we should buy at zee market and apothecary shop." He stopped and peered at the lad quizzically. "Can you write?"

She nodded. Finally, she offered something of value.

"*Bien*. Let us begin."

CHAPTER 21
TO MARKET

It was not long before Keelan and Marcel were weaving their way through the crowded aisles of the large market near the waterfront. Marcel stopped at one of the stalls and began to negotiate intently with a short, wrinkled woman over the price of ropes of garlic and dried peppers.

Keelan's olfactory senses were bombarded with fresh and rotting fruit, livestock of all kinds, and the sharp tang of humanity in general. Thankfully, a slight breeze wafted in from the sea and helped to dissipate the odors a bit. It was still humid, and the bandages serving to both protect her wounds and bind her breasts were already damp with sweat. She was grateful for the large straw hat Mrs. Schoen had given her. It protected her head from the merciless rays of the sun and hid her face from inquiring eyes. While confident with her disguise, she was not willing to press her luck.

"You there, boy!"

Her shoulder was jostled lightly, and she jumped back, grabbing her hat before it flew with the breeze.

Keelan looked up and gasped.

Standing before her was Simon.

It was the first time she had ever seen the house slave from Twin Pines appear irritated. In her presence, his face had always been a mask of somber servitude.

Simon frowned at her. "I asked you a question, boy. Don' you got the manners to answer?" He pulled out a faded green handkerchief and mopped his brow and cheeks as he huffed.

"Si—uh..." She caught herself quickly and gave him a slight bow, uncertain how she should act. "S-s-sorry, sir."

Simon put his handkerchief away. "I'm a looking for..." His expression froze. He leaned closer and peered at her face. "Miss Keelan? Dat *you*?"

She couldn't breathe. He'd recognized her! Now what would he do? The market was too crowded to flee. It was no use pretending. Best to just be honest.

She pulled her hat lower, totally deflated. "Yes, Simon, it's me."

The day the hurricane hit Twin Pines, she and Landon had been trapped in the cellar of an old cabin on the outskirts of the plantation. It contained a hidden passageway, and that day Simon had brought three runaways—a family—there to seek shelter.

The cabin served as a stopover refuge.

Simon used the cover of a violent storm to move the family. Later, she'd found out they were Pratt's runaways. The concept of slavery had never sat comfortably with her, nor had Pratt, for that matter. As a result, she and Landon had given the three escaped slaves what supplies they had and bade them a safe journey. She'd let them go and said nothing. Landon had kept the secret as well.

Simon lowered his voice. "What're you doin' dressed like *dat*? You all right? There's a bunch of strangers been by the house asking 'bout where you might be."

What should she say? She didn't want to tell him anything that would get either of them in trouble, but she needed to try to prevent him from telling anyone about her.

"Daniel and I are trying to avoid those people, Simon. They're pirates and mean us harm. Both Daniel and I are in disguise. We are preparing to flee Charleston. Please don't tell anyone you've seen me."

Simon's face softened a little as he sized her up and down. "You turned your head once for me, Miss Keelan. I can do the same fo' you, now."

She sighed in relief and whispered, "Thank you, Simon."

He bent down and murmured, "If'n you gets in a hard way, Mr. Schoen can help git you to a safer place. He at The Whistling Pig."

So, Daniel's intuition had been correct. The Schoens aided runaways. It all made sense to her now, after her experience in the tavern's attic.

Simon peered over her shoulder at the long row of stalls behind her and raised his voice a bit. "My Missus wants oranges and grapefruits, and our usual seller is all out. Did you pass any on dis row?"

"Yessir, we did, about halfway down." She pointed.

"Did you take a look at 'em?" Simon questioned. "It's a hot day, and I don't want to waste time and breath walking up and down the aisles if I ain't gotta."

"He was beginning to unpack a new crate," she answered, shifting her basket to the other arm.

"Ah, good. Thank you, boy. Good day to you." With a quick nod, Simon continued on his way without a backward glance.

Thank you, Simon.

She spied Marcel motioning to her from several stalls down and set off with her chin a little higher and a more confident step.

After a final stop at the apothecary, Marcel and Keelan made their way down a narrow alley as they headed back to the *Seeker*. Their baskets and leather satchels were filled with a wide variety of goods, as well as receipts for sacks of sugar, Indian meal, flour, and other heavier items, which would be delivered before dusk. It was a day well served, and now it was time to return to the ship, clean the galley, and make room for the supplies.

It had also been a long day, and she wasn't accustomed to the physical effort expected of someone in her new station. She wearily trekked behind Marcel through the streets of Charleston with her head down, watching her feet as she hopped around piles of dung and puddles of filth. They cut through a less crowded alley, offering a shortcut to the wharf.

Her mind drifted to Slaney, and she prayed the maid was safe and well. She should be nearing Philadelphia. How long would it take for her to find passage to England? Her thoughts were interrupted when she plowed into the cook's back. Her collision sent several packages from her basket tumbling to the street.

Mumbling a hasty apology, she squatted to retrieve the fallen parcels. A movement ahead of them drew her attention, and she peered around Marcel's legs and down the alley. Keelan's heart lurched as she caught sight of the gleaming metal of a long knife. The blade was clenched in the fist of a thick-chested man, who was standing a few feet in front of Marcel. A quick check behind her confirmed they were alone.

The man started to speak. "Ye'll hand over yer valuables, beginnin' with the purse on yer belt," he pointed his knife at the small bag of coins at Marcel's waist. "Leave yer goods on the street and keep yer hands where I can see 'em. Maggie will check yer pockets, in case ye forgot anythin'."

CHAPTER 22
THIEVES IN THE ALLEY

A scrawny, middle-aged woman with long stringy hair stepped from behind the man. She pulled a small, thin dirk from the folds of her tattered skirts. The couple inched closer while Keelan and Marcel placed their things on the ground. Marcel untied his purse and dropped it next to his feet.

The woman laughed humorlessly. "Look, Errol, he wants me ter come git it. Maybe he thinks while I'm down there I'll do 'im a nicer service, eh?"

The man growled and shoved the woman toward the purse. "Kick the coins to me and go through his pockets."

"Hell, no, I ain't gittin' too close to 'im." She walked around Marcel and pointed her dirk at Keelan. "You, boy, pick up the purse and bring it here to me, *now!*"

Keelan swallowed and reached down for the purse. She glanced up at Marcel's face. He winked, then flicked his gaze toward Maggie with an almost imperceptible nod. Her heart began to pound, and she gave a quick nod back. Apparently, Marcel was not parting with his purse without a fight. Sparring with Daniel had trained her for this type of situation, but she never imagined she would ever be forced into one.

From her crouched position, she quickly dove to the right. As her palms hit the ground, she kicked her feet in a wide arc parallel to the alley floor. She clipped Maggie's feet neatly from beneath her skirts and brought the woman crashing to the ground. Keelan rolled away, and then scrambled to her feet in time to give her adversary a swift kick in the jaw, knocking her out cold. On instinct, she pulled from her bootleg the dirk Daniel had given her.

Marcel stepped over his purse and goods and began to circle Errol with his arms wide. She raised her blade and without hesitation, threw it. It sank into Errol's shoulder with a sharp plunge of quivering metal. He screamed and dropped his own blade to clutch the knife handle. He barely glanced at his partner, lying prone on the dank stones, before he spun and ran, the knife still in his shoulder.

It was several seconds before Keelan's breathing slowed and Marcel's jaw snapped shut. Even after he closed his mouth, he kept opening it again to speak, but seemed to be at a loss for words as he stared at her in amazement.

After a few moments, he said, "You are most useful in a fight, young Mahdi."

He then walked over to Maggie's still form and picked up her dirk from the ground. To Keelan's surprise, he handed it to her. "To replace the one Mr. Errol ran off with," he said, gruffly.

She bit back a smile and placed the knife into the leather strap around her boot. They picked up their things, and Errol's hastily discarded blade, then exited the alley to head once more for the ship. Every few moments, Marcel would glance down at Keelan, then shake his head and mumble to himself in French. They made a quick stop at the courthouse to report the incident, and provided the location of the unconscious women they'd left in the alley, and then returned to the ship.

Henry hailed them as they approached the ship's ramp.

"Hoy Marcel! Got the galley stocked full yet?"

"*Oui*! By zee end of zee day, it will be."

Henry nodded toward Keelan. "How'd the lad do fer ye?"

Marcel grunted and set his load down. Rubbing his stiff shoulders, he gestured for her to board. "Go on and put zee load in zee galley. There iz no reason for you to stay and listen to me talk about your heroics. Your ego will expand beyond your chest's capacity to hold it."

Keelan hurried past the men, eager to be out of their sight and away from their stares. She paused at the top and glanced back. Marcel gestured madly with both arms, while Henry stared at him with his mouth agape. These men had fought battles with pirates and still seemed to be surprised that she could throw a knife. How old did they think she was? Twelve?

A memory floated into her mind unbidden of Landon placing his dirk in her hand and saying; *"Cock your wrist like so..."* Would he have approved?

Landon Hart.

Handsome, charming, vibrant.

Stubborn.

Yes, she'd lost her heart to the man. But did she truly know him? Perhaps he was no more than a dandy who excelled at seducing women and avoiding attachments. She had suspected as much that first time they'd crossed paths. The truth will out when they next met, depending — would he be glad to see her again when the two vessels joined back together?

More than anything, she wanted to know if he still wanted to marry her. Sail with her. Be with her.

She rubbed her sore shoulders and sighed in frustration. For the thousandth time she wondered if Landon had changed his mind about marriage. What if he wanted her as his mistress, instead? Would she'd have the fortitude to defend herself against the onslaught of seduction and the heady charisma Captain Hart used as weapons? Shifting her shoulders back, she lifted her chin.

Certainly, she'd become a spinster before she became any man's mistress.

She let her shoulders slump. Who was she fooling? So far, she'd lost the battle with that man's charm every time. She had no reason to believe her resolve had strengthened any in the past week.

She hadn't seen Daniel since earlier in the morning, so she quickly scanned the faces of the men on board as she made the trip to the galley. Several sailors paused what they were doing to watch her pass by. Her heart pounded nervously in her chest as she focused on hunching her shoulders and lengthening her stride in a more boyish fashion. It was one thing to simply look like a boy and quite another to act like one. It was even harder to remember to walk like one. Did she appear as nervous as she felt?

"Your actions and your gait are crucial to complete this illusion," Daniel had said. *"You must carry yourself like a young man. And you cannot shriek at such things as bedbugs or rats."*

Some sailors nodded or muttered a greeting. She did her best to respond in a like manner.

Sighing in relief, she dumped her things on the galley floor and sat down near them to catch her breath. It had already been a long day, and it was not yet noon. The ship creaked and groaned softly as it shifted in the quiet waters. She listened to the sounds of activity above as the crew went about their chores, readying the vessel for its voyage.

She was impressed by the cleanliness of the galley. She found several nearly empty bins, and it didn't take her long to unpack the supplies and put them away. Crocks of cane syrup and molasses fit neatly on a shelf in the pantry. Keelan took note of the tall lip on all the shelves, which obviously kept the contents from sliding against the cabinet doors when the seas became rough.

The sound of deliberate footsteps echoed down the steps. She straightened, expecting Marcel.

Instead, it was Daniel. "Good God, Miss Keelan! Are you all right?" he whispered in a concerned voice.

"I'm fine, really," she responded, glad to see him.

"Henry found me and told me what happened. He didn't want me to get a distorted version from the crew. Although he assured me my 'son' was unharmed, I had to see for myself."

Daniel's voice was as eager as a young boy's. "The news is all over the ship. According to Marcel, you single-handedly foiled two would-be robbers this morning!"

Keelan shrugged, trying to put Daniel at ease, but she couldn't hold back her grin. "It was almost like one of our training sessions."

Daniel reached out and squeezed her arm affectionately. "You did the right thing. I am proud of you." His next words brought a lump to her throat. "The commodore would have been *very* proud."

KEELAN WENT about the rest of the day dodging elbows and questions. Sailors who had stared at her earlier with wary gazes now seemed more at ease with her presence. The men were a mix of old and young, brown and white. Most were scarred and missing teeth or fingers, all were shaded darkly by the sun.

Henry had warned them of her healing back, so they were careful to keep their distance. A couple of them forgot themselves and reached over to give her a hearty clap on the shoulder, but she was able to step quickly away, eliciting winks and chuckles.

"Marcel said ye were faster than a lightning strike, and I can say I agree," one had said laughing.

The good-natured ribbing continued during the evening meal as the crew lined up with their trenchers. She responded to the banter with small smiles or bashful shakes of her head, nimbly hopping and darting away from jutting shoulders and knees while plopping spoonfuls of rice and beans, Indian meal, bannocks and meat on their platters. According to Marcel, the captain always fed his crew a small feast the day before they set sail, since they'd be without such luxuries while at sea, making her wonder how bad meals would be while they traveled.

After everyone had their share, she and Marcel filled a plate and wandered up on deck to find a spot to sit and eat. Noisy gulls circled overhead, hoping to catch a stray morsel. Keelan found Daniel and sank down near him to eat her meal. She enjoyed the way the sailors wolfed down the bannocks she'd made. Marcel had been pleasantly surprised at her level of culinary skill and had allowed her to make them unassisted while he finished his inventory list for the captain.

"Zee Captain feeds his crew better zan most. We are in dangerous waters often enough, and he wants his crew strong and healthy to fight zee pirates."

Like Gampo? "Do you often run in to pirates?" she asked.

Marcel grunted and shrugged, "Often enough. We are all expected to assist in defending ze ship. And we do just zat."

After most had finished their meal, Henry stood up and gave a shrill whistle. The chatter stopped as he glanced around at the crew.

"I hope ye enjoyed yer last mainland meal. The captain should be ready to set the sails at daybreak tomorrow."

The crew cheered.

"Ye know the rules." Henry continued. "Ye bunk aboard the ship tonight. We need a sober and alert crew in the morning. If ye decide to leave the vessel, ye do so at yer own risk. The ship'll not wait for ye."

He shoved his hands into his pockets. "The captain will be taking on a few passengers this trip."

A slight groan arose as some men voiced their opinion to this last tidbit of news.

Henry held up his hand for silence. "Ye are not to speak to

them unless they talk to ye first. Any argument requiring a judgment is to be brought to me quietly. Stay out of their way and be polite when tellin' them to git out of yers."

"Are there any petticoats?" a voice shouted.

"Ain't no business of yers who the captain takes aboard." He swept his gaze over the crew. "Now, git about yer tasks."

Keelan and Daniel rose and walked to the rail. A group of unruly seagulls squawked noisily overhead. "I wonder how many passengers the captain is taking," she murmured to Daniel.

"It can't be many because there are only two cabins still empty," Daniel replied. "The rest of the ship is stuffed with cargo."

She rubbed at her darkly stained skin, wondering how long the dye would last before she'd have to reapply it. Daniel had hidden a small bottle in his sack, hopefully it would last them as long as it was needed.

A soft breeze caressed her face, gentle as a butterfly's foot. She looked up and pointed her face in the direction of the wind.

"Aye, a good westerly is coming." Keelan and Daniel turned at Remus's voice. They'd not heard his approach.

He stopped near Daniel's shoulder. "Tomorrow's light will send us off under a good breeze, tho' the men will be wary until they catch sight of the passengers. We don't need no petticoats on this voyage."

"Why is that, Mr. Remus?" Daniel asked.

Remus leaned his bulk against the rail and picked his teeth with his fingernail. "Any salt who's been on the water will tell ye, havin' a woman aboard brings the bad luck." Nodding, he bade them good evening and swaggered away, whistling a nameless tune.

CHAPTER 23
UNWANTED PASSENGERS

Remus was right. Dawn broke the next day, clear and fresh. The wind had picked up a little, and the ship pulled at its anchor like a filly testing her reins, eager to run. They all broke the fast with leftover bannocks and Indian meal porridge and then went about with their various duties, getting the ship ready to sail.

Marcel had dismissed Keelan to the upper deck. "Go fill your head with zee last sights of Charleston, boy," he said. "And while you are up zere, find out who our passengers are. I like to know who I cook for, eh?"

Keelan pulled her hat low to shield her face from the sun, as well as from inquiring eyes, ever conscious of hiding her feminine features. Spying a box tethered to the side of the foredeck, she perched herself on it as the men lashed down barrels and loaded the last of the ships' supplies.

A milking cow lowed morosely as she was pushed and pulled up the ship's ramp. Two spry nanny goats followed, bleating their bewilderment. Half a dozen pigs had been brought aboard earlier and grunted to each other from the small square pen near the mainmast. Several chickens darted hither and yon among the feet of the crew. She hoped she'd find their permanent roost. Without one, it would be a bit difficult to collect the eggs, since she would have to hunt for their laying spot first.

The remainder of the purchases Marcel had made yesterday arrived. Remus and Johnny carried the heavy sacks of rice, dried beans and Indian corn meal below.

She couldn't help but worry if she'd be recognized or found out. Uncertainty at her ability to play the part of a galley boy without giving away her fairer gender pulled at her stomach. Daniel had done his best to tutor her on her new position as a cook's boy and crew member.

"You'll be expected to help with the labors of the ship in addition to your culinary duties," he'd warned. "As slight as you are, I doubt too much will be put upon your shoulders. However, when told, you must attempt to finish the task as best you can. In the eyes of the captain and crew, you are a young male laborer, so you must act the part."

Throwing one of those heavy sacks on her unhealed shoulders was going to hurt, but there was no getting out of her duties, which was why she was surprised when the men waved away her offer to help with this task.

"Ye'll just be in the way, boy," Remus said gruffly.

"These sacks weigh more than you do, lad," Johnny teased.

"Go tell Marcel to unlock his pantry," Remus suggested.

She nodded and went to the galley. Whether they meant what they said, or were sparing her still-healing back and shoulders from the chafing and the weight of the sacks, she wasn't sure. Either way, she was grateful.

The sacks were stuffed into barrels and sealed in an attempt to keep out rats and other vermin. Additional barrels stowed hogsheads of rum, ale and whiskey. Brandy, wine and port were stored in a special pantry built off the galley. Marcel shut the tight-fitting door and then locked it.

Keelan returned to her perch and enjoyed observing the activities on the waterfront. A few of the crew found spots along the rail as well.

According to Remus, after the ship had been released from dry dock and her leaking hold sealed, small additional repairs had followed. Then, the cargo had been loaded and lashed down. The last of the supplies and rations had been purchased and stored.

They now awaited their captain.

Relief and apprehension battled inside her. The *Seeker's* captain was already an acquaintance, but what if he recognized her and refused to let her stay aboard? He'd already seen her sparring with Daniel in her waif's clothes, so her current disguise might not work with him at all. She made a fast decision to remain out of Conal O'Brien's sight as best as she could until the journey was well underway. Then she'd find out if he knew of Landon's plan to seek out Gampo.

Remus confided, "Word has it he had unfinished business of some sort."

A landau moved along the waterfront, its pace restrained but determined. It stopped at the pier where the ship was secured. The driver stepped down, opened the carriage door, and extended his hand. A slender glove grasped it and a woman gracefully alighted, like quicksilver from a glass bottle. Her dress was a deep gray and a feathered hat was secured at a smart angle on her head. From what Keelan could see, the woman's hair was as dark as a raven's.

A low groan sounded from Remus, "Well, look who's joining us for another sail," he muttered, spitting over the rail.

"Another?" Keelan inquired.

Henry strolled up behind Remus and rested his elbows on the railing. "Aye. She sailed this same leg two years ago. Except she was aboard the *Desire*. Surprised to see her on the *Seeker* tho', eh Remus?"

Remus nodded at Henry's earlier observation and frowned. "She's the other captain's—Hart's—bit o' fluff. She's a bad omen, mark me words. Last time she sailed with him, a fierce storm hit an' washed Stuckey overboard, remember?"

The other captain.

Hart. Keelan's stomach clenched into a knot.

"She chased him hard," Henry agreed, willingly filling her in on the gossip. "Cap'n Hart was pleased enough to have her attentions now and then, but after a couple years she wanted him to give up his ship, marry her and run her daddy's plantation." Henry laughed. "Devil may doubt it, but the captain had no desire for that life to be sure. He's a seaman, not a lubber, anyone who knows him knows *that*."

Keelan swallowed. The notion that the woman and Landon had been lovers grated against her heart, even as she tried to steel herself against the sharp teeth of jealousy biting into her rational mind. She told herself it didn't matter. Hart was already sailing for Harbor Town on the *Desire*.

Remus added, "Cap'n sent her pretty little arse back home, in spite of it all. Ain't seen her again til today."

No new news there. Landon Hart had been gleefully unattached and unmarried when Keelan had met him at Twin Pines. Her mind took her back to Aunt Sarah's garden, the day he'd offered to free her tangled hair from a stubbornly rigid bush, in exchange for a kiss.

That kiss had been her undoing.

Or her awakening.

The memory led to a sensation of abandoned constraint and... longing. Landon Hart had kissed her, and from that moment forward she'd craved another kiss. Although she had done her best to resist the desire, when the opportunity had arrived she did not have the power or will to do so.

She was weak.

Henry nudged Remus in the ribs. "If Cap'n Hart rejects her, I wonder...what'll be her intentions whilst she's aboard?"

"Maybe she's set her bonnet on Cap'n O'Brien this time," Keelan replied with a half-hearted laugh.

Remus and Henry guffawed and slapped their knees at the suggestion. "Captain O'Brien likes him a skirt now and then, but he'd stay away from *that* skirt."

Keelan glanced down as the subject of their conversation stepped daintily to the base of the ramp from the pier. She gave a slight gasp when the lady lifted her head to inspect the ship.

The black widow, Annette Camsby, perused the faces at the rail.

Keelan's heart jerked in her chest. Annette and Landon.

Of course.

Now, she understood why they seemed to be so familiar with each other at Doreen's ball. Landon and Annette had been lovers.

Lovers.

Keelan scowled. That word, *lovers*, poked her throat like a stale biscuit. Were they still lovers? Would Landon have a difficult time resisting Annette's charms? Would Annette still want him?

She rolled her eyes and shook her head at the stupid questions. Of course Annette would want him. Why would she not? Landon probably rode straight to Annette's town house after witnessing that ridiculous kiss of Everett's on Uncle Jared's porch. A part of her heart crumbled. A dark, thick sensation oozed in and its weight pulled at her like a headstone.

So, this is how it felt to be jealous of another woman. This is what it felt like to have a broken heart.

So many questions and concerns flitted through her mind. How much of their journey did Landon's former mistress plan to make with them? What if Annette recognized her, as Simon had? Maybe she and Daniel should slip away unseen now, perhaps travel by land, if need be, to Philadelphia. It seemed possible. It would be infinitely better than sailing with the two of *them*.

She studied the pier and nearby boardwalk. People hawked

wares, some strolled casually, stopping occasionally to inspect an item or two, everyone seemed to be in motion, except...

A figure leaned against a piling near the mouth of the pier. Her heart lurched. Orvis Pike had his gaze fixed on the carriage and the lady who had alighted from it. He was probably watching to see if it was Keelan. If Daniel hadn't discovered Gampo's reward for her capture, she might have arrived in the same manner as Annette Camsby.

Keelan's shoulders sagged. The boat was being too closely guarded by the pirates for her and Daniel to make a successful escape. Even in disguise.

"God's blood, there's *another* petticoat," Remus said darkly.

A second woman, holding a small bag, emerged from the carriage. She was dressed much simpler, perhaps a servant. Her head was covered, her features masked.

Mr. Henry barked to the men loitering closest to the ramp. "You there! Johnny! Remus! Haul up the rest of these ladies' things. The biggest trunk is to go into the hold, but put it in a handy spot, in case they should require it."

The men pushed away from the rail and shuffled down the ramp like men headed for the gallows. "Aye, Mr. Henry."

She scanned the pier for Orvis.

He was gone.

A cold sensation gripped her neck. *Where did he go?* She studied the pier and the boardwalk again, but there was no sign of the man.

Keelan pulled the brim of her hat lower so she could inconspicuously watch Landon's lover stroll along the deck. She gave a small internal sigh of longing as she admired the perfectly coiffed hair, the beautiful silk gown, and the petite gloved hands. She was exceedingly aware of her own state of dress: boots, baggy breeches, Landon's linen shirt. She reached up and rubbed the collar. Uninvited, the image of Annette Camsby dancing with Landon tugged at the raw strings of jealousy within her chest.

They'd been beautiful together, two dark-haired figures waltzing around the room, talking, smiling...

Thinking of Landon also brought a lonely weight to her heart. At least if Orvis was still in Charleston, then so too, was Gampo, which meant Landon was safely sailing south on the *Desire,* either seeking the pirate or fleeing her. She gave a sarcastic snort.

If she'd listened to Slaney's advice and stayed away from the man, she wouldn't care if Annette Camsby was aboard. She pressed her lips together. The maid had been right about some things. Landon Hart was the kind of handsome rogue who could have a woman whenever and wherever he wished. He could easily make it a game to see how many maids he could woo, and leave swooning for his touch, longing for his kiss.

Unbidden, the hard warmth of his thighs against the back of her legs seeped in to her mind. His fingers on her wrist...

"Hold the blade like so..."

Warm breath against her cheek.

"Then cock your wrist and let it fly."

Hot moist kisses....his tongue probing her mouth with first tenderness, then desire.

Azure eyes pierced her mind.

Mocking.

Smiling.

Flashing in anger.

Clouded with concern.

Hooded in hurt.

Keelan's heart lurched. Now she ached with a kind of pain that pulled at her soul. For the past two-and-a-half years she had spurned countless suitors while making any number of excuses: too old, too arrogant, too uneducated, too poor, too melancholy, nose too big, belly too big.

Others had been refused by her parents because they were unworthy. She stifled a humorless laugh. Had a man born out of wedlock asked for her hand, he would have been laughed to the gate.

She pondered Landon Hart, the man who had once asked her to sail the world with him. He didn't seem like the type of man who cared much about what others thought.

Still...

Had he wanted me with him, she mused, *he would have taken me. Perhaps these circumstances are for the best. No matter how strong my affection, I will never stay with a man who does not love me, just as I would never want to be with a man I could not love.*

Yet...she *did* love. She loved Landon Hart whether she willed it or not.

The raw painful arrow of truth emerged through the bramble tangled around her heart like a crocus in spring. Much to the anguish of her flayed pride and common sense, she loved Landon Hart. When? How?

Oh, dear Lord, *why?*

She was being tormented by something she might never be destined to have. This was probably her punishment for being so cruelly selective with her previous suitors.

Her jaw tightened. It did no good to dwell on what could have or should have been. The past was the past. Her only hope was to focus on the future and the new path she must forge for herself and pray it would lead her home.

Perhaps without Landon.

A slow metallic ache spread through her chest.

She forced her mind back to her earlier reasoning. He'd left, so she had no choice but to follow his directions to sail north. Either he'd been striving to keep her safe because he cared for her, or he was trying to get rid of her.

So, he could be with his mistress.

Her gaze paused again on Annette Camsby, because apparently she liked torturing herself.

Remus had returned from his trip below and stood near

Keelan. He shifted toward her conspiratorially, "Well, she is now the *Widow* Camsby. It seems her third husband died of the fever last winter. She asked to see the captain first thing. Poor Henry had to tell her he's not yet boarded." He chuckled. "Barely got the words out before he had to duck a flying chamber pot."

Keelan was hit with a sense of immanent foreboding, like a dark thunderhead on the horizon.

Remus gave her an odd look. "Yer a bit green, boy." He peered closer, then nudged her with his elbow. "Don't worry, ye'll git yer sea legs soon enough."

She nodded. Better to let him think she was getting seasick. Although thinking about Annette Camsby made her stomach lurch almost as badly.

Remus grinned at her. "Tell ye this, young Mahdi, we're going to have a rough few days. If Madam Camsby's in heat and is shunned again, she'll be wantin' another warm body to take to her bed. A young buck like you might just suit her fine." He reached over and feigned to cuff her ear. She quickly dodged his swing and mumbled, "It won't be me. I wouldn't want to catch anything."

Remus threw his head back and roared with laughter. "Smart lad, ye are, but there's not many a man on this ship with the same sense in his head or his britches. They'd as soon lay the lass now and worry about the other later." He hailed Daniel, "Mr. Khalil!"

Daniel walked up, nodded a greeting to Remus and Johnny, and leaned his forearms on the rail.

"How are the beasts?" Johnny asked.

Daniel rubbed his shoulder and grinned at Keelan. "The mare is a bit spirited. She slammed me into the boards as I was changing the dressing on her leg this morning. She's healing well, though. Has the captain arrived yet?"

"Nay. Not yet. He should be here shortly," Remus responded.

"I was told to tell you and Johnny to report to the helmsman," Daniel said.

Remus nodded, and he and Johnny stepped away hastily to comply.

Keelan's gaze was drawn to another figure moving furtively toward the ramp. Even though he limped, there was something familiar about the man's gait. He carried a small trunk under one arm and a leather satchel under the other, similar to the medicine bag Dr. Garrison carried.

Dr. Garrison!

Keelan's heart pounded. *Dear God, please don't let him board this ship.*

God apparently had more pressing prayers to answer because Everett wasted no time lurching to the ramp like a startled stork.

Keelan gritted her teeth. She sensed Daniel stiffen beside her.

He bent his head and spoke into Keelan's ear. "We will have to make ready to leave this vessel as soon as we can slip away. It's not safe for you. I'll not have you on the same ship as Dr. Garrison."

Another surge of panic welled in her chest. A bounty on her head in Charleston, and Garrison on the same ship with her. How long would it take to find other transportation north? She glanced again to the spot where she'd seen Orvis earlier. Two different men had taken his place and appeared to be in casual conversation, but their eyes were fixed on the *Seeker*.

"Daniel," she whispered, "spies are watching the ship." She nodded toward the pirates. "It could be days or even weeks before another vessel is ready to journey north. And if war breaks between England and France, as Captain Hart and Uncle Jared predicted, it could delay our departure even longer. We must continue." She pleaded with the valet, "Please, Daniel. We can't risk the delay."

She couldn't leave now, she had too many questions. Why had her mother had a child with another man? Who was he? She clasped her hands together and stared at her stained fingers. What she really needed to know was if Landon had been serious when he'd asked her to join him, or if she was no more that a pleasant temporary distraction for him. Observing him and Annette together might give her the answer to that question. She couldn't leave until she knew for sure. Her mind told her to go, but her heart begged her to stay long enough to confront Landon and learn the truth from his own lips.

Really soft, really tantalizing lips.

Daniel closed his eyes and rubbed his forehead, as if his thoughts were causing him pain. "I promised the commodore I would take you to England and help you find your father. I will see my oath fulfilled and my duty done, Miss Keelan." He opened his eyes and his gaze sharpened. "But, not at the cost of your safety."

She supposed she'd feel the same way if their roles were reversed. "Henry said we'll sail from Harbour Town to Philadelphia. If you still think it is too dangerous, then we leave the *Seeker* and find a different ship northbound when we arrive in Harbour Town." She waited while Daniel contemplated their situation.

He gave her a reluctant nod. "It makes sense to stay aboard and then take stock in the next port."

A shout from Remus drew their attention to the dock below. "Hoy Captain! Yer late. Was she that good, or did she tie ye to her bed posts?" he called out jovially.

Conal O'Brien attempted a grin and nudged the shoulder of the man next to him. Keelan's breath froze in her throat as she gazed upon the stern and rather unmistakable face of Landon Hart, striding beside O'Brien.

Why wasn't Landon on the Desire?

Daniel grasped her arm. "What luck!" he whispered enthusiastically. "I'll have a word with Captain Hart as soon as I can meet with him privately."

They both observed Landon and Conal board the vessel amid additional shouts of greeting and raucous comments about activities ashore. The two simply waved them off, in good-natured fashion.

As Landon and Conal came closer, Keelan noted the weariness of their stride and the slump of their shoulders. The crewmen seemed to notice the stern set of their mouths and stifled any further ribald comments. Landon had dark circles beneath his eyes and a haggard look of worry blanketing his features. Keelan studied him. Relief and dread tangled together. In her heart, she was happy to see him again. Rather than wonder if he'd be happy to see her too, all she could think of was if he would seek comfort in Annette Camsby's arms again.

Annette Camsby.

Landon.

A thought hit Keelan like a slap to the face. His mistress was back aboard and had already asked for him. Annette had *known* Landon would be aboard the *Seeker*.

A loud rush of air filled her ears as the realization hit her. The trip to Harbour Town provided an excellent opportunity for the two lovers to rekindle their old relationship. How could Landon resist such beauty, especially if it radiated from a woman so willing to climb into his bed? Winning the argument with Daniel to stay aboard until they reached Harbour Town no longer had the same appeal it had a few moments ago. A darker question gripped her mind. After securing Keelan's passage aboard the *Glory*, had Landon sought out Annette to accompany him south?

Was that the reason he kept the *Seeker* waiting?

Keelan tried to swallow the rock forming in her throat at the thought of watching the two together.

Daniel nudged her. "I wonder what Hart's reaction will be when he sees Garrison aboard this ship." Daniel crossed his arms with a confidence she did not share. "My bet would be he's bound and turned over to the Charleston authorities."

She hoped not. "Daniel," she whispered, "if he's taken to jail and charged with kidnapping me, won't I have to bear witness to the charges?"

Daniel was silent as he pondered her words. "True enough," he responded. "'Tis better to keep our enemies close, where we can watch them. We have the advantage. He doesn't know we're aboard. Take care, Miss Keelan, to stay as inconspicuous as you can." He looked toward the main cabin. "I'll find a quiet moment to have a word with Captain Hart about our circumstances."

"Nay, Daniel, please don't!" The words fell from her lips before she could stop them.

He turned to her, surprise evident on his face. "In heaven's name, why not?"

Taking an unsteady breath, she stared at her clasped hands, not willing Daniel to witness her pain as she spoke. "I'd rather not burden the captain with my state of affairs at the moment. He might well feel obligated to take charge of my protection, and I will not be any more indebted to him than I am already. It's obvious to me much weighs on his mind at the moment, and I shall not add to his burden."

Daniel bent to peer at her. "It's my understanding the man cares about you deeply. Your protection would be less an obligation and more of a concern on his part."

Daniel had not seen Landon's interactions with Annette; he did not know their history.

She lowered her gaze and murmured. "I am uncertain of my standing with him at the moment, Daniel. It appears he has invited one of his previous mistresses to join him on his journey." She tilted her head in Annette's direction.

Daniel's features darkened briefly, then it softened in understanding. "We shall remain anonymous for a while then. At least until we can determine where everyone stands." He patted her hand affectionately. "It is unwise to make assumptions, Miss. Better to seek the facts of the matter."

As she pondered his words, her mind thrashed about in indecision. More than Landon's affection for her was at stake now. Her life was in jeopardy as well.

Daniel crossed his arms and nodded. "Let's bide our time for a few days and watch them. There will be plenty of opportunities to exit the ship in Harbour Town or even Philadelphia."

Keelan glumly nodded in agreement. She shifted her gaze back to the end of the pier and caught her breath.

Orvis was back at his post.

CHAPTER 24
WEIGH ANCHOR

K eelan had done her best both to help the sailors, and stay out of their way. Remus took her under his wing and gave her several specific tasks to perform. Unfortunately, she had to go to the starboard side to complete them, removing her chance to watch the pier.

When she went to back a couple hours later, she chanced a quick glance long enough to notice Orvis was no longer at his post. That should've given her some sense of relief, but instead, an uneasy shadow settled in her chest.

"Weigh anchor, lads!" Conal braced his legs, hands on his hips. "Hands to braces, set topsails, and let down the sheets!"

The anchor was raised, and the hoisted sails billowed full and urgent. The crew looked with satisfaction at the brisk gusts filling the canvas.

Landon stood near the helm, issuing additional instructions as sheets were adjusted and lashed. The sails snatched the wind, and the *Seeker* glided swiftly to open sea. Landon was as much a part of the ship as the mainmast. Standing with legs braced wide, the only disturbance in his countenance was the lingering look he gave to the Charleston harbor and the stoic expression on his face.

What was he thinking? Keelan glanced at the harbor and her heart suffered a brief pang of grief as she recalled standing by Papa's side the day their ship dropped anchor a couple years ago. She'd been grieving the loss of her mother.

Her life had been on a different path, then.

The wind gently moved them out from the waterfront and parallel to the shoreline. Charleston shrank quickly into the distance as the *Seeker* gained speed at the expert hands of her crew.

Landon stood straight and tall at the helm. So far, she had managed to stay out of his way, but eventually their paths would cross. A part of her yearned for it, as much as dreaded it. What would she say? *"Good day, Captain. I missed the ship I was supposed to board. Don't mind me, I'm just the cook's boy. Send my regards to your mistress."*

She swallowed, but couldn't squelch the prickly sense of foreboding that gripped her. How far would this charade take them? Would Landon recognize her before she was ready to doff her disguise? More importantly, how would he react? She clenched her teeth. Or would her presence ruin his plans with Annette Camsby (hopefully)?

After reaching deeper waters, the *Seeker* swung southward again, and the shore returned as a distant dark green line on the horizon. It seemed odd a ship should sail so far from the shore when it would soon make port again.

Henry had stepped up to the rail next to her, so she voiced her question to him.

He gestured toward the low line of land to the right. "There be a lot of sand bars and small islands along this coast, lad. Many a vessel has been run aground by less experienced captains. Easy pickin' fer the pirates then. Cap'n chooses to try to make them work a bit harder to catch us." He grinned.

Keelan gripped the rail nervously. "Do many pirates prey in these waters?" She thought of Gampo.

"Not as much as back when." Henry shrugged. "Blackbeard hisself raked these seas fer years. Why, Blackbeard's men stole ashore into Charleston one day and kidnapped a good number of prominent townsfolk quite a few years ago. He ransomed them fer medicine fer his crew." The man winked and then chuckled, "His men had the clap, ye see, and Captain Blackbeard knew they would not be able to keep their mind on their work if their cocks were itchin' like the devil."

The stain on her skin had better be masking the heat creeping up her cheeks. She ducked her head to hide her embarrassment and pretended to scan the shoreline. "Did he get the medicine?"

"Aye. He did. Put him out of business fer a while, still."

A flash of silver caught Keelan's eye, and the Widow Camsby floated by toward the steps leading to the helm. Landon' brow lowered at her approach, and he moved away from the wheel, permitting the helmsman to take over. He descended the steps and met her near the rail where Keelan and Henry stood.

Annette made no effort to lower her voice. "Good day, Captain Hart," she smiled sweetly over the frilly fan she fluttered before her face. "I sent word with your man before we set sail that I wished to speak with you privately, but alas, you never came. I am forced to seek you out instead." She pouted and angled partly away from him coyly and waved her fan at her chest. Keelan narrowed her eyes at the shameless flirtation.

Henry made a small choking noise. Landon shot a warning look over Annette's shoulder at the old sailor, even as a small smile tugged at the corners of his mouth. With an eyebrow arched, he then turned his attention to the young widow fluttering in front of him like a moth.

"Good day, Madame Camsby." He gave her a slight bow before gesturing at the activity around them. "As you can see, I have been a bit busy. Do you have a concern you wish to share with me?"

Keelan gulped and pulled the brim of her hat lower, while casting surreptitious glances at the pair.

Annette maintained her pout. "Well, yes, I do."

He waited, hands clasped behind his back.

"I had expected for you, as host, to see to the comforts of your passengers more appropriately," she chastised, in a hurt tone. "These voyages are extraordinarily boring. I need some companionship." She batted her long black lashes, then lowered her voice. "Join me in my cabin this evening. We'll sup together."

Landon's jaw ticked. He bowed graciously. "Forgive my poor manners, Madame Camsby. I would be honored if you would join me for dinner this evening at eight."

It was as she'd feared. Landon and Annette seemed to be rekindling their relationship. It was time for her to move away. She'd heard all she needed to hear.

Annette lowered her lashes as a slow smile seeped across her face. She lowered her fan and swayed it in a slow sultry motion in front of her very ample bosom, which was straining against the bodice of her gown.

Keelan had seen enough. Clenching her fists until her nails bit into her palms, she turned away.

Landon continued, "Captain O'Brien and I have yet to meet the other passengers aboard. Tonight's dinner will give us all an opportunity to become better acquainted. I will then be able to introduce you to your fellow passengers, so you will have others to talk with to break the monotony."

His words made Keelan pause. He'd given her a very subtle rejection. She chanced a quick sideways glance at Annette from under the brim of her hat.

Annette's pleased expression faltered a little, but she nodded her head. "I look forward to this evening." She slapped her fan shut and made to leave, then paused before stepping closer to

Landon. She placed her hand familiarly on his chest and murmured something to him. He shrugged in response, and she smiled wider as he offered his arm. They strolled away in the direction of the aft deck.

Keelan shoved her hands in her pockets and stepped away from the rail before she pushed Annette over it and into the churning sea below. Landon's reaction was more subdued than she'd expected. Not like a man happy to see his mistress. With those barbs tumbling around in her mind, she went below to check if Marcel was in need of her assistance. Pondering Landon's motivations and being near Annette's flirtations only gave her a headache.

KEELAN SPENT the next couple of hours helping the cook prepare supper for the captain, passengers, and crew, serving up rice and salted fish into various bowls and trenchers. She wasn't yet used to the bawdy comments and jokes the men tossed around, and her ears burned as she served helpings of Hopping John.

Marcel flew about the small galley like a fly in a jar, chopping sweet potatoes and stirring the pudding. He took a spoon, dipped it into the soup, and after blowing to cool it, took a sip. "Ah!" Marcel said, pleased. "Ze first meal at ze captain's table must be *perfect,*" he said with a flourish of hands. "All ze passengers will be dining wiz him and Captain Hart tonight." He cocked his head and peered at her more closely.

"You are most solemn, young Mahdi, is all well with you?"

Images of Landon and Annette together had been pestering her mind like a swarm of gnats flying around inside her head. She did her best to squelch them. It would not do for her to draw any extra attention from the cook. She had to keep her charade consistent and believable.

"Aye, sir. Just a bit off-balance. Remus said it might take a day or two before I got my sea legs."

"Ah," the cook nodded. "I have a remedy." He reached for a small tin and pulled out a dried piece of root. He sliced off a small bit and gave it to her. "Chew on this a while. It will help."

"What is it?" She eyed it curiously.

"Root of Ginger. Chew it."

She did as she was told and found the flavor unique and sharply pleasant.

Marcel pointed to the wooden box under the chopping block. "Pull out ze dishes and goblets from zat trunk over there."

Keelan opened the trunk and removed the woolen cover. Beneath it lay neatly stacked pewter plates, bowls, goblets and silver placed between layers of thick woolen squares.

The galley had two doors. One opened to a short hallway leading to the stairs and upper deck. She hadn't opened the second door. Marcel gestured to it now as he dunked a piece of bread into the sauce to sample.

"Set ze Captain's table. You will find ze linens in a cupboard in zere."

Keelan nodded and counted out the number of plates she would need. They clinked softly as she removed the cloth separating them and placed them in a neat stack. Nimbly stepping around the mumbling cook, she lifted the latch with her elbow and nudged the door open with her shoulder.

On the right was a desk strewn with papers and maps, as if someone had impatiently tossed them there. The desk was tightly affixed to the corner walls. Cupboards covered the rest. How many she would have to go through before she found the one housing the table linens? The opposite wall contained another door, perhaps a closet.

The table stood directly in front of her, its end bolted to the wall. The two long benches tucked neatly underneath were surrounded by a raised border of narrow planks, keeping them from sliding away.

She couldn't find the linens while holding the plates, so she moved back to the cluttered desk and gently shoved the papers and maps aside to put them down.

"I thought I was helping by clearing off the table."

She jumped, losing her grip on the plates. They tottered and began to slide toward the floor. The top two clattered on the wooden planks. A long bare arm reached over and steadied those that remained. Landon's handsome profile stirred a mixture of surprise, trepidation, and suppressed joy. He bent to retrieve the fallen items.

"I'm sorry if I startled you," he said. "You're the new galley boy, young Mr. Mahdi, correct?"

She hunched her shoulders, ducked her head and nodded, afraid to speak. She would have stepped further away if she could trust the rest of the dishes to stay put.

Landon collected the fallen plates and placed them on a bench. She glanced at his tanned back, and the muscles rippling beneath his skin with his movements. He straightened and pointed to the cupboard nearest the galley door.

"You'll find the linens in there," he said. "Please tell Marcel our guests have all accepted the invitation for dinner this evening."

She faced the cupboards, keeping her back to him, and listened as he walked away. It had never occurred to her his cabin could be accessed directly off the galley. She groaned. Now she would have to be ever vigilant to his comings and goings and not relax her charade even a little.

His voice startled her. "And, boy..."

She paused.

"The passengers are to be treated with the utmost respect, regardless of your personal feelings. Understood?"

Her stomach jumped as she shifted to peer at him from beneath the brim of her hat. Did he suspect anything?

Landon stood inside his cabin door, hand on the knob, and ran the other through the glossy black curls on his head. "While I have been told you are quite capable of taking care of yourself against thieves and ruffians, and it appears you have a keen ear for a yarn, I fear you might be lacking experience in the area of dueling with a woman's tongue and mood. Be warned that Mrs. Camsby tends to take out her anger on the nearest warm body." He glanced at her, a small pained smile played at his lips. "'Tis in your best interest to steer clear of her, as her mood on this trip may be quite dour."

Lips tightening, she nodded again.

"Good. Please tell Marcel to set out a bottle of Madeira. If I recall correctly, Mrs. Camsby has a liking for it."

She flinched and tried to ignore the sudden anger beginning to roil inside her. Of course he would stock his mistress's favorite wine! She clenched her jaw and nodding once more, didn't move or breathe until she heard him close the door. She yanked open a cupboard.

Steer clear of Widow Camsby, indeed!

She huffed at the notion that Landon Hart viewed her as a whipping boy. She'd like to see Annette *try* to strike her. Or was he warning her away from that gaudy piece of skirt like a prancing stag in rut?

"Sail away with him, huh!" She grabbed the tablecloth and shook it out with an angry jerk. "I am out of his sight for a fortnight and he is already strutting like a dandy to another. Lies, lies, lies."

His words were a farce, designed to steal a kiss simply for sport. With his lusts appeased, he would have left her for the next feminine form to catch his eye. Apparently, he preferred his beautiful mistress to accompany him on shorter trips.

She grabbed the plates from the desk and dumped them on

the table with a loud clatter. She moved around it, slapping them down as she went.

"The arrogant lout. Conceited cad."

An amused voice sounded from the captain's doorway. "Have the trenchers insulted you, Mahdi? From the din you were making, I was sure you had been attacked by an angry stack of pewter platters."

She jumped. Landon's head poked out from behind his cabin door.

"Nay, sir," she said in a low voice, as she placed the last plate on the table. "I am sorry for disturbing you." She briskly escaped through the door into the galley.

When she entered, Marcel pointed to two steaming buckets near the door.

"Take zem to Captain Hart. Ze bath iz filled but for zee hot water."

Scowling, she opened her mouth to protest and then closed it again, as she could give no good reason to avoid her duty without arousing the cook's suspicion.

Fine. She'd simply knock, deposit the buckets inside the room, and let the captain add them to his own bath. Content with her plan, she hefted her burden, nudged the galley door open, and crossed the dining cabin to his door. Still fuming, she knocked smartly with her toe.

At Landon's beckoning, she entered. The water sloshed to and fro in the buckets as she pushed open the door. His furnishings were tasteful without being ostentatious. A mahogany tallboy stood against the far wall, while directly to the left stood a bed of the same, cloaked with a simple navy silk canopy. Next to the tallboy was a closed door which had to lead to the outside hallway.

Landon's voice resonated through the room. "Just pour in the water, Marcel."

She turned toward the voice and almost dropped the buckets.

Landon was lowering himself in the tub, showing more of his natural state than Keelan wished to view. His hips were slim, his belly taut and flat. A thin line of black hair traveled downward—she squeezed her eyes shut, aghast at where her gaze traveled.

Thankfully, he did not look up, for if he did, he would have seen a heightened blush covering young Mahdi's face. Instead, he immediately reached for a slab of soap and rubbed it in his hands, then briskly rubbed the soapy suds over his face. He paused in his work and cocked his head to the side.

"The warm water, Marcel?"

Since there was no way to avoid her duties; it'd be best to take advantage of Landon's temporary blindness. Keeping her gaze carefully averted, she pitched the first bucket into his bath. In her haste to be done, she didn't think to divert the stream away from his body. The hot water hit him full force in the chest.

At his yelp of pain, Keelan froze, and it took her a fraction of a second before she jerked into action. She picked up a nearby pitcher and, to reverse the effect of the scalding deluge, flung the contents in the same general direction.

At the sudden blast of colder water on his lap, Landon's eyelids flew open. A bellow followed as soapy rivulets streamed in to his eyes. He hurriedly splashed his face to cease the merciless burning.

"*Damnation!*" he roared, rising from the water and reaching for a towel to mop his face. "Are you trying to maim me or geld me?"

Horrified at the sights he revealed, she stepped back as the sound of running feet approached from the hallway behind her. The cabin door flung open wide, hitting her full force on her backside and sending her flying headfirst onto Landon's chest. Momentum carried both man and waif back into the tall brass tub with a loud splash.

Conal's voice sounded concerned. "Landon, I heard—".

Her hips hinged over the lip and her feet flailed in the air as she made a desperate attempt to heave her upper body up and out. The smooth wet sides were slippery, and she couldn't push herself up. Her face plunged back in the water covering Landon's lap. She floundered madly to gain purchase and push herself upright. Landon finally grabbed her by the hair and pulled her face out of the water.

Sputtering and coughing, she braced a hand on his stomach and pushed herself upright. The realization of where her other hand rested put her into a mild panic. She fumbled to scramble from the tub, only to slip forward against his chest again. Fighting furiously to free herself from the proximity of his naked body, she shoved harder against him, this time eliciting a grunt of pain.

Landon growled, "In God's name, would you stop thrashing about before you succeed in making me completely useless to a woman ever more?" Frustration was evident in his tone, making Keelan cringe.

With measured patience, Landon stood up, grasped her around the waist, and made to deposit her out to the floor. However, both the boards and the tub sides were slippery. He lost his balance, causing his hands to slip up along her ribs.

She gasped and froze. His eyes widened, and his mouth dropped open at the soft curves beneath his hands. Their eyes locked and for a moment, neither seemed able to draw a breath. She jerked away from him, only to slip on the wet floor. There was no one capable of catching her this time. Her backside hit the wet wooden planks, causing her to expel a pained grunt.

Both Conal and Landon stood frozen with shock. Surprise and amazement give way to total disbelief as Landon's gaze slid over her body. The floppy hat had flown from her head when she fell in. Her hair had broken free of the tie, allowing it to hang in streams of wet, curly, ringlets. She chanced a quick glance down. In the struggle, her vest had come open. Beneath it, her soaked shirt clung to her like a second skin, leaving Landon a clear view of her chest. The silky white of her breasts contrasted sharply with the deep tan of her neck, face, and arms. Soft, pink peaks strained against the fabric bandages, leaving Keelan no secrets to withhold from his astonished gaze.

Likewise, Conal stood paralyzed in his tracks, jaw agape; hand still on the door latch. When he finally did find his voice, it came out as a lame croak.

"I'll... be... damned."

She scrambled away from Conal's surprised visage and backed against the far wall, snatching her vest closer about her.

Landon's voice was almost uncertain. *"Keelan?"*

CHAPTER 25
REVEALED

"Is it you, Keelan?"

Landon could hardly believe his eyes. Her skin was as dark as a native savage. Her hair had been cut and stained as well. If he hadn't felt the curve of her breast, he'd never have guessed the boy, Mahdi, was a woman. Although, if he'd looked closer, her eyes would have betrayed her. Those eyes haunted his dreams whether sleeping or awake, glittering emeralds with threads of gold in the center.

A weary air of defeat emanated from her like a sodden blanket. After a moment, she nodded mutely. Her shoulders dropped as she fixed her stare at the cabin floorboards.

"Conal," Landon strained to find his voice. "I must swear you to secrecy. Not a word of this to anyone, or Keelan's safety will be compromised. Please leave us."

"Aye, Landon." Conal's amusement was tightly contained behind the curt nod of his head. The corners of his mouth twitched. What the man found so bloody amusing was beyond Landon's comprehension at the moment. Keelan's presence on the *Seeker* muddled up his plan considerably. Annette Camsby's face filtered through his mind, and he mentally cringed at the added layer of discomfiture.

If both women had done what they'd been told, everything would have worked out.

The door closed; Conal's footfalls in the passageway died away. The air in the cabin seemed to sharpen and pierce his chest like a million needles in the rigid silence following the click of the latch.

Keelan continued to study the worn floor boards.

Did she have any inkling what she'd put him through the past couple of days? He couldn't find her. He'd slept little. He had feared she'd been retaken by Gampo, or worse, Garrison. He'd run out of places to search for her after she left the tavern. Schoen's maid had told him she'd gone with a dark man. The sun-bronzed skin of a seaman, of a pirate... of *Gampo*... had contaminated his thoughts, and he found he was unable to form a strategy. Conal dragged him back to the *Seeker* to settle for a bit and think things through. They had a route schedule to keep; lives depended upon it and to be late could be deadly. He'd wanted to track Gampo, the bilge rat.

Things made a little more sense now. The dark man the maid saw was likely Daniel, who would have stayed with his mistress.

The more Landon stewed, the angrier he became. Combined, the lack of sleep, worry, and frustration added to the relief at seeing her alive. It all churned into a roiling, turbulent swirl of emotion. Before he could stop himself, he grasped her shoulders, gave her a jolting shake, and brought his scowling face inches from her own. "What are you thinking, you little minx? Do you realize what you've done?" He shook her again. "You should *not* be on this ship!"

Her eyes widened, then narrowed. "Unhand me," she hissed furiously as she attempted to jerk free of his hold. "Your fingers bite into my wounds."

He immediately released her but did not move from his

stance. Was all this a game to her? She remained frozen, rooted to her spot, her gaze on his face, eyes flashing green fire. Landon clenched his fists and shook his wet head in frustration. He snatched a towel and secured it about his waist, and then, in an attempt to cool his ire, paced the cabin.

"Conal and I have been searching for you. I received a message from Commodore Hall, belatedly, stating he was urgently summoned north. He feared he couldn't deliver you safely, so he chose to leave you behind. Schoen's had informed me of Gampo's offered reward, so I went back to The Whistling Pig, where we were informed you had left the day prior, although the maid knew not where. We rode to Jared Grey's town house, then to Twin Pines, to find it half burned to the ground, as was Garrison's residence and office here in town."

She gasped and her eyes widened. "Uncle Jared and Aunt Sarah, are they—"

"Unharmed," he said, quickly. "They were in Charleston at the time. Garrison's place burned down the night I found you at the warehouse. One of my men saw the doctor loitering about the livery and followed him here, to the *Seeker*. When he booked passage, we allowed it with the hope he might lead us to you." He continued to pace, expending the energy generated by hours of worry and fear. "Every place we searched and did not find you, tore at my peace of mind, nearly driving me mad," he said hoarsely.

Pausing in front of her, he gripped her upper arms again in torment. "My God, Keelan, I feared Gampo took you. I feared you *dead*!"

KEELAN LIFTED HER CHIN. "Oh? You were *so* concerned for my welfare, you almost forgot about Annette Camsby's madeira!" Yes, she was acting stupid and jealous, but at the moment all rational thoughts seemed to have abandoned her, blast it. She peeled his fingers from her arms. "It would seem your anguish over my well-being took flight the moment she planted herself with such familiarity on your boat!"

"It's a ship, not a boat," he muttered, the edge of his mouth tight.

She poked his chest with her finger, wishing it were a dagger instead, so he'd feel the same sting. Dear Lord, just hearing his voice was painful for her. "You black-hearted snake! You wanted me on Commodore Hall's *ship*, because you had a liaison planned on *this* one with one of your mistresses. Your tender words and warm promises are worth less than the ocean water beneath this *boat*."

He actually looked chagrined. *Ha.* He'd been caught. At least he had the decency to be embarrassed. She'd wanted to hear the truth, and now she had. She'd been such an idiot. A naïve little fool.

No doubt he regretted the truth being outed more than his recent actions.

She propped her fists on her hips. "Sail away with me, Keelan. I want you with me, Keelan," she mimicked. Angry tears threatened, and she whirled away from him before he could see how deeply she had fallen for his ploy and how dupable she'd been. "I was nothing more than another conquest to you, a gullible maid, easy to fool. It's obvious you changed your mind and decided against taking me with you. Rather than being man enough to tell me yourself, you simply planned to toss me aside and flee." She strained to prevent her voice from breaking. "You put me on a ship heading north, while you intended to travel south with your mistress." She brought her fists up to her chest, and pressed them over her heart, but the pain and humiliation only sharpened when he didn't deny it.

Landon spoke in an even tone behind her; an edge of anger

laced his words. "The *Desire* was too closely monitored, Keelan. Gampo heard us talking at the warehouse. He'd find you by following *me*. As a diversion, I sent my vessel south, thinking you'd be sailing the other direction with Hall. It was my hope Gampo would abandon seeking you out in Charleston, and think you'd left on the *Desire* and follow her to Harbour Town, which would have taken him even farther from you." A pause. "Dammit Keelan, I was trying to *protect* you! Choosing this scheme has only put you in more danger," he growled.

Strong fingers gripped her shoulders again, and he spun her to face him. She closed her eyes so he couldn't tell how badly she was hurting. He'd put himself and his ship in jeopardy by offering both as a decoy, which was admirable, if it were true. She wanted to believe him, yet feared the pain he'd inflict on her heart if she was wrong again. While his argument sounded logical, it could be a convenient lie. Annette Camsby was still aboard, probably preparing for dinner. Probably expecting to be served her favorite wine. Probably anticipating Landon inviting her into his bed.

It was too big a risk.

Keelan, gesturing to herself and the surrounding space, whispered angrily, "Daniel, and I had no choice but to choose this *scheme*." She pushed the dripping ringlets of russet and brown-streaked hair from her face. "We couldn't risk being discovered. Gampo's men seemed to be everywhere, watching every vessel. After the *Glory* departed, his men came to search the tavern, so we had to flee first and worry about the destination later. This was the first ship in the harbor set to sail."

Unbidden and unwanted, the image of Landon and Annette strolling about the deck earlier permeated her mind. Her throat constricted as if a stone were caught in the middle of it. She'd have to steel herself against seeing the two of them together during the voyage to Harbour Town, although she wasn't sure how. She'd sleep in the pantry, or in the hidden compartment with the runaways down in the hold.

The waves of power and anger resonating from Landon were beginning to become unbearable. She had to get out of this small space. Stepping back in the direction of the door, she drew a deep breath. It was time to push him out of her heart. It wouldn't be easy, but the first step would be keeping physical distance between them, starting now. "Please, just stay away from me. I'll depart when we reach Harbour Towne. I won't say anything to Mrs. Camsby, and I'll leave the two of you to yourselves."

He returned her gaze with one of hot, blue fire. In two strides he stood before her, his chest inches from her own.

She swallowed. This wasn't keeping with her plan to maintain distance between them.

Wide shoulders blocked the rest of the cabin from her view. Although she wanted to bolt like a frightened hare, she stood her ground.

Landon shook his head, a bewildered expression on his face. "Little fool," he muttered. Circling his arms about her, he brought her full against his hardened frame and her breath would have left her in a *whoosh* if she hadn't gasped in surprise first.

His lips captured hers, demanding, *insisting* she respond. This was madness. She had to be stronger than this! Keelan tried to pull away, but found herself paralyzed by his touch. His arms, like iron bands, held her immobile. His lips moved against hers in a way that made her forget where she was. His fiery kiss radiated a heat which spread through her body and warmed the core of her soul. His hands slid down her sides and slipped around to caress her buttocks, pressing her to him; the hardness of his passion pulled forth a yearning from deep within her belly. She wanted this, yes. She wanted *him*. Part of her wanted to shout with joy. He wanted *her*. But wanting wasn't enough, not for her. She needed him to want *only* her.

She desired him, yes, but not like this. Not with the possibility he wanted her, but didn't actually love her as she loved him. Especially not with his mistress here.

How was she supposed to defend herself against an assault like this? Landon's tongue played with hers in an exotic dance. The sweetness of his mouth tormented her self-control. Memories swirled in her mind like a tornado... The two of them, trapped in the small tattered cabin during the storm, his hands on her calves, his lips tracing fire on her thigh, the musky scent of him mixed with leather and rain, the beauty of his face, eyes like the sky. She was unable to hold on to one vision long enough to complete it before another took its place.

Except for one memory.

Landon and Annette standing close... her hand on his chest. Was he using Keelan for his own temporary satisfaction? Or Annette? Was he using *both* of them? Dear God, she was still unable to stop kissing him; her free will had vanished along with her common sense. Her affection for him was deeper than she wanted to admit, and although her mind told her to stay away from him, it was impossible to retreat when he was this close.

This warm. This passionate. This vibrant.

Still, she managed to bring her hand to his chest and weakly push against it. Curiously, instead of shoving him, her hand spread over hardened muscles rippling beneath her fingers. She gasped as his hand found her breast, then groaned as his fingers brushed away the fabric binding them, tracing a sensual circle around the taut rosy peak he had somehow freed from bondage.

His kisses traced a fiery trail down her throat, and she drew a ragged breath. As the air rushed into her lungs, her head sought to clear itself from the passion her heart and body so eagerly sought. She wanted more of this, but what if the end result was more pain? Would he be kissing Annette like this later tonight?

This time, she pushed harder against his chest.

"Landon," she breathed. "Stop!"

He stopped but didn't release her. His eyes bored into hers, a glowing, smoldering light visible in the deep blue depths.

"Don't you understand, sweet Keelan?" He traced the line of

demarcation between the darkly stained skin of her chest and the creamy white of her breasts. "My allegiance is to you and you alone. Why would I seek another when my only desire is for you?"

Were these silky words simply a means to get her into his bed? How could she possibly believe him when he'd obviously planned on sending her to Philadelphia while sharing this leg of his journey with Annette? Landon danced with Annette Camsby at Doreen's ball, her hand on his chest, his arm on her waist. He seemed willing enough to endure her touch and affections then. What had changed? Anything? Nothing?

She couldn't afford to be enchanted by his charms and sensual kisses, but oh, how she wanted to be. She wanted to beg for it.

Although it took every bit of emotional and physical strength she could muster, she managed to push herself away from him.

"Keelan, don't—" he whispered hoarsely.

Disappointment and regret swirled into anger.

"You have succeeded only in convincing me you are no more than a rutting dog," she said woodenly, squeezing her eyes shut once again. "Now, unhand me at once! And please, don't do that again. Ever."

Distance. Distance. *Distance.*

His arms were slow to comply, but eventually he released her and she jerked away from his heat and penetrating gaze. She focused on repairing her appearance as best she could, given the condition of her sodden garments. The wet linen strips which served to both protect her wounds and bind her breasts were useless; they'd dropped around her waist in their soggy state. She groaned in frustration as the bindings ignored her fingers' demands.

"Perhaps I can lend some assistance," Landon quietly offered from behind her. Was that disappointment? His ruse didn't work, and she had discovered his scheme.

Keelan shook her head as she glanced over her shoulder and

fought to keep her voice from trembling. "I doubt any assistance you offer will benefit me in any way."

He had donned his breeches and was rummaging through the lower drawer of the tallboy. "I might surprise you." He removed a long knife, a folded piece of soft doeskin, and a long leather lace. "Although I would prefer otherwise, under these circumstances I am forced to aid you in your quest to hide that soft feminine form of yours, which I have come to crave so deeply."

He placed the soft leather on the floor and then proceeded to carve several holes along the short sides of the rectangular hide. The muscles in his shoulders and back rippled with his movements, and she hated herself for admiring them.

"My original intent was to have this made into a pair of gloves. However, I believe it now must serve a greater calling." His sensual lips curved into the slightest smile. He moved to stand before her, holding the short sides of the doeskin in his fingers.

She eyed him warily. "A corset? I fail to understand how wearing *that* will benefit my disguise," she questioned, lifting a skeptical brow.

"It is not intended for that purpose, love," he replied, an amused glint in his eyes. "Remove your shirt."

"I will *not!*" she gasped, horrified. She was quite proud of herself for fighting off Landon Hart and his mesmerizing lure. Granted, it took her a few moments, but now that she'd managed to push him far enough away, she didn't dare jeopardize her position. She was weak, *too* weak to test her resolve so soon.

"This will cover you better over the bandage," he explained patiently but firmly. "Now, trust me and do as I say."

"I don't need your help. I can do it myself." The pitch of panic in her own voice made her clamp a hand over her own mouth.

"Keelan," a quiet note of exasperation permeated his tone. "I intend for this to be laced over your chest to disguise your—curves—better." He held up the leather and cord. "One of us must hold it together while the other threads the tie. Now, please, remove the shirt."

Realizing there was little she could do to dissuade him from his mission, she presented her back and shrugged out of the shirt which had once been his.

Despite the dark stain applied, Keelan was positive her skin still reddened at what she was about to do.

CHAPTER 26
TRUCE

Landon's gut churned and his flayed pride smarted at Keelan's words. *A rutting dog?*

He'd bared his soul! He'd told her about the sacrifice he'd made by sending his ship ahead to Harbour Town instead of Philadelphia. Up north, he would have delivered the rice and indigo for a delicious profit. Harbour Town had no need for such cargo. They had their own rice plantations and indigo mills.

He'd even *told* her he desired only her, not Annette. She didn't *believe* him.

How could she not believe him? He'd never lied to her before, had he? Snatching his shirt from his chair, he clenched his teeth together to prevent any ill-timed words from falling out of the mouth that still ached to kiss her again. Her kiss had been tender and full of longing. He could sense it. The heat from her body ignited a fire within his. They'd experienced a rush of passion *together.* Somewhere deep in the delicate recesses of his soul, a sensation stirred in a withered hollow he'd believed had been destroyed long ago.

In his past, loving a woman had only brought on pain and

humiliation. It had made him weak. He'd squelched it. Never again. At least that is what he promised himself.

But...he not only wanted Keelan, desired her; he *needed* her. He needed her by his side. She made him feel strong, confident and *whole*. A tiny thought wheedled its way into his mind, itching like a mosquito bite.

She didn't trust him.

At all.

Trust between them was crucial now, if they were going to be together. He had to be able to trust her to keep his secrets. If they were ever exposed, his life—along with many others—would be placed in jeopardy. How was he supposed to do that in confidence when she obviously didn't have faith in him?

Keelan took off the shirt, her movements jerky, like a wary doe. She'd put a barrier between them, more fragile than thin china. She feared he would shatter it.

He could. Easily.

But...what would that accomplish, other than give her a reason to call him a bully? What could he do to gain Keelan Grey's elusive trust? This was a new problem he'd never had to deal with before. His crew trusted him with their lives and their welfare. *Not once* had he ever been required to prove his worth or honor. To *anyone*. If anything, she should have to convince him *she* could be trusted.

The shirt dropped to the floor and his gut tightened as he stared at the angry slashes along her delicate back and shoulders. Fury welled in his chest. He'd spent days seeking an informant who'd reveal Keelan's kidnapper. He'd found nothing. Even the few men captured at the warehouse didn't know the true identity of Gampo's employer. The man was nothing more than a shadow. Landon would have liked justice to be done upon the bastard, but he couldn't find him, dammit. And Gampo escaped. Again.

Keelan adjusted the bandages, then crossed her arms over her breasts and peered timidly over her shoulder.

He placed the soft doeskin against her back, and then reached the ends around her chest, pausing as his knuckles gently grazed hers. She tensed and sucked in her breath.

Ah, then. She might not trust him, but she desired his touch, nonetheless. He could work with that.

"Would you care to hold the ends, my love?"

◌◌◌

KEELAN SNATCHED the ends of the leather corset from his hands, and pulled them tightly against the center of her chest, determined to repel his charm. He peered around her shoulder. Smiling almost lewdly, he dangled the long lace before her eyes. "Would you have me apply the ties, or perhaps hold the leather, so you can string the laces?"

The cause for his amusement was quite clear. If he held the ends, she would have to trust him to keep them snug over her chest. She'd just as soon let a fox in to the chickens' roost. If she permitted him to string the lace, she'd have to endure the touch of his fingertips as he threaded it through the holes. As humiliating as the second choice was, it was definitely the lesser of the two evils. Hopefully.

"Proceed with the lace, Captain." She narrowed her eyes and added sternly, "But try to be a gentleman about it."

He gave her a gallant bow. "I am here to serve, my dearest."

"I ponder your comprehension of the term," she replied dryly.

Landon indeed took his leisure in threading the lace through the holes in the hide; one by one, despite the glowering looks she threw his way. He threaded each eyelet with extreme care and slow, deliberate movements. When the task was complete, she snatched the laces from his fingers and angrily tightened them.

"Scoundrel."

He gave her a lopsided grin as he allowed his gaze to roam at will. "I take pride in the fact I complete all my tasks with perfection."

"Bah!" She bent down to retrieve her shirt from the floor, missing the admiring attention he gave to her slender hips and backside.

"What am I to do with you, sweet?" Landon inquired softly.

She gave a sarcastic laugh as she buttoned the shirt. "Leave me alone. You have enough distractions as it is."

"Ahhh, but my love, that is impossible. It's imperative for you continue in your guise as 'young Mahdi' to keep you safe," he mused. He took in every detail of her appearance, from the snug fit of her breeches to the green fire of her eyes. "But, I cannot allow you to hang your hammock in the hold with the crew at night. Too risky. You'll have to sleep here."

She stared at him, aghast. *Was he mad?* "I will not!"

"You must," he stated firmly. "Keelan, you can't keep a hammock in the hold with the crew. You're bound to be discovered. It will only be a matter of time before one of the men joins you in the head, or surprises you at a most inopportune moment. At least here, you'll have privacy."

She bit her lip. In truth, her thoughts had traveled the same path earlier. Sharing sleeping quarters with Landon Hart, however, would be disastrous. "I will not play the doxy to your lusts," she said angrily. Best to get that point through his thick skull. "Instead, I shall leave that duty to Annette Camsby."

Landon stared at her a moment, the tiniest hint of a smile playing about his mouth. Then he shook his head. "I will harbor no arguments, Keelan." Landon said sternly. "With Garrison aboard, your safety depends on your identity remaining secret for a while longer."

He knew? She fixed an accusing glare on him. "You knew he was aboard this ship?"

Landon shrugged casually. "Had I known *you* were here, I would never have allowed it. This was an opportunity for me to watch him. I have my suspicions about Garrison, and I had intended to test them."

Doubt tugged at her mind. She wanted to believe him and trust him, but she was torn. He wanted her in his bed. He used concern as a ploy to weaken her guard. There had been no mention of marriage vows to accompany all the things he desired of her. By-blow or not, she wouldn't play the part of a mistress for him. Or anyone, but especially not him.

Ugh. Who did she think she was fooling? One touch from Landon Hart would melt whatever wall she managed to construct between them. She had to find a way to be stronger than that. Keelan clenched her jaw in firmer resolve. She would not allow his handsome features and beguiling charm to sap her resistance.

She would *not.*

Landon reached for his shirt and shrugged it on. "You'd best get back to the galley. Marcel will wonder what has become of you." He grinned. "No doubt, he'll think I saw fit to see to your bath, as well as my own." Landon's eyes sparkled with laughter. "He'll never realize how truthful that assumption would be."

That man! Keelan snatched up the buckets and stomped out. Landon Hart was not going to make this easy.

Well, he was about to find out she was stronger than she looked.

CHAPTER 27
GAMPO'S SPIES

E verett studied the scribbled note.
I know where she is. Meet me in the aft hold. <u>Now.</u>

Something seemed off. Maybe it was the tattered piece of handbill upon which the message was written. Maybe it was because not many people knew he was aboard. He raised his voice as loudly as he dared, "Who gave this to you?"

The man shrugged. "Someone came up behind me and whispered into my ear. Told me not to turn around. Put the paper and a shilling in my hand and then told me to give it to the tallest man on deck. That be you." He moved on before Everett could ask another question.

Sweat beaded along his upper lip. Had one of his contacts found Keelen? Problem was, his fortunes had recently changed, and he was unable to pay the reward he'd promised. Perhaps the man would be desperate enough to negotiate. He pushed off from the rail near the aft deck and sauntered toward the hatch. He swept his gaze around the ship. Annette Camsby stood near the helm beside Captain O'Brien. The plainly dressed woman who'd accompanied her stood nearby. She glanced his way and gave him a slight smile, which he returned with a quick nod to indicate all was well.

KEELAN APPROACHED the helm like a child tasked with cutting her own switch for her punishment. Annette was there chirping at Conal O'Brien like a spring bird. Time to tell Conal to return to his cabin so Landon could apprise him of "the situation."

The situation being her.

As she took the first step, a movement caught her attention, and she glanced over in time to catch sight of Dr. Garrison ducking below deck. It wouldn't have merited her consideration if the petite woman who'd accompanied Annette aboard hadn't dashed over to follow him.

There was something familiar about her.

Keelan stopped and peered more closely. The young lady paused to cast a furtive look about before she descended. For a brief second, her face was visible from beneath her bonnet.

Doreen!

Keelan had left a letter for Uncle Jared, telling him he could find his daughter with Mrs. Camsby. Did he read it? Was Doreen accompanying Annette or the doctor? She sucked in a breath. Both?

She started to follow her cousin, then remembered her prior task. She darted up the steps to the helm, found Captain O'Brien, and quickly delivered Landon's message. Annette's irritated expression at the interruption lifted her mood somewhat. At the captain's nod, she spun and headed below deck.

The lower hold was dark and reeked of old, wet rags. It was separated into three sections. The cargo was dispersed based on weight and destination. Sounds of a muffled conversation rose above the wooden beams, encompassing the hold like a giant ribcage. It took a moment to adjust her eyes; the light was thin, coming from a single lantern somewhere near the center of the space.

Keelan snaked her way between barrels, bales, and crates, following the low hum of murmured conversation. A high shriek, suddenly cut short, froze her in place. It was followed by a soft *thud*. Heart pounding and fearing for Doreen's welfare, Keelan crept forward, then paused at a familiar voice.

"So ye thinks ye can steal away without paying yer share to Gampo, eh?"

Orvis Hatch!

"I did no such th-th-thing," Garrison responded. "There were no shares. The plan failed. What do you want? Why are you aboard this vessel?" His voice rose to a treble pitch.

"Seein' as how Gampo couldn't find the wench what killed 'is first, I was instructed to take vengeance from yer hide instead, since ye be the one who paid us to bring 'er in." A pause. "Unless ye can tell me where to find 'er. Me bones tell me she's aboard here somewheres."

Keelan's entire body went rigid. Her intuition had been right; Everett Garrison had been responsible for the kidnapping. It made her wonder more about his claim that Doreen had misunderstood his instructions, and had given Papa too much medicine, killing him. Her mouth became dry. Somehow, she didn't think it was Doreen's mistake.

She peeked around a large crate and bit back a gasp. Doreen was slumped on the floor. Orvis had a knife at the doctor's throat and had him backed up against a wall of crates next to Doreen's motionless form. A trickle of blood darkened the floor beneath her cousin's nose.

She backed away to get help, then paused. If she left, she might return too late. Orvis looked eager to draw blood. She slipped the dagger from her boot and circled around to the other side of the large crate, hoping to stay out of sight a bit longer and get closer to insure a more accurate throw.

Dr. Garrison raised his hands, palms out. "I don't know where she went. After she ran from the warehouse, I couldn't find her either. I'm sorry."

Orvis drew his eyebrows low. "Gampo don't take lightly to them what's backed out on an accord. Them warehouse goods weren't no easy takin's like ye said they would be, and in the end, we didn't get no shares from our labors, neither."

The doctor's hands shook and his chin trembled. "Tell—tell Gampo I'll make it up to him. I—"

Hatch gave an incredulous snort of laughter. "Like I said, he wants it to come outta yer hide," he sneered, gripping Garrison's hair with his free hand. His blade flashed, and the doctor shrieked.

Keelan froze in terror. Orvis now held a bloody piece of the doctor's scalp, hair still attached in his hand. With a dark snarl, he raised his knife again. She jolted into action and moved from her hiding place to get a clearer shot. The ship pitched slightly and shifted her balance enough to cause her shoulder to bump the crate. Orvis sliced his head toward the noise.

He'd seen her. With no other choice, she drew back her dagger, and took the only option she had, which was to go on the attack or at least attempt to appear threatening. "Move away from them." Her voice sounded unnatural in her ears.

Instead of doing as she demanded, the pirate gave her a distorted grin that was more like a grimace, considering his face was still swollen and discolored from their earlier engagements. Everett stumbled to the side as Orvis drove the blade into his torso.

"No!" she screamed.

Orvis whirled, pulling a second blade from his belt, and strode toward her. "I'll have yer eyes fer fish bait, boy."

In a panic, she threw her dagger, but it went wide, slicing off a piece of Orvis's left ear. He flinched and howled. Behind him, Dr. Garrison struggled to pull out the blade buried between his ribs. Finally succeeding, he pushed himself away from the wall and staggered toward the pirate. Orvis grinned at her and raised his blade as he moved closer. Behind him, Everett lurched forward and with a desperate heave of effort, buried the dagger in Orvis's back.

The pirate fell face down and didn't move.

His strength expelled, Garrison began to collapse.

"Dr. Garrison!" She ran to help him, but his weight dragged both of them to the floor.

Doreen stirred and pushed herself to a sitting position. Her eyes were wide, and she numbly swept her gaze from side to side until she found Garrison crumpled in a heap on the floor. "Everett, my darling, what happened?" Doreen whimpered as she crawled toward them, oblivious to the blood dripping from her temple and nose.

The doctor had his hand pressed against his ribs; blood was still streaming between his fingers. Keelan ripped off her vest, wadded it into a ball, and gave it to him to press against his side.

He didn't look up from his task. "I need my medicine bag and some bandages." His words were choppy and pained. He glanced at Keelan. "It would help, boy, if you would press this wound firmly. I'm finding it hard to apply enough pressure on my own."

"Yes sir," Keelan replied and quickly replaced his hand with hers. For all he'd done to the people she'd held dear all her life, she couldn't ignore his injury. The doctor had just saved her from being attacked, and probably from being killed.

Doreen teetered to her feet. Keelan pressed harder to stop the blood from seeping and glanced at her cousin. "Make sure you have someone inform Captain Hart or Captain O'Brien what's happened."

Doreen's head snapped around in her direction. Keelan stilled. She'd forgotten to lower her voice.

Did Doreen recognize it? She quickly directed her gaze back to the doctor. The exchange between Orvis and Dr. Garrison had reaffirmed the decision to travel in disguise had been a good one. The pirates continued to seek her out. She couldn't risk another recognizing her like Simon had. Her heart pounded in her chest, and she felt Doreen's stare boring into her back.

Her cousin paused a long moment before she responded, "I will."

Dr. Garrison had pulled a handkerchief from his pocket and was pressing it against his wounded head. Keelan wiped the blood from his eyes with the corner of it. Two emotions warred in her chest. The first, anger at Garrison. The second was a grudging gratitude. She glanced at the still, face-down form of Orvis Pike lying a few feet away. If Dr. Garrison hadn't prevented Orvis from attacking her, she'd be dead. She'd panicked, and it had almost cost her life.

Everett grimaced as he readjusted the handkerchief. "Thank you. If you hadn't distracted him, I'd probably be dead, and so would Miss Grey." He glanced toward his side where her hand pressed. "Can you tell how deeply the blade went in?"

Keelan lifted her hand long enough to peek. "It went in at an upward angle under your ribs."

He closed his eyes. "Not too much damage then, only pain. I can instruct Doreen—Miss Grey, to dress it. I will need whiskey and bandages."

"I'll see you get them," she replied.

The sound of running feet interrupted their conversation, and Daniel's voice rang out in the dim light, "Mahdi, where are you?"

"Over here!" she called.

Conal, Landon and Daniel rounded the large crate and skidded to a stop.

"Are you hurt?" Landon's gaze swept over her body as she stood.

Keelan shook her head. "Dr. Garrison's been stabbed." She related the earlier conversation and events.

Landon's mouth thinned and his eyes glinted with something dangerous as she finished. "We'll lock the doctor in the rear hold until we reach Harbour Town." He gestured to Orvis and murmured to Conal, "It's doubtful he boarded the ship alone. Until we find his cohorts, tell Johnny, Remus and Henry to be extra vigilant around the newest hands we hired and report any suspicions to us."

Conal nodded grimly. "There's less than ten new hires, I'd figure. I'll have them move their hammocks together. Easier to keep track of them when they're off duty."

Doreen's voice warbled up and down as she scrambled around the crates. "I'm here! I'm back. I have the medicine bag," Her face was blood-stained and her hands shook as she brushed a handful of hair away from her eyes. She shouldered her way between the men, dropped to the other side of the doctor's prone form, and let out a shaky breath. "I've been assisting Dr. Garrison for the past several months. I know what to do."

Doreen removed a clean cloth and a whiskey bottle. She nodded to Keelan to remove her hand and when she did, Doreen doused the wound, causing the doctor to suck in his breath. A strong odor of spirits wafted in the closed air of the hold. Doreen immediately pressed the clean cloth over his wound. "Continue to put pressure on it," she instructed Keelan, without glancing at her. Keelan complied and Doreen rummaged through the bag again.

Garrison flicked his hand toward the bottle. "Whiskey. To dull the pain," he said hoarsely before squeezing his eyes shut.

Keelan reached for the bottle, but Doreen stopped her.

"Wait, I have something better," she mumbled, still rooting through the bag. "Ah, here it is." She pulled out a small, unlabeled brown bottle and scooted closer to Dr. Garrison's head, which she gently put on her lap, as if handling thin glass. "Everett, drink this." She put the bottle to his lips, he opened his mouth, and took a gulp. His eyelids flew open.

"That... wasn't whiskey! What did you give me?" The panicked pitch of his voice bounced off the wood hull.

Doreen's eyes shone with tears. "Don't fret, darling. It's the pain medication you purchased for Uncle George. The bottle you told me would take away the worst pain."

His face paled further. "No..."

Doreen stroked his forehead and reapplied the handkerchief to his head wound. Tears streamed down her cheeks and dripped from her jaw. "You said it was terribly expensive and only for severe pain, but I can't allow you to suffer like this. I care too much for you."

Everett Garrison's face contorted as he struggled to speak. "That's... not..."

He convulsed and Doreen let out a startled cry. "What's wrong? What's happening?"

Garrison arched and thrashed, jerking away from her. Keelan grabbed the bottle from Doreen's grasp and sniffed. It wasn't whiskey or vinegar. Her chest constricted as she put together all the pieces. Dr. Garrison hadn't just given Papa the wrong medication. He had instructed Doreen to administer poison to Papa the night he died.

The same realization stuttered across Doreen's face. "Dear Lord!" she cried. "Why? Why did you have me give this to my uncle?" Her eyes were wide with shock and terror.

"He killed my Rachel. My love," he choked. "She and my family... were on the ship he sank." He fumbled with the pocket of his coat and withdrew the tattered letter Rachel had written, accepting his marriage proposal. His hand trembled so badly, the letter almost fell apart. He pressed it over his heart. "My Rachel needed to be avenged." An odd gurgling sound emanated from his throat. He gasped and convulsed again, then his chest stilled.

"Oh dear God, please forgive me! Forgive me!" Doreen wailed, covering her face with her hands.

"It's not your fault," Keelan said softly, kneeling beside her. "You thought you were helping him. You didn't know." Doreen collapsed into her arms and Keelan held her even as tears welled in her own eyes. "You didn't know."

CHAPTER 28
A SECRET REVEALED

Keelan scurried through the hatch as fast as her quaking limbs would take her. She jumped up the steps and on to the deck. She had a desperate need for fresh air to clear her head. Her mind screamed in torment from the brutal realizations pummeling her. She paused at the rail and gulped in several deep jagged breaths. She'd had her suspicions, but deep down she didn't want them to be true. Deep down, she had known.

Garrison. Murderer.

They had trusted him. Papa had helped and encouraged him to develop his practice. He'd preyed on them and their charity. *Garrison* killed Papa and hired pirates to kidnap her. Those actions had nothing to do with infatuation as she had errantly surmised. In the several months prior to arriving in Charleston, he'd played the part of an awkward physician with ease. She shuddered.

She had viewed him as a harmless, clumsy gawk of a man, who tried her level of tolerance as would a pesky fly. How wrong she had been.

She placed a hand over her heart and tried to will it to slow to a normal rate. How foolish of her to be so blind to his charade.

She had been so concerned with her own problems, like avoiding a marriage to Pratt; she had missed what was happening beneath her nose. She clutched her hand against her chest. The locket and ring dug into her skin and reminded her of their presence.

Keelan pulled the ribbon, lifting the two items from the crevice between her breasts. She stared at the signet ring, a welcome distraction from the grisly scene below deck.

In the rosy, golden light of the setting sun, she gently traced her finger over the crest, wondering idly about the man who'd sired her. Was he a good father to his other children, her half brothers and sisters? She had always prayed for siblings. Would they accept her? Probably not, but she would still wish for it to be so. What other secrets awaited her in the darkness of George Grey's old trunk? Whose family's blood surged through her heart?

The man in the miniature stared back at her. What features did her true father's seed give her? The eyes? Her father's smiling green eyes sparkled at her as if they shared a secret. Her mother's eyes were gray, so perhaps, yes, the eyes. What of her warm russet tresses? Her mother's hair was a pale brown, her father's a shiny black. Whence came the red curls? Perhaps another relative, a grandparent, maybe?

She straightened. Pondering her heritage would not reveal her mother's secret any quicker. The probable presence of another pirate spy aboard made her quest more dangerous. Even so, she would see it through to the end. If her father's house did not welcome her, so be it, but the desire to meet her kin would drive her there, in time.

The ship's bell sang with a mellow tongue as it marked the end of the last dogwatch. Another shift of seamen would soon rouse from their hammocks for duty until the hourglass had been turned four times and the ship's bell rung eight.

A quiet voice rose above the creaking ship and the gentle splash of the sea against the sturdy hull. "You've had a rough time over these past few weeks. How do you fare?"

Keelan jumped, then managed a small smile as Conal O'Brien stepped forward and leaned his forearms against the rail next to her. His eyes were kind. She relaxed. "I'm alive. Considering the fate which has fallen on the rest of my family, I feel blessed, but I worry about the other pirates amongst us."

"As the captain is also the ship's master, I can see justice met for any offense aboard this craft. If we find them, I can have them put in irons and punished." He shifted his position. "Since they're likely wanted by the law, we'll deliver them when we make port in Harbour Town and let them meet their fate at the short end of a rope."

The shoreline had become a distant black line, and the sun began its inevitable descent. Wind snapped the sails, and the ship responded with a groan, ropes whining in the sheaves. "You have my sympathies on the death of your father," O'Brien said quietly.

Keelan swallowed. "Thank you. However, the man was not my father," she said hoarsely, fighting back the tears threatening to spill. If Landon hadn't already told him, he probably would soon. The two were fast friends. At least she'd be able to scrutinize Conal O'Brien's reaction to the news. She continued, "Not truly by blood, but he raised me as his own. I should have suspected Garrison was poisoning him. If I had paused to ponder the situation, I would have seen the entire puzzle laid out." Anger welled in her chest. Why hadn't she seen it?

"He fooled everyone." He put his hand on her shoulder and gave it a small comforting squeeze. "You can't blame yourself."

Her throat constricted. Keelan shrugged her silent thanks and wiped her nose on her sleeve.

He chuckled. "You're becoming used to playing the boy, Mahdi."

Realizing what she had just done was far from ladylike, Keelan gave the captain a chagrined smile. "So it would seem."

He rubbed the back of his neck, as if pondering a question before he finally spoke. "Ye said something that confused me.

And I beg yer pardon if it offends ye in any way. Ye said Commodore Grey was *not* yer sire?" He left the question hanging.

A solitary tear broke free and began a lonely trail down her cheek. "On his deathbed, Papa told me he could not give my mother a child, so she went to another man... One who could... who could give her..." Her voice broke and she paused for a moment to gather herself. *Stop being silly. Crying about it won't change anything.* She should be happier. Now, she had the opportunity to choose her own path. That thought provided a bit more comfort.

After wiping her eyes, she showed him the locket, dangling on the ribbon with the ring. "My mother took a lover who sired me. And years ago, he looked like this."

O'Brien bent low and studied the miniature.

A young man. Dark hair. Green eyes.

His eyes widened with shock, then hardened with fury. "Where did you get this!" he demanded, snatching the locket from her fingers. He stared at it, then his gaze followed the red ribbon to the ring dangling at the end.

She stepped back at the unseemly reaction and eyed him warily. "Papa gave it to me. He said my mother cherished it." She studied him. His jaw was clenching and unclenching sporadically. "Why does it disturb you? Do you know him?"

He stepped close and looked hard at Keelan. "Yes, I know him," he said.

Her mouth dropped open. Could it really be this easy to find the identity of her sire?

O'Brien stared at the locket, then shoved it back to her. "And now, I think I understand the purpose of Uncle Fynn's meeting with Commodore Grey. He must have suspected."

"Suspected what?" Hart and O'Brien had visited Twin Pines to speak with Papa, but she knew not the topic. Her mind swirled with questions. "Who was your Uncle Fynn?"

His jaw tightened. "My mother's brother." He jabbed a finger at the miniature. "I have seen that portrait before, as well."

"You—you have actually seen this *same* portrait?" She stared at the miniature. "In God's name, where?"

"It hangs on the parlor wall in my parent's home, next to my mother's," he stated flatly. At her curious stare, Conal O'Brien inhaled sharply and then continued.

"That man is my father."

CHAPTER 29
A SHIP ON THE HORIZON

Conal O'Brien braced his hands wide along the rail and leaned forward, letting his head drop. "Uncle Fynn must have suspected you were sired by my father. It was probably why he wanted to meet with Commodore Grey, to confirm it." He gave Keelan a sideways glance. "The Commodore told us he didn't know Fynn, but thinking back on it, neither Hart nor I felt he was being entirely forthright."

Keelan wasn't sure what to say. While she was euphoric because the search for her father's identity was completed so quickly, Conal had to deal with his obvious anger toward the man as well as his desire to protect his mother.

He shook his head. "If ye hadn't had the ring, I wouldna of believed ye. My da has always worshipped my mum. I canna believe he…" He looked away and stared at the sea flowing quickly past the hull. Bursts of spume sprayed in their wake.

It was easy to understand the turmoil of emotions swirling in Conal's gut. The same ones had assaulted her the night Papa died. Keelan untied the ribbon around her neck and removed the ring. She held it out to him. "This belongs to you, then. It is your family's signet ring, your crest, is it not?"

"Aye." He opened his hand, and she placed it on his palm. He held it up in the fading light and studied it a moment. "The four lions represent deathless courage in battle by four brothers. The wheat is a symbol of plenty. We are a clan descended of sea warriors." He gave her a small smile. "And more recently, sea merchants." He slipped the ring on his finger. "Thank you for returning it."

Her fingers curled over the locket half. "May I keep the miniature?" Papa said her mother treasured it because her father gifted it to her. It was the one thing she had which connected both her parents.

Conal nodded, his nostrils flaring. "My mother has one of her own, more recently painted." He dropped his head again. "I'm sorry. I shouldna have spoken to ye that way."

"Don't apologize." She wanted to comfort him, but wasn't sure he'd welcome her pity. She touched his shoulder with her fingertips. "I understand how you feel. It's been difficult for me to digest all this information as well. My life is suddenly not what I thought it was."

He swallowed and lifted his head to check the sails. "'Tis no fault of yours. It shouldn't be held against ye."

She looked out over the ocean at the sun, burning red near the horizon, uncertain how to ask the question burning equally hot on her tongue. There was no easy way to ask it. Perhaps she should simply blurt it out. "Why would your Uncle Fynn need to confirm my existence with Papa—Commodore Grey? I can't think of a reason why such information would be important to him."

Conal shrugged. "Fynn was never one to comply with popular opinion. He followed his own compass. There were many times I challenged his reasoning, but he always had a firm plan and in the end, it usually worked his way." He glanced at her through long, auburn lashes. "He and my father were tight as kin, although he was my mother's brother. I want to believe his interest in the commodore wouldn't cause my mum pain in any way." Conal pushed away from the rail. "There's no telling now. He took his reasoning to the grave with him." He bid her a good evening and excused himself.

The cow lowed forlornly from her pen. A nanny goat bleated a sympathetic response.

Keelan stood alone, still in shock.

The ocean waves broke against the ship's stern, the sails clapped and inhaled the breath of the wind. The sun had descended closer to the horizon, as if fleeing the thick clouds chasing it. Her mind swirled with the rush of recent events.

Everett. Murderer. *Monster.*

Conal. Captain. Friend. *Half brother?*

Her father—his father? What wicked, twisted trick of fate was this? How could the world be so small?

How could it be so cruel?

Her musings were interrupted by the dogwatch's cry. "Sail, ho'!"

Conal's voice boomed a short distance away. "Where away?"

"Near two points off the starboard bow, sir!" came the reply.

O'Brien strode across the deck. "Johnny, take the glass and go aloft. Try to make out what she is."

They all waited while Johnny scampered up. Impatience tinged O'Brien's voice, "What do you see, man?"

"Aye sir, 'tis a schooner with dark sails. She looks like the *Dragon*!"

Conal's voice barked through the evening mist. "Call all hands and make sail for her!"

A sudden flurry of motion arose from the deck.

"Mahdi!"

She jumped and shifted her gaze from the man clinging to the ropes at the top of the mainmast to the voice harkening her. Conal's piercing green gaze captured her own. Eyes like hers.

Tussled, russet locks curled against his forehead, lifted by the wind. Russet locks like hers.

"Find Hart!"

She scampered below the deck. As Keelan neared the galley, low voices made her pause. Daniel and Landon. She couldn't make out what they were saying. As she was about to creep closer to listen, Landon strode past the door in the direction of his cabin and then paused at the sight of Keelan standing near the steps.

His face softened. "What is it?"

"A—a sh-ship," she stammered. "A ship has been sighted!"

His mouth tightened at the news, causing her stomach to twist. They were in trouble. Without a word, he flicked his hand, motioning her up to the deck before him. She wordlessly complied, fear pricking her skin.

Gampo had caught up with them.

৩৯৪

LANDON ADMIRED Keelan's pleasantly curved backside as he followed her up the narrow steps. At this angle, he would have to be a fool or a blind man to not notice the womanly shape in front of him. He scowled and made a mental note to find her a longer jerkin to wear.

Landon's new concern was keeping Keelan's identity secret until Orvis Pike's cohort was revealed, removed from the ship and placed in the custody of Harbour Town's sheriff.

He mentally ran through the new faces he'd seen on the *Seeker's* decks. Orvis had done a good job staying out of sight; otherwise, Keelan would have recognized him long before the confrontation in the hold. Everyone must remain watchful.

He refocused his attention to the issue at hand and cursed. He'd hoped by sending the *Desire* southward early, Gampo would follow, taking him and his thirst for revenge further away from Keelan. A nervous twinge shot through Landon's stomach. Keelan was supposed to be journeying north, away from danger, not south toward it. The sighting of another ship made him anxious, but he'd wait until he had a chance to view it through the glass before he'd worry about Keelan's safety.

As long as it wasn't a schooner with dark sails, they'd be fine.

CHAPTER 30
DARK SAILS

"It's a schooner with darkened sails," Conal said. "Although they fly no flag, I'd bet my last pint of grog that it's the *Dragon*."

Keelan caught her breath and gripped the rail until her knuckles stretched thin and white. Gampo! Why did he come after the *Seeker*? Did Orvis or the other pirates find a way to signal them? Her heart stuttered. Or had Gampo known all along she'd been aboard?

"Aye, it looks to be her," Landon responded, his mouth set in a grim line. He snapped the glass shut. "We're heavy with cargo. However, they approach leeward, probably returning from following the *Desire* to Harbour Town. They must have discovered Keelan wasn't on her. We make the port in less than a day. I suggest we start with half the water barrels since we can replace them quickly and then lose the rations."

Conal stared at Landon a moment before he sent orders to the crew. "Lighten the load. Unlash and pitch over the water barrels."

"Aye, sir!" Several crew mates jumped to action.

"Clear the lashes and load!" Conal shouted. His order was repeated and echoed in relay. Additional orders were relayed as the cannons, called guns on a ship, were primed to fire. He flung a command at Keelan. "Take Johnny and Remus down to the galley and haul up the heaviest contents of Marcel's larder."

Sails were hauled high and guns loaded. Men carried up crates of smaller weapons, such as rifles, pistols and swords and lashed them to the masts. Conal and Landon continued to shout commands while Keelan hurried to locate the two crewmen.

She found Remus and Johnny and after relaying the captain's instructions, the three headed for the galley.

Marcel met them at the galley door. "What eez—" At the sight of the three of them, he shook his head and sliced the air with his hand. "Non! Take ze water first! I spend too much—"

"The water has been let go, Marcel," Remus shouldered his way into the pantry. "We'll start with the salted fish and rice."

They hauled large barrels and sacks of other staples up to the amidships deck. Marcel, Keelan noted with amusement, grudgingly pointed to the items he was more willing to part with and greedily protected those he was not.

"You will not take my citrons!" The red-faced cook grabbed the burlap sack half-filled with bright, yellow lemons and clutched them to his chest. "Throw the goat instead!"

"You can't throw the goat overboard!" The words were out of Keelan's mouth before she had time to think.

Marcel and Remus stopped arguing and stared at her oddly. She almost froze in panic. A galley boy probably wouldn't have said that. What would he have said? "Take the molasses," she suggested. "At least it will not kick you."

Remus grinned and nodded. "Aye. That makes better sense. 'Tis easier to toss, too." He took the crock and headed up the steps.

Marcel, however, continued to stare long and hard at Keelan. "Why would you care about a goat?"

Keelan swallowed. "It's not the goat I care about," she replied, fearing the frenzied beating of her heart was visible in the pulse of her neck. "The captain ordered water barrels overboard. We'll need the goat for the milk."

Marcel narrowed his eyes After a second he nodded and shrugged. "Makes sense."

With as much calm as she could muster, Keelan wiped her nose on her sleeve, grabbed a bag of onions, and swiftly followed Remus to the upper deck. She'd come dangerously close to giving herself away. After noting Marcel's reaction, she wasn't sure she was safe from discovery just yet.

Above deck, an active crew had readied the guns and unfurled additional sails. The pirate ship maneuvered to intercept them, tacking back and forth like a serpent.

"There's a second vessel!" The call came down from the watch. "Ahead on the larboard side!"

"A second?" Conal reached for the glass and put it up to his eye. "A cunning trap. I wonder if she's a prize crew or is part of Gampo's fleet."

"Prize crew?" Keelan had never heard the term.

"The former crew what's aboard a taken vessel," Remus answered. "It's what *we* don't want ter become."

Conal shifted his stance, lowering the glass. "Johnny, eyes on the larboard sloop!" Conal barked. "Call out if she changes course."

"Aye, Captain!"

The second boat was ahead of them and in-between the *Seeker* and the pirates. If they slowed and turned toward them and the *Dragon* swooped in behind, Conal's ship would be raked across the stern and aft, as well. The small portable guns the sailors set up fore and aft couldn't possibly defend them against two other vessels raking them with their broadside guns.

Conal focused on the pirates and their darkened sails, the ominous look on his face making Keelan catch her breath. Worry seeped into her limbs. He didn't have to tell her this was bad.

Landon's earlier observation had proven worthy. The *Seeker* sailed with the current and the winds. The pirate ship was approaching from the east and starboard side. By the time it was able to position itself along the same path, the *Seeker* had begun to gain speed.

☙❧

A PUFF of smoke from the *Dragon* caught Keelan's attention. Immediately, a sailor gave a warning shout from the crosstrees before the report echoed over the water.

Conal whirled. "Helmsman! Hard to leeward!"

"Aye, sir!" The crewman spun the wheel to the left.

Landon barked another sharp order and a small sail was shifted. The ship changed its course, turning away from the dark sails.

To Keelan's relief, the cannonball landed well short, with a rather unimpressive splash. Elated, she whooped her cheer along with the crew.

Conal made an observation. "We're in range of their guns. We might not be able to lighten the load fast enough to outrun both of them," he said. He locked gazes with Landon, his gaze steady and predatory. "You know my take."

Landon crossed his arms. "The guns are ready." He held Conal's gaze a moment longer. "We have women aboard. We have to outrun them as best we can and pray we reach Harbour Town first."

Conal nodded. "I realize that." He glared at Gampo's ship. "I'd give my last drop of water to see that schooner sink to Davy Jones locker."

Landon merely nodded. They would not confront him today. Sails were trimmed, and the *Seeker* made another sweeping turn westward. The crew began wetting the canvas so it would hold more wind. Keelan carried buckets of seawater from the rail to Johnny, who handed them to another shipmate. Her shoulders burned under the strain. Although she tried to be careful, water sloshed to the deck, making the walk back and forth a slippery one until someone scattered sand over the boards.

"The little sloop has lowered her mainsail!" a sailor shouted.

Keelan's heart lurched against her chest in a mild panic. The *Seeker* bounded over the waves and would soon pass the smaller boat. Gampo's vessel still approached from farther west, and if it didn't alter its course, it would ram the smaller sloop broadside.

"What the devil is Gampo doing?" Landon leaned forward and focused on the other two boats. "Is he using the sloop as a shield?"

Conal scowled. "We won't attack the other boat, and he knows it. He'll come around then bolt out of her cover, ready to fire his port side guns."

Damage and destruction to the *Seeker* seemed inevitable. Keelan reached down and checked for the dagger strapped to her boot, hoping its presence would bolster her bravado.

It didn't.

"Keelan."

She jumped, startled at the sudden voice in her ear. She spun around and expelled a breath. "Landon, you almost frightened me out of my skin."

For a moment, concern left his face as he gave her a lopsided grin. "My apologies," he murmured softly. "I would never be able to forgive myself if I frightened you out of your skin." He paused while his gaze traveled from her eyes to her throat. A strange tightening in her belly moved with his perusal as it continued downward. "Not long ago," he continued, just audible, "while attempting to bathe, I found the feel of your skin most appealing."

"Captain," she could only breathe the words. "You have no scruples."

"Nay." He smiled devilishly. "I haven't a single one."

She wanted to walk into his arms and let his strength calm her fear. However, that would be counter productive to her current objective, which was *distance*. He stepped closer, and she caught herself breathing him in.

Stop it.

This was not being strong. This was being weak. This was definitely not keeping a safe distance. *Was* there a safe distance? Landon reached his arms around her and she almost jumped back, fearing he was about to embrace her in front of the crew. A stiff leather belt pressed against her hips as he buckled a pair of pistols to her waist.

His voice remained low, barely a whisper, while he focused on his task. "Keelan, we will not surrender this ship. If we have to engage, you are to lock yourself in my cabin. They'll have to make it past the crew and me to get to you." He placed his hands on her shoulders, his crystal gaze intense. "These pistols are only good at a short distance. Best at close range. Don't fire unless you have *no other choice*." He swallowed, his expression a swirl of emotion.

Concern. Fear. Despair.

Yet also...courage, ferocity, and determination. He would battle to the death for his crew.

For her.

She suddenly understood. If they were defeated, she would have a choice to make. She could let the pirates assign her fate, or she could determine her own. She stroked the cool, dark gray metal. Would she have the courage to use both of them? She couldn't find the words to speak, so she just nodded.

"My sweet—"

His voice barely reached her ears over the wind and the sounds of the ship flying over the water. She lifted her face and met his gaze. The pirates could only board the *Seeker* if they disabled her. They could only get to Keelan if Landon... The thought of him lying cold and motionless on the deck of the *Seeker* paralyzed her breath. A swirling gray cloud permeated her mind. Images of Landon cut through the fog, giving her a brief glimpse of each memory before it faded: Landon discovering her hiding spot in the garden... on his horse with her riding bonnet perched on his head and a leering grin on his face... fighting with ferocity sword to sword with Gampo in the warehouse... his eyes darkening to a deep blue just before kissing her...

The fog dissipated when he placed his hands on her shoulders and gave them a gentle squeeze. "Keelan, I love you."

Their eyes locked, and in that moment the wavering uncertainty skittering through the surrounding air calmed. Sounds became muffled; motion seemed to slow. In this single slice of time, she had an acute sense they were connected by a power stronger than fear, more resilient than the possibility of impending death. From the cadence of their breath to the rhythm of their heartbeats, they were bonded.

She raised her chin and took a deep breath. "I love you, too."

Whatever Fate had in store for them... let it come.

They would fight together.

CHAPTER 31
BATTLE AT SEA

L andon stood on the uppermost deck as the *Dragon* chewed away the sea separating the two vessels. Her hull was painted a blood red. Several sails were the same color; others were various shades of grey, blue, green, or white with numerous patches, making them appear more like a ragged quilt.

"It's him." Conal ground out the words as if they were pieces of gravel.

"Yes," Landon answered warily, his voice soft and even, as if he raised it but a little, the air around Conal would catch fire.

The sharply angled boat rushed to engage the *Seeker*. Landon stood at his friend's shoulder. "We're not murderers, Conal."

"I know that." Conal's jaw clenched hard. "However, I believe Lady Justice has earned her due." He stood still as a rock, except for the sea breeze lifting his hair from his broad shoulders. It was the first time Keelan had seen him without it neatly pulled back.

Landon leaned a hip against the rail, a figure of casual indolence, but Keelan knew better. Underneath he was tense and rigid, ready to spring into action if called upon. "True enough." He nodded. "But can you be sure the crew is willing? Can you be certain no innocents will be lost to satisfy the vengeance Gampo has earned? That second vessel might not belong to him." He pointed to the sloop. "Look, even now they seem to be trying to haul up her mainsail again, although I'm still at a loss why they dropped it in the first place. It wasn't something a seasoned crew would do."

Conal's gaze was fixed on the dark, two-masted vessel, which sliced through the waves toward them, but his shoulders dropped a little. "You're right," he finally answered.

Keelan noted the hard line of his jaw and the surrounding tightness of her half-brother's eyes. He was a man of honor; that realization made her happy and proud.

Landon nudged Conal's ribs. "We've outrun him before, we'll do it again."

Conal inhaled deeply through his nose and blinked. "Aye."

A distant boom made Keelan jump. She watched in horror as the small sloop's foremast shook, then broke in half. The top section folded down over itself and the sail fluttered crazily beside it.

"Perhaps it's not Gampo's prize ship after all," Landon mused.

"Well, she's about to become one, unless we can detain, or at the very least, distract the *Dragon*," Conal said.

"Ho, Captain!" came a shout from the crosstrees. "The sloop's foremast has been crippled, but she's still hauling up her mainsail. The *Dragon* is almost clear of her."

Conal snapped to action. "Clear the braces! Man the port side guns! As soon as she passes the sloop, fire!"

Landon turned to Conal. "The second and third guns are filled with grape shot, one and four are armed with bar shot," he said, his voice confident and firm.

Conal nodded. "Send them a volley of grapeshot. Pepper the

Dragon's mainsail and slow her down. Avoid sweeping the decks, if you can. Disable her sails. Aim high."

Landon strode across the poop deck. He'd strapped a saber to his hip and a gun belt around his waist. Long dark curls whipped behind his broad shoulders and her breath left her lungs.

He's magnificent.

And he loved her. *Her.*

Landon shouted to another man standing by the main deck hatch. "Two and three guns, at the ready! Aim high lads, aim high! We want to shred the canvas as best we can." The order was relayed below to the men manning the ship's guns. Keelan nervously tapped the handle of a pistol as she tried to follow the activity on the main deck below.

A puff of smoke from the *Dragon* warned the crew of an incoming shot. A cannonball ripped through the top railing of the *Seeker*, flew past Remus, bounced off the main deck, and then plopped into the sea. The entire ship seemed to pause for a breath while everyone checked to make sure all body parts were still intact.

Landon broke the silence. "Fire as you bear!"

"Aye, sir!"

A loud *boom* sounded, making the deck boards shake beneath her feet. She grasped the rail, and was enveloped by a cloud of acrid smoke, which made her cough. She pulled her shirt up over her nose. When it cleared, she scanned Gampo's boat for damage. Her eyes were watering so much, she couldn't tell if the sails had holes from the grapeshot. By the sight of men scrambling on deck and the sudden bobbing of the vessel, enough damage had been done to slow down their progress, somewhat.

Landon reached for the spy glass. "Looks like the small sloop has finally reset the mainsail." Conal placed it in his hand, and Landon peered through it for a few seconds. "Who the devil is commanding that boat, I wonder? They've released the jib the wrong—"

Another smoke cloud from the *Dragon* shot out from the broadside facing the small sloop, followed by a muffled boom.

"Looks like he's switched his sights from us to the boat," Conal braced his hands on his hips and rubbed the back of his neck. "I was wrong in thinking it was part of Gampo's fleet. She just happened to be in the wrong place. We canna help her now."

"If we fire the bar shot and take down one of the *Dragon's* masts, it might give her time to sail out of range," Landon said.

At Conal's nod, Landon raised his voice and gave the orders, "One and four guns, at the ready. Aim for the mainsail, boys! An extra pint of ale to the gunners who split it in two!"

As Landon's orders were relayed to the gun deck, the rest of the crew crowded around the rail to watch.

"Fire four gun!" Landon shouted.

Keelan was more prepared this time and covered her ears with her hands. At the shudder of the gun firing, she closed her eyes to the thick smoke. The breeze had picked up and soon whisked it away from the deck, and after a second, she dared open her eyes. The *Dragon* now had a drooping triangular sail near the front of the ship.

A shout rang out on deck, "A hit to the main gaff tops'l!"

Landon sent out another command to the gunners. "Fire one gun!"

Another shuddering boom jarred the deck. The wind drove the smoke ahead of the ship and she caught sight of the bar shot, just as it reached the schooner. Both fascinated and terrified at the same time, she watched it crash through the top of the forward lowest square sail and splinter the mainmast about midway way up. Then, the upper foremast slowly toppled and folded in half.

"Huzzah! Huzzah!" The sudden cheer arose on the decks of the *Seeker,* and the distance again grew between the two ships.

Landon's voice held a note of pride. "Good work, lads! A hit through the fore lower tops'l and foremast! Reload and stand ready. Load your guns and run them out!"

Keelan remained beside the helm as the crippled pirate ship forfeited the chase. Elation washed over her like a shower of sunshine, and she found herself laughing with glee. Landon grinned at her, and she couldn't help smiling back at him. Conal turned his attention to the wind in the sheets. "Helm a quarter point to starboard! Lay aloft and take in two reefs!"

"Aye, Captain!"

A flurry of other commands shot across the decks, and the crew moved with amazing agility to accomplish them. Sails were trimmed, and the *Seeker* shifted away from the *Dragon*. The smaller sloop limped toward the shore and crossed over their wake behind them.

"At least the smaller boat has an opportunity to flee," she said.

Conal peered through his glass at the sloop. "Small crew. I don't see any wounded sailors. It looks like there's damage to the foremast and sail. Unless they're lubbers or daft in the head, they should be able to make it to port using the mainsails before Gampo can ready his boat to give a chase."

Landon raised his brows and shook his head. "I'm not so sure of their skills, they should've never lowered the mainsail."

The *Seeker* continued to gain speed, and the wind snatched a wisp of hair from under Keelan's hat. If she hadn't fastened the chinstrap tightly, it would have probably flown away with the breeze. A loud clapping rent the air, and she followed Conal's sharp gaze to a loose mainsail, flapping faster than a sparrow's wing. A commotion soon followed near the main mast. A sailor scampered like a monkey along the topgallant spar. A second perched on the spar below and sawed at one of the sheets holding the main topsail.

Keelan held her breath. If they fell, it would surely be to their death. It almost appeared as if they were intentionally trying to cripple the *Seeker's* sail.

"Lash down that sail! Sheepshank the rigging best ye can, lads. Hop to it and with a will!" Conal turned, pulled his pistols from his belt, and fired a shot into the air. He aimed the other one at the two sailors aloft. "Either come down now or test the steadiness of my hand."

They froze for a moment and then reversed back to the ratlines to begin the climb down. Remus and Johnny, along with another dozen mates, were waiting and wrestled them to the deck. After a slight scuffle, the men were subdued.

"It appears we've flushed out the other spies," Landon observed. To Remus and Johnny he said, "Secure them in the hold. Keep them under close watch."

"Aye, sir," Remus responded. To the pirates he growled, "Move on, ye bilge rats. Ye'll git yer due soon enough. It's been a while since we got to see a good keel haulin'."

Both men paled and exchanged terrified looks before Remus and Johnny shoved them toward the hatch.

Conal glanced up at the crewmen, who worked fervently to repair the damaged rigging. "We're losing speed, dammit." His expression remained stoic, his mouth in a harsh line.

Landon clamped his hand on his friend's shoulder. "The *Dragon* is no longer in a position for a chase. We'll have our chance another day, my friend, when we have all three ships at hand." He jerked his head in the direction of the hold. "I'd like to have a conversation with our pirate guests below. Perhaps if we're persuasive enough, they'll share the location where Gampo roosts when he's not at sea. Then we could pay a personal call after our stop at Harbour Town."

Conal nodded in agreement. "Let's give them some time to contemplate their current situation. They might be more talkative after a time locked in the bilge with the ballast."

He issued orders to tack back and make a wide sweep, retracing their earlier path, but staying well outside the range of the wounded schooner's guns. Several members of the crew grabbed grappling hooks and stood at the rails. They made a sport of snagging items tossed overboard earlier, making wagers on who could recover their target first.

The *Seeker* continued its starboard arc until it was once again sailing south toward Harbour Town. Keelan breathed deeply, savoring their victory and giving thanks no one was hurt. The dark-sailed pirate boat bobbed on the water, and the little sloop still limped eastward toward the shoreline.

She hoped to never see them again, but she had a strange tingling along the back of her neck, and suddenly the distance from the two ships couldn't widen fast enough.

CHAPTER 32
A PROPOSAL

The crew repacked and stowed the ammunitions and other weapons. The guns were once again tightly secured, powder and balls replenished and made ready for the next time they were needed. A light rain started, and was soon accompanied by a thin mist, which muted the usual sounds of activity aboard the *Seeker*. The vessel would soon arrive at Harbour Town, South Carolina. Everett and Orvis were both given a brief sea burial, during which Doreen had locked herself in Annette's cabin, tormented by guilt.

Keelan's heart filled with pity for her cousin. She'd talked with Doreen at length earlier, and as she suspected, her cousin had indeed recognized the sound of her voice while they were in the hold. Keelan told Doreen about Gampo and his desire for vengeance, and Doreen promised to keep her identity and location a secret. Her cousin had sobbed on Keelan's shoulder until her tears were spent.

"I'm so sorry, Keelan," Doreen repeated.

"Shhh... you can't keep the burden of this blame on your shoulders, Doreen," she'd replied. "Your intent was never to harm either Papa or Dr. Garrison. The fault belongs to Everett, and God will judge him now."

The daylight waned just as a fog drifted in. Within the hour it had thickened. It was not long before Conal ordered the anchor lowered. "Too many outer sandbars and shoals to navigate in the mist," he noted. "'Tis better to wait 'til it lifts than risk running aground."

From her post near the mainmast, Keelan made out the vague outline of the ship's stern. Most of the crew went below deck to hang their hammocks and turn in, except for the few who sat around an overturned crate, and played cards by the dull yellow glow of the night watch's lantern.

The desire for some privacy to ponder her own thoughts, made her wander to the aft deck near the main cabin where she leaned against the rail to stare out into the gray curtain. The fog hid both ocean and horizon. She extended her hand, and the thick, wet mist swallowed it. Fog covered the ship in a translucent darkness, holding both Keelan and the *Seeker* captive and paralyzed. She shivered as its moist breath crept across her bare neck, unable to shake the trepidation skittering down her spine.

What of the hammock hanging in Landon's cabin? The strokes of his long, lean fingers on her skin, and the urgent demand of his kisses could easily bend her to his whim. If he but *touched* her, she would be powerless to resist him. Her heart pounded with need even as trepidation tingled in her stomach. She drew in a deep breath of calm, her path clear now.

He loved her. The knowledge made her light as a sparrow. He didn't ask her to marry him, though. A heavy fist of sadness settled in her heart next to her joy. Her intentions, while admirable and virtuous, had been no match for the intense and powerful lure of Landon Hart.

She loved him. He was cocky; so sure of himself that the fates acquiesced to his whims because it was too much trouble to argue. He loved adventure and changed directions with the tide and the wind, whether or not others could keep up. He was brave and strong and hungry for life. Yes, she loved him.

Falling in love with Landon was sure to lead to inevitable misery and heartbreak. Her will had not saved her; she had fallen anyway. A solitary tear broke free and crept down her cheek. She loved him and wanted to trust him with her heart, but she was afraid.

The promise of marriage seemed less likely now, and even less important. Another deep sigh of defeat swirled the air around her. He loved her *now*, but would he eventually break her heart? According to her mother, there was always another woman, another port city somewhere along the way to steal a mariner's attention and his heart. Whatever she and Landon had today, this hour, this minute was ethereal. Was it meant to last? She didn't know. He loved her today, and today would have to be enough.

Perhaps today should be enough. Who was she to demand more?

"Keelan."

The apparition of her thoughts walked toward her. The mist swirled around him as he strode through its vapor like a pirate ghost, unhindered by the same gray blanket holding her captive. The silver saber strapped to his waist stood out starkly against the black breeches and boots. The white linen shirt almost glowed against his darkly tanned skin. The top ties were unsecured, revealing his bare neck. Her pulse leapt as Landon stepped closer, and she desperately resisted the temptation to reach out and run her fingers over the broad expanse of his chest. Her gaze slid involuntarily up over his strongly boned jaw and paused on the small scar on his chin before lingering on his lips. Thinking back to the fiery kiss he had dealt her in his cabin earlier sent a flurry of awakening within her. Her breasts tingled from the memory of his touch and a strange ache began to pulse in her lower belly. She expelled her breath in a soft pant and finally found the courage to meet the scorching heat of his gaze.

Was he replaying the same memory?

Sapphire eyes flashed like blue steel with something

combustible and a little unsettling. For a moment, she could not breathe. If he touched her, she'd surely melt.

LANDON'S HEART CLENCHED, and he reached up and tugged the strap holding Keelan's hair in a queue at the base of her neck, freeing her short auburn curls. He could not keep his fingers from delving into the soft tresses. Is this what it was like to be under a spell? His breath caught as her irises grew dark and limpid, like liquid emeralds. Her lashes fluttered then lowered to her cheeks, and she leaned her head into his fingers. He wanted her more than he had ever wanted any other woman. This desire was different; it was not only more powerful, but more possessive as well. Unlike past dalliances, he did not want his time to end with this woman—waif—sprite— imp.

Ever.

Keelan would always fight to forge her own path, with or without him. He could never ask her to compromise her morals or forsake her upbringing to be his mistress. She had already voiced her opinion on that matter, vehemently. Worse, she didn't trust him. What did he need to do to change that? He wanted her trust and devotion. He craved it. A wave of realization struck him like a storm surge from a gale.

He'd never be able to force her to trust him. He, of all people, should know that trust is earned, not demanded. If he wanted to keep her, he would have to do more. Be more. This line of thinking should have him running the other direction. Yet, for the first time in many years, it wasn't unpleasing. If anything, it drove him more strongly to her.

In Charleston, when he'd feared her lost, he'd been staggered by the emptiness surrounding him. Now that he had her, he wasn't about to be separated from her again.

Ever.

He needed her to stay with him. He needed her by his side. He needed *her*.

Tonight, this knowledge provided a calm sense of purpose rather than an intense desire to flee. But at the moment, he couldn't think of a single word to say to sway her favor to him. His grip on her hair involuntarily tightened, and his lips were on hers before he knew it. She was a fresh spring breeze kissed by the salty sea air. Her body leaned into him, and he wrapped his arm around her waist, pulled her closer and held her until their bodies blended together.

The thump of her heart against his, the whispers from her lips, the smell of the ocean in her hair, all combined into a heady spell which left him powerless and exposed.

And he didn't care.

❦

KEELAN'S HEART pounded as Landon's arms wrapped possessively around her. She inhaled his scent as his hardened frame pressed against hers. Leather, salt air and musk drifted in her nostrils. His tongue teased her mouth open, tasting. Within the swirling the mist, their passions twirled and melted together. Nothing existed except his lips, his touch, his scent. Where there was Landon, there was warmth, comfort, strength.

Fire.

She pressed against him in an uncontrollable attempt to ease the sudden ache which began to spread, first within her belly... then lower. If he wanted her, she would give herself to him and allow herself to be loved for whatever span of time he willed it. Yes, it made her weak, but she didn't care. No man would ever match Landon's passion and power. She'd savor this small slice of paradise for as long as she could. The events of the day reminded her of her own mortality. Perhaps it was time to live for the moment.

His grip around her tightened, and his hand slid up to cup the firm roundness of her breast. She sighed as his mouth moved to her neck, leaving little molten impressions in its wake. It was impossible to complete a single thought. A low moan escaped from her throat, and her fingers instinctively buried themselves in his hair. She heard his voice in her ear, low and husky with emotion.

"Keelan, I need you with me. I cannot stay locked on land, yet neither can I bear to be separated from you." He cupped her face gently with his strong hands. Even in the near darkness his eyes glittered with something that made her want to dive headfirst into them. "I can't imagine living the rest of my life without you by my side." He rested his forehead against hers and his voice dropped, raspy and tortured. "However, I am a man of the sea, not the type to run plantations or city shops."

She swallowed, but the tangled mass of emotion in her throat stayed. It's not as if his words surprised her. In fact, hadn't she expected this? She'd been thinking the same thoughts seconds ago. "Yes, I know," she whispered, covering his hands with hers. "And I am not a woman who'd be content to stay home alone and await a man who is gone at sea. You know this as well."

Landon's voice lowered into an almost anguished whisper, as if he was both afraid to speak and afraid not to. "Yes, I know."

He'd asked her to sail with him once. Had he changed his mind? No matter. She would take tonight, and whatever amount of time they had until they dropped anchor in Harbour Town. She was a woman, and his crew believed a woman on a ship was bad luck. What more was there to say?

Landon grasped her hands and took a quick breath. "Keelan, I want you by my side, always. Will you sail *with* me, love? As my wife?"

CHAPTER 33
FREEDOM RUNNER

The shock of pure joy froze every muscle in her body. Did Landon Hart just request her hand in marriage? This man? This untamable sea captain? His words sunk in, reforming the foundation of her doubts, changing the framework of her soul. Keelan's jubilation was so powerful her heart seemed suddenly to pause in mid-beat, or maybe it simply exploded. Landon's hands framed her face, and she could only stare at the midnight eyes holding hers prisoner. Her vision of Landon, the handsome dandy of a sea captain, with a beautiful woman in every port city, dissipated before her eyes. In his place was this fearless, strong-willed man ready to love her, cherish her, and grow old with her.

Keelan responded the only way she could. Her slender fingers slid up and pulled his head down. This time, she captured his lips with hers, seeking the warmth and softness pressed against her mouth. His fingers traced the frame of her face, dancing over her skin, before cradling her jaw in his palms. He moved his lips from her mouth to her cheeks, kissing away the tears of joy, then moved up to her eyelids, brows and forehead. He slipped his arms around her and pulled her against his chest, and she nuzzled her face against his shoulder and hugged him back.

"There is something I must tell you first," Landon murmured.

Keelan stilled. She tilted her head back and looked at him. She already knew his past. What else was there? He'd been married once before. His wife had died giving birth to another man's child. "You already told me about your first marriage."

He shook his head. "It's not that." He paused as if to contemplate his next words. "I think I already know, but I want you to tell me how you feel about those who aid escaped slaves."

His question took her by surprise. Her mind went back to the Whistling Pig, and the suspicion she'd had about the Schoen's, Simon's warning, and advice to seek the couple out at the tavern if she needed help to flee Charleston.

There was also the runaway family trio who had escaped from Pratt's plantation and sought refuge in the cellar of an abandoned cabin where she and Landon had sheltered from a storm a few weeks ago. She had tended their wounds and Landon had left them the provisions he had in his saddle bags. Provisions that, truth be told, had been unnecessary to bring along for a short meeting with her Uncle at twin Pines.

Suddenly she understood.

"You help them escape, don't you?" she whispered.

He nodded, watching her every movement. "Fynn had started helping runaways years ago, after he himself had escaped his pirate captors. The Schoens, Simon, from Twin Pines, and the Ahern Merchant Fleet are all part of a small clandestine group of coastal residents and merchants who help slave families flee by transporting them north, to Philadelphia, then on to Canada."

He pulled away and took her hand, entwining his fingers with hers. "It's more dangerous aiding families than it is individual runaways. The three slaves we found in the cabin cellar a few weeks ago hid in the *Desire's* hold for several days. Because of repairs and stolen cargo, I was unable to leave on time for Philadelphia. Then, when Gampo put a price on your head, I had to send my ship to Harbour Town as a decoy. I must still take the

Desire back up the coast to Philadelphia, where Fynn's family and friends will move them, and the others northward."

He stood silent and tense, waiting.

Keelan brought his fingers to her lips and kissed them. "I'm glad you help them."

A shadow floated away from Landon's face. The tense worry lines around his eyes softened. He pulled her into his arms and held her. No words were spoken. They stood together for a moment or two, and then he took her hand.

"Come with me," he whispered.

He led her to his cabin and opened the door. Conal and Daniel were already inside and turned toward them as the door clicked shut. She paused, confused. Before she could ask, Landon knelt before her. Keelan's heart stuttered at the intensity of his gaze and even more at the humility in his countenance. Where was the cocky grin? The seductive perusal?

He opened his mouth, closed it, and swallowed before taking a gulp of air. Heaven's breath, he was terrified. His eyes turned a deep shade of blue, like a midnight sea.

"Keelan Grey, I give my oath before the eyes of God and these witnesses to bind myself to you until death parts us. Before the eyes of God and these witnesses and upon my honor, I pledge my love, loyalty, and fidelity to thee for the rest of my living days. When we arrive in port, I pledge to seek out a priest to bless our marriage and confirm it is legally binding. If you will consent to have me as your husband for the rest of your life, place your hand in mine and join with me in a handfast, to bind you to me, and bind me to you."

Without breaking his gaze, he lifted his hand and offered it to her.

Kneeling at her feet, proud, guarded Landon Hart, now raw and exposed, offered his heart to her in the presence of her half-brother. Landon Hart, the man who'd said marriage didn't suit him. When had he decided to risk his heart again? It didn't matter. He trusted her to love him and love him she would. Landon's eyes shone with an indigo light that warmed her as only the truest love can.

Her legs trembled and wordlessly, she sank to her knees and placed her hand on his palm. His fingers closed over hers and he placed his other hand on top. Her eyes welled, and she fought to contain the tears. The emotion seeping into her chest made it almost impossible to utter a single word.

"Landon Hart," she said, her voice catching, raw with emotion. "I place my hand in yours before the eyes of God and these witnesses and bind myself to you as your wife. I pledge my love, loyalty, and fidelity to thee until death takes me from your side."

Landon's long, lean fingers gently uncovered her hand. He slipped a sapphire and diamond crusted ring on her finger. "My grandmother's."

She stared into those hypnotic, blue eyes, which glittered like the jewels on the ring and fell in love again. And again.

"My Keelan. My love. My wife." Landon brought her hand to his mouth and kissed her fingertips. Her heart skipped as he cupped her face in his hands.

"Congratulations, my friend!" Conal clapped Landon on the back, sending him tipping forward against Keelan. So, of course, he took the opportunity to kiss her.

Laughing, Conal hauled her to her feet, and then offered his hand to Landon and pulled him up as well.

"And, as ship's captain, I pronounce you wed! Best wishes, Mrs. Hart, for a lifetime of happiness." Her half brother grinned and kissed her hand.

"Thank you, Conal, for agreeing to bear witness," Landon replied, clapping Conal's shoulder.

Conal gave her a small bow before he turned to open a bottle of wine. Daniel took her hand and bowed over it. "I wish you a long and fruitful marriage, Mrs. Hart."

"Thank you, Daniel." Keelan looked up into her husband's sparkling blue eyes. He gave her a slow smile before his lips dipped to briefly capture hers.

"A toast!" Conal pressed glasses into everyone's hands. He raised his glass and the others followed. "May the seas of marriage be calm, the winds be swift, and the current amiable!"

Keelan laughed and raised her glass with Landon's in salute.

Conal pressed a hand to his chest. "And, on behalf of the O'Brien family, I welcome Landon as me brother by marriage, as well."

"It is an honor." Landon stepped forward, clasped Conal's outstretched hand and shook it.

"And, therefore, I give my consent," Conal continued with a grin, "for you to name your firstborn son after me."

They all laughed. Keelan threw her arms around Conal's neck and kissed him on the cheek, gaining a surprised smile from her half-brother. "It would be the very least we could do," she said.

"I believe," Daniel broke in, "our part in this grand affair is complete." He stepped to the door before giving Keelan a brief bow. "My lady, best wishes to you and Captain Hart."

"Aye to that!" Conal said, as he plucked the bottle of wine from the table. "Come, let us celebrate the day's events beneath the shelter of yonder mizzen mast with this bottle of fine wine and a deck of cards. By the way this bank of fog is acting, we won't be doing much else for at least a day or so."

Daniel opened the door and Conal stepped outside, giving the valet an exaggerated nod of thanks as he passed. The door closed.

They were alone.

Landon raised his glass, and she raised hers. Together they finished their wine. He plucked the stem from her fingers and placed it on the table before taking her into his arms.

The world floated away as his lips leisurely played upon hers. She joyfully returned the kiss, and he tightened his arms about her waist, pulling her closer. Their kiss deepened, fanning the fire kindled weeks ago in a garden in Charleston, on a fine spring morning in June. He broke the kiss and touched his forehead to hers.

"Since the day I gazed upon you floating on the lake, a beautiful, naked water nymph," Landon's voice sounded hoarse, "I have wanted to touch you in all the places my eyes admired. I'm like a man starved. I crave your touch, I crave your heart. I crave the energy from your presence."

They were drawn to each other, the two of them, like a bead of water seeks a dry edge of linen. "I'm yours forever," she finally whispered. "I can't imagine living another day without you."

Landon leisurely removed her shirt and breeches, taking his time to place kisses on her shoulders, her ankles, her knees, until she stood naked. Keelan's senses erupted as the warmth of his hand found the firm rounded swell of her breast, his thumb stroking until her nipple grew hard and aroused.

His other hand caressed her hip.

Keelan's heart had been pounding a staccato rhythm in her chest, but now it lurched erratically. Landon was about to make her his wife in body as well as spirit. It was expected. It was the nature of things, after all. It was what a husband and wife normally did on their wedding night. It was terrifying.

She longed for it and feared it at the same time.

"Keelan, my love, your image has haunted me, even in my daydreams, plucking at my thoughts, drawing my attention away from every task. For so long, I have wanted to have you near me, to hear my name fall from your lips, knowing I was forever in your heart."

"You've been in my heart longer than you realize, Captain." She could hardly take a breath as his hand pressed her hips against his. Her lips tried to form the words whirling through her head, but it was impossible. She could only breathe his name and curl her fingers into his hair, pulling, urging him closer.

Again, his lips descended upon hers, but this time they were soft and tender. Her pulse quickened, and a lovely warmth swirled inside her. His tongue beckoned hers to a dance in the moist warmth of her mouth.

"I taste honey and wine," he murmured.

After adjusting the light from the lantern until the cabin was bathed in a faint, orange glow, he lowered her to his bed. Her gaze followed his movements in timid admiration as he undressed. Broad shoulders gave way to a narrow, tapered waist. There was no doubt Landon was in excellent physical form. Crisp hair lightly covered his broad chest; his belly was flat. She caught her breath as her gaze skimmed lower. Landon's male reaction to her stare brought a sudden hotness to her cheeks. She quickly blinked and raised her gaze to his face. How would she possibly survive being impaled by that? She swallowed and for a moment, the panic swelled.

Sensing her unease, Landon gently brushed a wisp of hair from her cheek. "I'll be gentle, love. Trust me, soon you will hunger for this as much as I do." He traced her jaw line down her throat with light kisses. He made a slight detour to a soft, sensitive spot behind her ear and she almost forgot what year it was.

"Your skin is silky, like rose petals," he whispered.

His softly stroking fingers sent another shiver down her spine, eliciting a breathy sigh from her. This part was wonderful. Kneeling on the bed, he drew her up against him and captured her mouth in a soft, tender kiss. Keelan's heart pounded erratically as he stroked her skin with reverence, as if savoring every touch from her neck, down her arms, over to the small of her back, and down her backside.

A hot gasp escaped her mouth as he pressed her hips harder against his. His kiss deepened, and his inquisitive tongue distracted her from the unfamiliar hardness. His hand returned to her breast. Waves of heat swirled around her, then threatened to erupt when his thumb once again rubbed tight circles around the rosy peak. Her throat vibrated with a deep moan of pleasure.

"You like when I do this?"

She nodded, or at least she thought she nodded. He cupped her other breast and repeated the delicious caress, making her sway into him from the sheer pleasure of it. There was more, there had to be more. Something was building inside her, urging her to him, looking for more. The sensation pushed all rational thoughts from her mind, and she covered his hand with hers and pressed it more firmly and he responded by kneading her breast, making her knees weak. His lips moved to her neck, then on to touch the delicate tip of her ear. Keelan could breathe only in small fragments, and the air around her seemed to thicken as his caresses became bolder.

"If you like that, then surely you'll enjoy this even more."

He kissed his way down to her breast, then took her nipple in his mouth. The wonderful sensation had her fingers convulsing, and she delved them into the curls at the nape of his neck. Flames licked at her core as his hot, moist lips brought her near the brink of insanity. His hands wandered along her calves, moving behind her knees in a soft caress, up her thighs to the soft inner hollow near her womanhood.

Just when it seemed she would implode, he pressed her back to his bed and then began to leave a trail of molten kisses across her belly. "My God, you are so beautiful," Landon's voice was husky as he murmured against the pale skin of her stomach. "Like a goddess, bathed in gold and dipped in diamonds."

CHAPTER 34
LOVE BOUND

Her skin tasted like wild cherries and sunshine. Landon inhaled the jasmine mingling with her womanly scent. When had he fallen in love with her? At the ball, when she had tried to fool him into thinking she was in love with Everett? Perhaps in the garden, when he had stolen a kiss under the guise of a payment for his silence, only because he could not resist the temptation of her sweet, full lips, which had fallen open in astonishment when he'd called her from her hiding place. Or was it in the early June morning, after dueling with Daniel, when she tore the blue scarf from her head and had given him a spry mocking salute before disappearing into the pines? Her look of brave determination when the *Dragon* had attacked?

Keelan.

His jewel. His love.

She was soft and strong, pliant as silk and strong as the tide. He wanted to hold her, love her, protect her and cherish her.

But more than anything, he wanted to devour her.

Her kisses drove him insane. It was all he could do to hold himself in check and not toss her on his bed and plunge himself into her just to ease his own long, smoldering hunger which had consumed him for weeks. He wanted to love her gently her first time. She arched against him and he sucked in his breath. If she'd let him.

The dew-kissed moistness of her mouth was sweeter than nectar. He brushed his fingers over shoulders, her skin like soft satin. She was everything he desired. The only one he desired. How could have she not seen it?

"Landon?"

Landon raised his head and lost his breath at the image before him. His gaze moved over his new bride's body. Fiery tresses teased by the sun fanned across the pillow beneath her head. Dark, auburn lashes touched her lightly flushed cheeks and her full, deep red lips parted in silent, passionate wonder. Firm, pink-tipped breasts curved gracefully to a creamy porcelain stomach. Lithe, shapely legs met at a tightly curled amber nest of wet heat. Her pupils had widened with desire, then went soft as his hand caressed her thigh and then slipped further to touch her warm moistness. His desire to have her was so powerful, he had to remind himself to keep his movements slow, his touch soft. He paused to kiss the other tender pink peak, and it pleased him to hear her swift intake of breath. Here was the most valuable treasure he'd ever seen, and she was his. All it had cost him was his heart. He smiled. It was a good trade, a good trade indeed.

KEELAN'S WORLD was spinning through thick waves of pleasure. She ran her hands up along Landon's hardened ribs, across his shoulders, and pulled him to her. *Closer.* There was no control, now. Her body reacted without a thought to guide it. He needed to be closer so she could breathe him in, envelop him.

"I love you, Landon," she could only breathe the words.

His eyes became hooded, voice thick with emotion. "I love you, wife. I don't want to hurt you, but I've been told the first time..." He shifted gently and pressed himself against her opening and the tender shield of her maidenhead.

She stiffened and her eyes flew open. "*Landon*..."

His voice was low and calm in her ear. "Shhh... Keelan, my sweet love, relax. Let me love you. I promise that I will make you crave this." He caressed her breast then slide his palm down to cover the wet nest of curls joining her thighs; his fingers slid into her folds and she closed her eyes at the bliss she suffered from his fingertips. His caress deepened, and she moaned.

He spoke in a low, gravelly whisper. "You are so wet for me, Keelan. So warm, so soft."

His lips touched hers, and her hands slipped convulsively over the hardened muscles of his back. Her fingernails dug into his skin as the pleasure swirled and rushed through her like a mighty wave, curling then crashing into the core of her soul. Something needy and restless churned in her core. When the pleasure exploded within her, he pressed further and eased inside; the pressure mounted until the thin membrane broke. Pleasure and pain. And a sense of fullness. Inhaling swiftly, she buried her face into his neck. Her breath shuddered.

He stilled. The heat from Landon's body enveloped her; she kissed his shoulder then paused. The pain had subsided. Instead, she was filled with a warmth and a need she couldn't describe.

Landon's hoarse whisper brushed her ear. "Keelan, look at me, my love."

She leaned her head back and stared up into the deep pools of blue. His eyes were dark and sensual as midnight velvet, and she found herself falling into them like a petal into a glassy lake. His heartbeat was hammering against her chest. Or was it her heartbeat hammering against his? It was impossible to tell.

"I love you, Keelan Hart. You possess my heart, breath and soul."

A knot of emotion tangled around her heart. Her chest

squeezed tight and warmth spiraled through it. "I love you back, Landon Hart."

His gaze imprisoned hers as he slowly, slowly started to move within her. There was little pain now, only movement, and her body took control, meeting his gentle, rhythmic thrusts. He filled her, fitting inside her as if his body was made for hers. They moved together in an even rolling motion, like the tide moves to and from the shore, with no beginning and no end. A deep hunger began to grow within Keelan's belly, and a soft moan escaped from her lips. Reaching up to Landon, she slid her hand behind his neck, and he responded by crushing her mouth to his. His thrusts quickened, and she rose to meet him. Landon's breathing became ragged, and he whispered her name. Urgent pulses of sensation flowed through her into Landon and from him into her until they were connected by something stronger than sinew and flesh. Their souls entwined and melded together in a golden flare of light. Little explosions detonated deep inside her and they both cried out with pleasure as he spilled himself deeply within her.

Fate brought them together.

Love bound them for life.

THE CRADLE-SOFT ARMS of Morpheus seemed to have just rocked Keelan to sleep, when a harsh, brutal pounding sounded upon the cabin door.

"Captain Hart!" An urgent voice penetrated the early morning quiet. "Sorry to intrude, sir, but you're needed on main deck straight away."

Keelan did not recognize the voice heralding her new husband from her side this morning, but she was immediately resentful. She wasn't ready to relinquish her husband, her companion, her source of warmth, comfort and strength, so soon.

Landon acknowledged the intrusion with a growl, "What is it, man?"

There was a slight pause. "The prisoners locked in the hold have escaped, sir. They have stolen one of the canoes. Cap'n O'Brien's fumin' mad and means to give chase."

CHAPTER 35
ESCAPE

Landon tensed at the news of the pirates' escape. Keelan's chest tightened. If the escaped spies reached Gampo and revealed the location of the *Seeker*, even the dense fog wouldn't keep them safe. Gampo had made it clear he meant to avenge Crowe's death personally. Since he blamed her for it, he'd come after the *Seeker*, putting people she loved and cared about in danger.

She still wasn't sure if Gampo had pursued them from Charleston because he'd found out she was aboard, or followed simply because the *Seeker* was part of Fynn Ahern's fleet, Gampo's long-time rival. She snuggled closer and Landon reached his arm around her shoulder.

"What started this feud between Fynn and Gampo?" she asked.

Landon took a deep breath, scrubbed his face with his other hand and gave a baffled laugh. "Those two salts had been at odds for the past twenty-five years, although no one seems to remember why. Fynn always remained tightlipped about it. His only plan of action was to do as much damage as possible to Gampo's ship without killing anyone." He shrugged. "Gampo seemed to have the same intent. Both did their best to hinder the other's business and disrupt each other's trade, like a couple of old, toothless dogs."

"Have many people died?" she asked. A light shadow of whiskers covered his jaws. Curious, she traced her fingers along his chin.

"No lives were lost in all those years. Brendan, Fynn's son, said Fynn died because he was hit by falling debris from a splintered mast. In truth, Gampo's shot had been high. He didn't rake the deck with grape shot, which tells me he had no intent to kill."

She moved her hand to his chest and marveled at the ripple of muscle beneath her fingers as he shifted to turn toward her a bit more. She raised an eyebrow. "Now, you've lost Fynn and Gampo's lost his first mate and his sister. It's become a blood feud, hasn't it? Gampo is still pursuing the fleet, so it doesn't seem like he's ready to call a halt to it." She was a part of this now. It wasn't because she married Landon, it was because he had married her.

Landon stared into her eyes for a moment, contemplating. "Conal and Brendan are determined to see him hang for causing Fynn's death."

"Where's Brendan now?"

"He's waiting for us in the harbor with Fynn's ship, the *Reward*."

There was something else bothering her. In fact, it had been lingering on the fringes of her mind for the past few days. "When we were in the warehouse, Gampo mentioned something about his sister. He seemed to believe Fynn had somehow wronged her. He mentioned Fynn would know how much a Persian would pay for me," she said. Although she felt safe in Landon's arms, she couldn't suppress the shiver that skittered across her shoulders.

He hugged her closer. "Fynn has never engaged in the slave trade, rather, he's done much to foil it. His group of Freedom Runners is proof."

"Gampo seems to be convinced Fynn sold his sister," she said.

"Gampo is mistaken." Landon smoothed a stray strand of hair away from her face and kissed her forehead.

"How did you come to be on Fynn's ship?"

"My parents died when I was twelve. Then Fynn took me in. I was lucky."

⊛

WHEN HE WAS YOUNG, it had taken wits and strength *and* luck. Landon twirled his finger in a lock of Keelan's hair. "Fynn had recently lost his brother to the same fever which killed my parents on the journey to America from Ireland. Although Fynn and Risa had children of their own to care for, they took me in and raised me as their own." He stroked his fingertips along the soft skin of her arm. "That old salt told the best yarns."

Fynn's stories invoked images of daring rescues, duels, and true love. He moved his fingers in small circles up to the silky skin of his wife's shoulder.

"When Fynn's wife, Risa, was a young maid, she was taken prisoner from a prize ship and sold by the pirates who'd captured it. Gampo gave the pirate captain a small fortune prior to the sale to buy her before she was placed up on the block."

"It seems odd that Gampo is outraged that Fynn might have bought and sold his sister when it appears he has his fingers in the slave trade as well."

Landon leaned close to her ear and breathed in deeply before he continued. Jasmine. Keelan always smelled like jasmine blossoms. She moved her hand from his chest up to her shoulder where his hand rested and wove her fingers with his. Her breasts brushed against his arm, and he fought to remember what he wanted to say next.

Ah yes, Uncle Fynn's new bride.

"Fynn had been enslaved by the same pirate ship. By the time it made port, he'd fallen in love with Risa. Before Gampo arrived to collect his prize, Fynn sneaked in and helped her escape from the pirate's gaol."

Keelan's eyes widened. "She was in a cell? Was she in love with Fynn, too? How did he release her?"

He smiled a bit roguishly. "No. She was most definitely not in love with Fynn. She was a Spanish aristocrat's daughter. He was a young seaman. He freed her by outwitting her guards. However, *that* is a story for another day."

Keelan looked down at their threaded fingers and hesitated. What was on her mind? She was contemplating something important. He waited.

After a moment, she raised her gaze back to his, and he was almost rendered powerless by the intensity of her dark green stare. A ring of gold rimmed her pupils and then flared out into the emerald irises like an exploding star.

"Did she eventually fall in love with him? Did they travel together? Did they love each other? Were they happy?" she asked.

"So many questions." He pictured Keelan as a young girl, small and thin, strong and impetuous, desiring the love and compassion of a mother and a father, yet left bereft. In his mind's eye, he could see her holding a babe in her arms, smiling. He wanted her to have a family because when he looked at her, it was all he could see.

Family.

Keelan desired to know her sire, and by damned, he and Conal would make sure she met him. Even better, she'd become part of a family the two of them would create together.

Bound by love, forged in their hearts and unbreakable. When he looked at her, he saw his future, his life... *happiness*.

Landon brought their hands to the small space between their bodies and brushed the pink buds of her nipples with his knuckles, and marveled at how her pupils widened and her breath shortened.

He continued, "Yes, and they were happy. Fynn and Risa sailed together. It was unconventional, even cursed by other sailors, but the two did it, anyway. They loved each other and nothing kept them from spending their lives together." He locked his gaze with hers. "Just like you and me."

Keelan smiled. "Yes, just like you and me." She kissed his knuckles. "Tell me, did they marry?"

"Yes," Landon admitted. "And when he sailed, Risa stood firm by Fynn's side. They had two sons, Brendan and Ronan, and both grew up on the ship. When Fynn sought horses from Persia to trade, Risa rode with him over the desert." Landon took a long, pensive breath. "It was Risa who offered shelter to two runaways and then wrote to a friend to help deliver them to safety. Fynn then organized an alliance. To this day, we still do our best to aid families seeking to escape to their freedom."

"Fynn must have loved Risa very much," she said softly.

Landon kissed her shoulder. "Fynn said Risa was the fairest gem he'd ever met and that he'd never encountered another woman like her, nor would he ever expect to find another again. She was his light. His star. Just like you are mine."

❧

ANOTHER LIGHT RAP on the cabin door reminded them of the business at hand. "Sir—Captain Hart. Sir?"

"I'll be right there," Landon finally answered. He pressed his lips against the hollow of her throat, then trailed kisses up her neck before whispering in her ear. "As much as I would wish otherwise, it appears we must dress and take care of the issue at hand." He smoothed his hand over her side and down to her thigh, sending shivers through her lower belly. His palm moved between their bodies, tracing a fiery path upward. Gently probing fingers caressed the moist curls before slipping past her folds and making intense circles around the little island of pleasure nestled there. "Although, I would rather dally longer here, as my husbandly duty demands."

This man. The things he could do with his fingers made her forget her own name. She pressed her hips against his hand and trailed her fingers over his lips, down his neck, and across the taut muscles of his chest, struggling to speak. "Then... when time... permits, I shall expect you to fulfill your duties as... demanded," she breathed, happy she could at least form the words. Her breath came and went in soft pants, his strokes against her sending swirling eddies of delight through her lower belly.

He caught his breath as her hand moved lower. "Indeed."

❦

KEELAN KNOTTED the scarf behind her head and gave a small sigh. "Although this disguise is easy to move in and comfortable, there are times I wish I could wear a gown again and enjoy the more feminine life I used to live." As she had earlier suspected, he was indeed a scoundrel when it came to keeping the ends close enough to tie together.

Landon chuckled and finished securing the leather corset. "I distinctly recall you garbed in something very similar to this when we first met."

She could only shrug. He had a point.

He gave her a wink. "I must admit, I'm enjoying the respite from the need to defend you from love-struck sailors. 'Tis hard enough to disguise your more womanly curves as it is." He tweaked her bottom.

She gave him a mock scowl before she shrugged into one of his old shirts, then pulled up and fastened her trousers.

He traced the line of demarcation, stretching across her chest. "Hopefully, it won't be for much longer." He plopped a worn, floppy straw hat on her head and gave it a secure pat. "Your bonnet, my lady."

He chucked her under the chin before planting a lingering kiss on her lips. "We can't take the risk of Gampo confirming you are aboard. For now, you must remain Mahdi, the emerald-eyed, cook's boy and son of a Persian horse trader. Next to Lin, Jorge, Renaldo, Hugo and Sakura, you should blend right in." He winked. "You'd be the only one with all your fingers and toes still attached. I hope no one notices."

Landon strode across the deck toward the small group of crewmen gathered by the main mast. The fog still hung about the ship like a sodden, gray blanket, muffling the sighs of the sea and the voices of the crew. The fog had kept them from moving the ship closer to Harbour Town's docks. Conal still felt it was too risky to navigate.

It helped to have the scarf; it restrained her curly cropped hair. The moisture in the air would have made it even more unruly. The sailors tied scarves around their heads much like Ruth, the plantation cook, had done at Twin Pines. Depending on the head, it either kept hair out of the way, or scalps from burning under the early summer sun. She'd had done her best to imitate the style. However, as comfortable as her clothes were, she still longed to enjoy other womanly pursuits.

Needlepoint, she could be content without, but a fragrant bath...

"Three of Gampo's men easily managed to gain access to the *Seeker* as deck hands; it's unnerving," Landon muttered.

"It would have been worse had they been successful in sabotaging the sails," Keelan answered as they came upon a cluster of men gathered in a circle near the main mast.

"How in the hell did they escape?" Landon ran his fingers through his hair in frustration.

At the sound of Landon's voice, the crewmen parted to reveal Conal squatting near Henry, who was groggily trying to sit upright.

"Near as I can make out," Conal answered, "a few minutes after the change of the watch, Miss Grey came around with a jug of wine she'd stolen from the galley. Somehow, she managed to persuade Marcel to unlock the pantry. She told the men on watch she was grateful to them for saving her from the pirates, and she wanted to reward their bravery."

Landon's eyebrows rose. "Are you telling me a single jug of wine inebriated the entire watch?"

"It weren't no ordinary wine, Captain Hart." Johnny stepped forward from the group. "The wench only offered us a wee bit. Barely two fingers worth in a tiny cup." He shoved his hands into his pockets. "Next thing I knew, Remus was tryin' to shake the teeth outta me mouth."

"Well, ye was quiet as a stone, man!" Remus retorted. "For a minute, I thought ye was dead!" He scratched his head and muttered, "Johnny's never missed waking me to take my turn. When I woke up on me own and the rest of me watch still in their hammocks, I knew somthin' wasn't right."

Johnny rubbed his temples. "Still feels like I was hit in the head with a rock hammer."

Conal gave Landon a humorless smile. "It seems Henry asked for two shares before he was to climb up to the crow's nest. We found him tangled in the rigging about halfway up. He's still fairly out of sorts."

"Remus and Johnny, take Henry to his hammock," Landon said, a hardened edge to his voice. "Where's Miss Grey now?"

"We found her tied and gagged in the hold below," Conal answered.

"But, why would she help them?" Keelan asked. She was both outraged and bewildered. Doreen's current actions seemed out of place. She'd changed on this voyage, and for the better. Something wasn't right.

Conal took an angry breath. "She was threatened. One had freed himself during the night. She'd been on her way to the deck to empty the chamber pot when he attacked her. He told her if she didn't help them escape, they'd kill her and sabotage the ship, so Gampo could take it. Miss Grey said she made the decision she believed would save lives rather than place them in danger. She felt it was her only choice."

"So she drugged the watch to keep the pirates from killing them?" Keelan asked.

"Yes." Conal said.

Poor Doreen. That thought stopped her. There was something she never thought she'd think about her cousin. "I believe she has an aunt here in Harbour Town," she said.

"I'll offer to provide an escort there for her," Conal said. "She's with Mrs. Camsby at the moment. She was quite shaken. I'm hoping Mrs. Camsby can comfort her and help her regain her composure somewhat."

Johnny and Remus returned, and the Conal directed his next order to Remus. "Prepare a longboat," he ordered. "Johnny's men can go ashore first, along with Marcel, who needs to replenish some of our galley supplies. I'll prepare a missive regarding the two renegades, which we can deliver to the authorities."

Remus spoke up. "T'would seem the bilge rats might be only an hour ahead of us. We could catch 'em!"

Landon nodded. "Aye, they have only two men rowing, and one is wounded."

"There is another piece of good news," Conal added. "According to Miss Grey, one of Gampo's men mentioned that once they were back aboard his ship, Gampo would head for his home on an island off the coast of Jamaica."

Landon caught Conal's gaze and his eyes gleamed like a cat ready to pounce. "He's holing up. We can catch him when he makes landfall."

"I'd like nothing better than to watch him swing." Conal spun on his heel and tossed over his shoulder, "Remus, tell Madam Camsby we shall take her and Miss Grey ashore within the hour. Johnny, get the men ready to depart before the next bell, only the next watch stays aboard. I want to find those men." To Landon, he said, "Let's meet with Brendan to discuss setting a course for Jamaica. Together, we have a score to settle with Gampo."

AT LANDON'S BECKONING, Keelan slipped through his cabin door, and placed on the table a small breakfast tray of bannocks, jam, and tea she'd assembled in the galley. The activities they shared last night left her famished.

Her husband stepped forward, closed the door, and took her in his arms. Husband. A soft sensation hugged her heart. She slid her hands around his neck. "I brought us some breakfast."

"The nourishment I seek is not on that tray." Landon's eyes glowed warmly as he gave her a slow seductive grin. "In truth, the sustenance I crave only *you* possess." His head dipped and his lips found the pulse now pounding erratically in her throat. The food could wait.

Keelan caught her breath and murmured hoarsely in his ear, "But, all I possess, I have already given to you."

"Then I want more of the same."

He moved to her mouth and kissed her deeply. Keelan's fingers dug into the firm muscles of Landon's shoulders while his hands traveled freely down her sides and around her waist, before slipping in the back of her breeches.

He trailed kisses along her jaw to that sensitive spot behind her ear. "I will forever demand one more kiss, one more caress, one more night of enchantment," he murmured in her ear.

"Good. I shall be happy to provide it." She smiled.

Keelan's own hunger grew deep within her belly, and she arched against the hardness pressed against her. A low growl rumbled in Landon's chest, and he skimmed his palms against her naked backside before pulling her hips against his.

"Well, I guess I should have knocked!"

Keelan jumped at the sound of Annette Camsby's voice and

attempted to disengage herself from Landon's embrace. His arms only tightened around her and he whispered into her ear. "Stay put, Madam, unless you wish to show her the effect your proximity has had on me."

Keelan ceased her struggles immediately. However, their display witnessed by another caused a hot blush to suffuse her cheeks, and mild panic to well in her chest. Would Annette blurt out what she'd seen to the crew?

"Yes, a knock would have been appropriate, Mrs. Camsby," Landon responded coolly. He slid his hands from her breeches and then casually caressed Keelan's back. She half turned to face Annette.

Annette's eyes flashed at the formal address given by Landon. She swept her hand toward Keelan. "So this is why you have refused to visit my bed?" she asked flatly.

Keelan caught Landon's gaze. Calm. Warm. Ornery.

"You've ignored me because, you have turned your lust to young *boys*?" Annette's voice dripped with disgust. "You're sick in the head."

Keelan bit back a sudden snort of laughter.

Amusement warmed Landon's eyes as he grinned down at her. "Not necessarily," he said.

Annette sauntered forward, hands on her hips. "Tell me, *Captain*, what does the crew think of this? Or do they not yet know? Because I assure you, your dirty little secret will be out within the hour unless you and I can come to a mutual agreement." She pointed commandingly to Keelan. "You may go. Landon and I are going to have a private meeting."

Although Landon managed to remain calm under Annette Camsby's attack, Keelan bristled at the woman's obvious threat against her husband. She whirled and faced the widow. "Whatever 'dirty little secret' you're prepared to tell the crew would be a complete lie."

"Really!" Annette exclaimed in mock surprise. "Let me see if I understand your argument. Or have you already forgotten I have just seen you in his arms, kissing him like a *lover*!"

Landon chuckled and leaned forward to whisper in Keelan's ear, "Well, she's right about the last."

Try as she might, Keelan could not hold back a giggle.

Annette became more incensed. "You dare mock me!"

"Madam Camsby." Landon intervened. "I believe it is time for the appropriate introductions to be made. Allow me to introduce to you, my wife: Keelan Grey Hart."

Annette's jaw dropped. "Wha—what did you say?"

Landon stepped from behind Keelan and bowed formally. "This is my wife, Keelan Hart."

"*Wife*!" Annette sputtered. "This is preposterous! You're not married! I have *met* the woman, and I assure you, sir, this is not she!"

Landon continued smoothly, unaffected by Annette's outburst. "Keelan, please allow me to introduce Madam Annette Camsby, late widow of Mr. Edward Camsby of Charleston."

Keelan pulled away the scarf hiding her hair. She closed half the distance between Landon and the stunned woman and spoke softly but with a cool firmness, "Although we both attended my cousin Doreen's cotillion ball, I assure you, we have never been formally introduced." She took great pleasure watching Landon's former mistress' mouth freeze open and gape in ill-concealed shock.

Landon moved to Keelan's side, grasped her hand, and then raised it to his lips.

"Tell us, Mrs. Camsby," Keelan asked, sinking into a formal curtsy, "exactly what do you intend to tell the crew?"

CHAPTER 36

THE REWARD

After demanding her trunks be loaded immediately on the longboat, Annette Camsby soon beat an irritated retreat to the main deck to wait its departure.

Landon placed a kiss upon Keelan's smooth brow. He was much comforted and proud of the strength and confidence radiating from his wife's gaze. "While Conal and I meet with the authorities, you and Daniel can accompany Doreen safely to her aunt's home."

Keelan gave a small sigh of pleasure. "I must admit, I cannot wait until I can and enjoy a nice, warm, relaxing bath with lavender oil and fragrant soap and—"

Landon chuckled and squeezed her tighter. "Let's stay the night in town. I'll find a room at the Harbour Town Hotel and we shall bathe *together* this evening. We'll dine with Conal and Brendan. When we board the *Desire*, I intend to introduce you to the crew as my wife."

The delighted sparkle in her emerald eyes warmed his heart. She pulled his head down and her lips beckoned his. She kissed him with the sweetness of Jamaican sugar cane. His hands moved over her buttocks and up to capture her breasts. The heat grew inside of him as her nipples hardened against his touch and her breath turned into a gentle breath of desire. Lifting her into his arms, he strode across the cabin and lowered her to his bed.

"I believe I have an obligation to fulfill," he said, a hint of a smile tugging at his mouth.

"You certainly do," Keelan said, grinning impishly, "and the delay will cost you extra."

༄༅

THEY FOUND the stolen canoe tied to a piling near a dock. The fog was still a thick grey wall, although it seemed to be thinning somewhat. The *Seeker* was nothing but a faint shadow in the distant mist. Anchored just offshore, Landon could vaguely make out the shadow of his ship, the *Desire*.

Conal followed his gaze. "The fog should burn off by evening. Let's plan to shove off at high tide on the morrow."

Landon nodded as he gestured to one of the men to haul up Keelan's new trunk. He wanted to surprise her. He brought the trunk containing the dress he'd purchased for her in Charleston up from the hold and smuggled it aboard without her noticing. She might not be able to dress as Keelan Grey Hart in public, but he'd make sure she would be married in a gown worthy of a bride on her wedding day.

Conal jostled the shoulder of one of the men tying off the longboat. "Make sure the men are ready to re-board as soon as the *Seeker* is anchored at dockside and flying the Blue Peter."

"Aye, sir."

Landon was certain Keelan was already anticipating her warm, scented bath. He smiled. He had another surprise planned for his new wife.

After sending Keelan and Daniel to deliver Doreen to her aunt's house, Landon and Conal spoke with the local constable. They reported both Gampo's attack and the assault and attempted sabotage by the three men who'd stowed aboard the *Seeker*.

Next, the two men stopped at the church on Baker Street and made the necessary arrangements for Landon and Keelan to be married. The priest kindly offered to marry them the same evening. The hefty purse Landon had left with the little man might have provided additional impetus to get the deed done, along with the knowledge Landon and Keelan had taken the ancient vow of a handfast and thus had already consummated their marriage. A low vibration resonated within Landon's chest and it took a moment before he realized he was humming.

Humming.

He ignored Conal's quizzical brow and curious look and strode forward to the docks. Locating the third ship in their fleet, the *Reward,* anchored dockside, he hailed her captain Brendan Ahern, who bade them to come aboard.

A tall three-masted barquentine, the *Reward* was the largest vessel in the Ahern Merchant Company fleet. A newly replaced mizzen mast stood shiny and bright against the scarred hull and ship's deck. The scent of freshly applied pitch lingered with the salty air of the sea. Muffled sounds of low waves, slapping the ship, mingled with the blunted voices of men aboard and other translucent activity in the early morning fog.

Fynn's eldest son shook Landon's hand warmly. Fynn's untimely death had been hard on them, but Brendan had taken it the hardest, of course. He'd seen the mast explode when the bar shot hit it, and although he said he had bellowed a warning, he'd been unable to reach his father in time to save him from the deadly shards which had rained down.

"The new mizzen is in place, I see," Conal observed, shaking his cousin's hand.

"Aye, and has been for nearly a fortnight," Brendan responded. "Anxious I am, to get her underway. I feel helpless as a spring lamb anchored dockside for so long." His jaw clenched as he flung his arm in the direction of the open sea. "While that rat, Gampo, is out there somewhere, probably seeking a hole in which to hide his cowardly arse."

Landon and Conal exchanged hooded looks. Brendan hated being bored, which occasionally led him to act before thinking, since to him, action was always better than stillness. Like Conal, Brendan believed in an eye for an eye and was obviously biting at the bit to get his hands on Gampo.

Would Brendan find peace if he avenged his father's death? Although it was quite possible, he simply seized the challenge because it demanded a call to action. When Landon had lost his parents, he had been too young, too stunned, to understand how grief paralyzed the limbs and the mind...suspended one like a hawk on an updraft. Thankfully, before he'd been dashed on the ragged shoals of death and loss and loneliness, Fynn had saved him.

"Yer like a shark, you are," Conal said to Brendan as they followed to his cabin. "Always on the move, ye can't stand to be still a single second." He clapped Brendan on the back. "It's a good thing we've arrived then, eh?"

Brendan gestured them inside and strode over to his desk, moved aside a tattered leather-bound book and pulled a bottle of whiskey from a drawer. "Aye to that. What kept you? I'd been just about to set sail for Charleston to seek you out when the *Desire* arrived and I received Landon's letter. I waited as instructed, but the information provided was bloody thin."

Conal picked up the old book from Brendan's desk. "What's this?"

"It's one of my father's journals," Brendan answered. "Odd though, it wasn't with the others." He pulled open a desk drawer and gestured to the gap in the back. "It was hidden in here. I haven't had a chance to read through it yet." He pushed the drawer shut. "Tell me what happened in Charleston."

Conal put the journal down. "We went to Twin Pines to meet

with Commodore Grey, as Fynn had planned. However, Grey was unable to tell us why Fynn had arranged the meeting." Conal accepted a whiskey from Brendan. "Although Landon and I both suspect he wasn't being entirely truthful."

Brendan sat, picked up his glass and took a sip. "So you visited Grey. That couldn't have caused such a long delay in returning here." He cocked a questioning brow.

Landon leaned against the doorjamb and frowned. "We ran into Gampo in Charleston. He followed us and managed to make off with some of our goods. It took time to reclaim it." He tossed down the drink and scowled at the empty glass. "I almost had him, Brendan. He took Keelan. He'd bought her, just like he did your mother. I almost had him."

Brendan splashed a bit more whiskey in their cups. Conal added, "The hurricane interfered with the delivery of the additional cargo our friends from Philadelphia commissioned us to acquire."

Brendan rolled his shoulders, leaned his head back, and took a deep breath. "And the additional cargo is where?"

Landon pressed his lips into a thin line. "Part's in the hold of the *Desire*, the rest is still in Charleston." Transporting runaway slaves north to freedom was always a big risk, but to Fynn, it was more of an obligation. His merchant business might have been a little less profitable than it could have been, but Fynn didn't care, claiming it made him a wealthy man in mind, body and spirit.

Conal observed Brendan carefully. "It's not what you'd hoped to do, but we have to go back to Charleston, and retrieve it, and then transport it to Philadelphia straight away, before it's discovered. We're risking all our necks as it is."

"Blast. I really wanted to set sail for Jamaica." Brendan paused with his glass halfway to his lips. "Who's Keelan?"

CHAPTER 37
MYSTERY TO LIGHT

The sun was up in the sky somewhere, shining its noonday rays. The fog seemed to be conceding its grip on the harbor somewhat.

Landon touched the small of Keelan's back to signal they were leaving. Normally, he'd offer her an arm, but it would cause quite a few heads to turn, since Keelan was still dressed as Mahdi.

He glanced at his bride. The glimmer in her eyes when they talked about sailing to South America or Asia made his heart swell. She was as excited as he to begin their journey together.

In less than a day, they'd be legally married. Conal had agreed to stand as a witness. Brendan promised to attend as well.

His stomach rumbled. The breakfast tray Keelan had brought to their cabin earlier had gone untouched after Annette's intrusion. The feel of his wife's bare bottom had lingered near the forefront of his mind after Mrs. Camsby departed. He'd whispered the need to revisit the encounter, much to Keelan's amusement, then eager agreement.

The trio stopped at the tavern across the street from the hotel and ordered a small feast. A short time later, warm bread, cheese, and various cold chunks of meat arrived, along with tankards of ale. Keelan took a sip of her mug, wrinkled her nose and pushed it toward Conal, who accepted it joyfully. Laughing, Landon signaled for the tavern maid and ordered a glass of spiced wine for her instead.

He wanted to reach over and grasp Keelan's hands and inwardly cursed the circumstances which forced her into disguise. He wanted to tell her about the wedding ceremony he had arranged. He wanted her eyes to light up that he'd kept his word. She had doubted him, but he had kept his word.

When he had pledged his heart to her, he'd meant it. With the simple handfast promise, he could have lived the rest of his life, content. Yet, something more drove him to seek the legal documentation; it was one last bridge of trust they had to cross together. She had to fearlessly join her life with his, with absolute conviction, and believe with her entire heart he was a man of his word.

The tavern door opened, and he glanced up. Brendan paused and scanned the room; his gaze found Conal, and he weaved his way around a few tables until he reached them. He clutched a ragged tome as if it were a wounded bird. It was the old journal of Fynn's he'd had found hidden in the desk.

Landon nodded toward the door. "Brendan has decided to join us, I wonder what—"

"Conal!" The catch in Brendan's voice made Landon stop in mid-sentence.

Conal raised his mug. "Hoy, Brendan! Pull up a chair and join us. There's someone I'd like you to meet." He glanced at Keelan and grinned.

Brendan seemed not to hear as he grabbed a chair. "Conal, you have to read this."

Landon leaned forward and grabbed Brendan's forearm, then nodded toward Keelan. "Brendan, this is—"

But Brendan was already talking to his cousin. Landon sat forward and placed his chin in his hands. Apparently, this was important enough to cause his friend to forget his good manners.

Brendan continued, "I started to read bits and parts of my father's journal." His eyes were focused on Conal. "It's about the stolen child Da used to talk about, remember?" He looked at Landon, then grabbed his shoulder and shook it roughly. "Remember, Landon?"

"Yes, we remember." Conal responded first, even as Landon was nodding his head. "Kidnapped from the crib while my family was visiting my aunt in London. I know that much, I was a wee lad at the time."

"Yes, but there's more," Brendan's eyes gleamed, and he squirmed in his chair like a young boy in church. "A few years ago Da overheard a conversation in a pub. A bo'sun was talking about the coin he'd made stealing a babe from the lady who jilted his disgraced commander, and how he was feeling guilty about the deed."

Conal gave Brendan an exasperated look. "Ye can't possibly think—"

"Just wait a moment, Conal, let me finish," Brendan began flipping through the pages. "Listen to what my Da wrote." He pressed open the journal and began to read.

Curious, I offered to buy the man a drink to hear his tale. Since he was already half in his cups, he spilled his story quite liberally. According to the man, he was instructed to enter the residence of a home at the same cross street as my brother-in-law's in England.

The child he took was approximately a year in age with curly auburn hair and an energetic temperament, (the same as young Cailyn's). It would be too great a coincidence that my niece Cailyn and another child, baring the same age, hair and character would be stolen from the same cross street. I'm convinced I've found the man who has taken my sister's child from her cradle.

I did not let on I was in any way involved in the matter, as I didn't want to scare the man away. So, I inquired about his commander.

When I asked his commander's name, the gentleman became quite agitated, saying his commander had been a good commodore and lead an effective crew. He wouldn't divulge the name. However, I later found out the man was none other than Commodore George Grey.

Several years ago, Grey had doggedly pursued my sister's hand and took the matter quite badly when she refused him. He eventually married and purchased a small country house and a shop in Chatham. He wrongly ordered an attack upon a civilian passenger ship a thrice of years ago. Unfortunately, Grey disappeared shortly after his court martial. The bo'sun mentioned the name of a titled gentleman who'd been good friends with the commodore. I shall research this further, but my first assumption is that Grey had Cailyn kidnapped as a means to punish my sister for refusing his hand in marriage years before.

Upon hearing the name *Commodore George Grey*, Landon glanced at Keelan. Her face had paled beneath the fading dye and her gaze flew to his and widened. With a shaking hand, she fumbled for her wine and knocked the glass over, interrupting Brendan's narrative. Landon tossed his napkin over the spilled wine and gestured for another glass while keeping a watchful eye on his wife.

Brendan shoved the book across the table to Conal and jabbed the next page. "Read this."

Conal began reading, then turned the page. He paused, flipped the page back, and reread it, then looked at Keelan and swallowed. It was a long still moment before he spoke, gesturing to the book. "Uncle Fynn believed the bo'sun expected there would be a ransom. He took a gold ring and a locket as proof of the child's identity and gave them to Grey when he handed over the child."

He turned the page and continued reading.

"The bo'sun described the locket as a miniature portrait of a beautiful woman with hair like a sunset on one side and a dark-haired gentlemen on the other. He broke the locket in two, leaving one half in the empty cradle and wrapping the other half in the blanket with the child.

Conal removed the ring from his finger and put it on the table. "*Along with a ring which had four lions carved on the crest.*"

Keelan reached inside her shirt and tugged the red ribbon holding the locket miniature and pulled it over her head. She placed it next to the ring, causing the table to go silent. Brendan looked from the ring to the locket to Keelan, and a sudden dawning of realization rippled across his face.

Landon leaned forward and put his hand on Brendan's shoulder. "Brendan Ahern, please allow me to introduce you to my wife, Keelan Grey Hart, of Chatham, England, raised as the daughter of the late Commodore George Grey of the Royal Navy *and* I believe, your cousin."

CHAPTER 38

FAMILY

"C'mon, Landon." Brendan said irately, taking in Keelan's clothing and darkened skin. "I'm being serious."

"As am I," Landon said.

"He's telling the truth," Conal said, staring at Keelan. "I witnessed the vows. She's in a disguise to protect her from Gampo's assassins."

"Well, I'll be..." Brendan leaned back in his chair, cocked his head and studied Keelan for a moment, then studied Conal, who hadn't taken his eyes off Keelan since he placed his ring on the table.

"We'd all given up," Conal said hoarsely, shaking his head in disbelief. "But Fynn hadn't. He promised my ma he'd never stop searching. He finally found you. He found our sister." Conal's eyes glistened with tears.

Keelan's throat constricted at his words, and her lungs felt twice their normal size.

Sister.

She was a *sister*! Her ears started to ring. Conal had said *our sister*. She had more than a father. She had a mother and Conal, and Brendan, her cousin.

She had a *family*.

A large tear fell unchecked to the table, followed by another. Conal wiped the third away from his chin before it could fall, his eyes still wide. "You're not my father's illegitimate daughter. You're my baby sister, Cailyn. The one who was stolen from her bed when I was a tiny lad." His face broke into a wide smile. He slapped his hands on the table, then jumped to his feet.

Conal lifted Keelan off her chair and enveloped her in a tremendous hug. They were both laughing and crying at the same time. Conal pulled Landon up, hugged him, clapped Brendan on the back, then grabbed Keelan again and kissed both her cheeks. She laughed and her heart swelled with both glee and love for her husband and her brother and the family she had yet to meet. Never had she dreamed her life would turn out this way. She was with the man she loved. She was part of a family. She was finally *home*.

"Now, dear one," Conal was saying, pulling her hand, "sit ye down again and let me tell ye about your younger kin. You got yer lovely red curly locks from our mother. In fact, I'm a bigger idiot, fer not seeing the resemblance, except for your eyes and chin. Those come from our da. Now, about your younger, twin sisters. Ciera, she's married with a wee one of her own. Carina is... well... she's an adventuresome sort." He shifted in his seat as if he'd just sat upon a burr. "She's not home much, and it'd probably be best if ye learned about her later. Then there's Aislyn, she's almost sixteen. Lastly, there's our brother Ian, who ought to be thirteen by now."

Brendan cleared his throat and Conal quickly added, "And there's Brendan, of course, and his brother, Ronan, your cousins. I'll not go into the rest of your cousins just yet, it'll only confuse you."

She had so many questions! Where to start? "Where do they live in Ireland?"

"Most of our family lives in Philadelphia now," Conal said,

eyes brightening. "As soon as this fog lifts, our fleet is heading north. You'll meet them soon. I canna wait to see their faces when they see you."

Keelan couldn't stop smiling. It was like a dream. Better. Reaching over, she gripped Landon's arm, and he nudged her with his knee under the table in response.

Conal and Brendan talked to Keelan for almost an hour about her kin. Landon added a story here and there where he could before he finally stood and gestured to Keelan.

"I made a promise to my bride that I would arrange a wedding and provide legal documentation of our marriage." He took Keelan's hand, not caring who noticed. "And I have done so."

Her heart nearly stopped. A wedding?

Conal nodded. "Good, then. I knew ye'd make good on yer promise to me, sis."

A moment ago, she didn't think she could feel happier, yet she did.

"We are to be married at Christ Church at dusk." He nodded at the two other men at the table. "I'd be honored if the two of you would join us as witnesses."

"Of course!" Conal picked up his mug in salute. "I'll be havin' to give away the bride, of course."

Keelan grinned at her brother. "Then, I beg your leave, to prepare for the ceremony."

Brendan and Conal stood. Brendan grinned and stuck out his hand to Landon. "Congratulations, my friend, I wish for you and my cousin a long and happy life."

Conal wasn't looking as happy as Brendan. He took in his own stained breeches and scarred boots. "This won't do. I have a much finer coat and breeches in my locker on the *Seeker*." He glanced at Landon. "If I take the canoe, I can get to the ship quickly and retrieve my best." He chanced a sideways glance at Keelan. "Our ma would expect it," he added in a chagrined tone.

Brendan was staring at Conal's boots. "Do you have *any* boots with a shine on them, Conal? If not, I can lend you a pair of mine."

Conal frowned. "Of course I do, you lame-brained dolt. I bought them the same time as you bought yours." He froze, then gave Keelan a sideways grimace. "Yer pardon for me language, Keelan."

He looked like a guilty child, and Keelan couldn't hold back her laughter. "We shall await your return," she said. Keelan caught Landon's gaze before she continued, "I'm sure Landon will demand a longer soak, since his last bath was disrupted most tragically."

Conal chuckled while Brendan sat back, looking from one to the other in confusion.

"Aye to that," Conal responded, laughing. "Aye to that."

CHAPTER 39
NEVER TURN YOUR BACK ON A
PIRATE

Landon was true to his word, and Keelan enjoyed a long, leisurely soak at the hotel. At least, it was leisurely until he joined her in the tub. It was some time later before they emerged, quite flushed and well-pruned. To Keelan's delight, the additional time in the bath had soaked off several shades of the dye, leaving her skin the color of clover honey, and her wet hair a deep amber.

Thanks to Landon's nimble fingers and patience, she stood before the mirror at last, in the grey satin gown her husband had purchased for her in Charleston. The natural tint of her hair was beginning to show, and the result was agreeable, much better than the tiger stripes.

Landon wore black breeches, shined boots, a new white linen shirt, and a deep navy waistcoat. He'd contained his dark satin locks with a black ribbon. For a second, Keelan forgot to breathe as she studied her husband. He was so handsome, she could hardly believe he was hers. Her love for him, which pulsed with every beat of her heart, seemed to be the only source of balance in her body. She closed her eyes and took a deep breath.

"Keelan." Landon's deep baritone broke into her reverie and she lifted her lids. The apparition standing near her could have been a Persian prince with crystalline blue eyes. "You're so beautiful," he said. Taking her hand, he spun her to him. The warmth of his lips on her fingertips made her stomach quiver. "This isn't a traditional path to the altar." He gave her that boyish grin which used to infuriate her. "However, you and I haven't had a traditional type of courtship, have we?"

She smiled, shaking her head, then reached up and touched his cheek. "No, we haven't and I'm glad."

"Well, our vows will be more traditional when we speak them before the priest," he said, tucking her hand under his elbow. "It's only a short walk to the church from here. Conal and Brendan will meet us downstairs and then we'll walk to there together."

When they descended the stairs, Brendan was already sitting at a table in a corner and sipping a mug of ale. Upon catching sight of Landon and Keelan, he rose to his feet and gestured for them to join him. He had on tan breeches and tall chestnut-toned boots. A light grey waistcoat and darker jacket outlined his broad shoulders and tapered waist. She made a mental note to ask Conal about family stature. How could she be so petite when her brother and cousin were as big as trees?

Landon reached out and shook his hand. "So you really *do* know how to dress for an occasion. I must admit, I was skeptical."

Brendan laughed. "You'll find I have a few polite characteristics, as well." He gave Keelan a deep bow. "Greetings, Mrs. Hart. May I say you look radiant today?"

Keelan curtsied and bestowed a brilliant smile upon him in return. "Thank you, sir. You are quite dashing yourself."

"Very smart boots," Landon added.

Brendan grinned. "I expected you'd be jealous. It's the reason I purchased them. Wait until you see Conal's. You'll turn greener than a field in May."

Landon pulled out a chair for Keelan, then ordered a couple glasses of wine and another ale for Brendan. Raising his glass, Brendan said, "A toast to the happy couple on this special day."

Keelan raised her glass. A shadow fell across the table.

It was Henry. He was disheveled, as if he'd just been roughly awakened. Were the effects of the drugged wine still taking its toll on the poor man? She paused mid-sip. Hadn't they left him aboard the *Seeker* to rest and rehabilitate?

"Captain Hart, Captain Ahern," Henry nodded to each man then snatched his hat off his head as he faced her. He stepped forward and squinted his eyes, as if she wasn't quite in focus. After a second, he blinked and gave her a slight bow. "Uh... Hello, Miss."

Landon cocked his head. "What is it, Henry? You look a bit rough. Is something wrong?"

Henry dragged his gaze from Keelan and nodded vigorously. "Yes, sir! A band of pirates have taken the *Seeker,* sir. They put most of us on longboats and set us adrift, pitching the oars over the starboard side of the ship. It took us quite a while to fetch 'em then row ashore."

This information sobered both Landon and Brendan, and they sat forward in their chairs. "*Most* of the crew? Where's O'Brien?" Landon asked quickly, setting down his glass.

"Still aboard the ship," Henry said, shoulders slumped. "He was caught unawares when they came aboard. They trussed him up along with Remus and his watch."

Oh no, Conal! Keelan's hand crept to her throat.

Brendan was already on his feet. "I'll prepare the *Reward* to give chase immediately." He paused, concern creased his face. "The cargo bound for Philadelphia..."

Landon took a deep breath, then took Keelan's hand. She wanted to go after her brother. But Landon had an obligation to deliver the runaways; they were depending on him and had placed their lives in his hands. She gave him a slight nod. He had a duty to perform. She wouldn't interfere.

"I'll see it delivered, then join you in your search." To Henry, Landon asked, "Did you happen to note the bearing?"

Henry rocked from one foot to the other, wringing his hat in his hands. "Didn't need to. They made it no secret they were heading to Jamaica and needed the cargo in the belly of the *Seeker* to use as a tribute to the Pirate King."

Brendan stiffened. A flash of panic crossed his face before he nudged Landon. The two of them walked a few steps away and spoke for quite a long time. She couldn't hear what they were saying, but by the expression on Landon's face, it was grave.

Landon reached for Keelan, and she stepped into the shelter of his arms. He hugged her tightly before he spoke, "I'm sorry, love, we won't be able to exchange wedding vows this evening. We'll be hard-pressed to get Brendan's ship underway fast enough to catch sight of the *Seeker*." He tried to give her a small reassuring smile. His eyes, however, were flooded with concern.

"Don't apologize," she said. "Our wedding is secondary to the issues at hand."

He nodded. "Brendan will be able to set sail immediately, since the *Reward* is ready to depart. We'll sail the *Desire* back to Charleston and arrange for our cargo to get to Philadelphia using another Freedom Runner. Then, I'll be free to follow Brendan to Jamaica, and join in the search for Conal." He kissed her fingertips. "I wish I could join the chase right away. However, with other lives on my shoulders, I must fulfill my prior obligations and promises. We'll only be a few days behind."

"I understand," she said. Turning to Brendan, she placed a hand on his forearm. "Find my brother."

Brendan covered her hand with his and squeezed. "I will." He turned his attention to Landon. "I'll leave word for you with the harbormaster in Baracoa. There are a couple of crew mates still there, I'll put their location in the note for the harbormaster. I dropped them off to recover from their wounds after the last attack with Gampo. If they're healthy and healed, I'd like you to bring them along." He tossed some coins on the table and left.

"Baracoa?" She'd never heard of Baracoa.

"It's a Cuban coastal town we use as a stopover port on the way to Jamaica," Landon explained. A strange light flickered in his eyes and he smiled. "I think Brendan has been keeping secrets, but we won't know for sure until we drop anchor at port."

Offering an arm to Keelan, he took her back to the hotel. Within the hour, they had changed, retrieved their things and joined Henry and his men in the longboat. Keelan was once again dressed as Mahdi. Although it was unlikely the pirates returned to Charleston, the reward offered for Keelan was likely to be still active. She'd have to remain disguised until they were well away.

She'd have to reapply that dreaded dye. In fact, she'd probably need a really good reason to eat ham ever again.

A slight breeze had kicked up, and the fog appeared more translucent than it had earlier. The *Desire,* as well as other ships in the harbor, seemed more clearly defined. While the men rowed, Keelan glanced over to where the *Seeker* had been. The empty space looked wrong and uneven, as if the vessel had tried to leave a sign that she was unwillingly dragged away. Even the gulls seemed disconcerted, their cries sparse and muffled.

As soon as they boarded the *Desire*, the crew hoisted the blue flag and rang the ship's bell, alerting the crew the ship would soon depart. Landon took Keelan on a tour and introduced her to several of his men as Mahdi. He sent Henry to interview the newer crew mates.

"If Gampo has spies on this ship, I'd like to flush them out before we're underway," Landon told her. "Henry has a way of asking questions that can make an innocent man feel guilty. If a man shifts his eyes at the wrong time, Henry will pounce on him like a hungry cat." He headed toward the hold. "Follow me. It will be a short while yet before we can be away. I have something to show you."

Below, he lit a lantern and took her hand, leading her toward the aft section of the hold. Freshly cut wood, livestock, and hay wafted through the air. Of course. Landon had purchased a horse,

Orion, from her uncle. A loud snort confirmed her suspicion. There were two new timber stalls in the center of the hold. Landon paused at the first one, and Orion immediately poked his nose between two slats in the side. Landon laughed and walked around the corner and opened the top half of the stall door.

"How was your first sea voyage, my friend?" Landon stroked the stallion's neck.

Orion gave another snort and nuzzled Landon's pocket. He winked. "I think he's more interested in meeting his neighbor."

"His neighbor?" She glanced at the other stall. "Did you buy another horse?"

Landon nodded. At the sound of Keelan's voice, a set of hooves rustled the straw next door, followed by a low whicker. Her heart leapt. "That sounds like..." Keelan reached over, opened the second stall door, and peeked inside. "Juliet!" She reached in and rubbed the mare's nose, then laughed with glee. In the shadows wobbled her dark-eyed, young foal, peeking at Keelan from behind his dame's hind legs.

Landon moved behind her and slid his arms around her waist. "This is my wedding gift to you, my love." He kissed the top of her head and then let out a frustrated huff. "And I promise you, there *will* be a wedding, soon."

"Oh, Landon, thank you for buying Juliet from Uncle Jared. I feared I'd never see her again." She turned in his arms and put both palms on either side of his face and kissed him. He tightened his hold around her waist and pressed her body against his. His hands traced a path up her side to her breasts and gently stroked her until her nipples tingled and her lower belly ached.

"My gift makes you happy?" He leaned his forehead against hers and she found she liked this little show of his affection.

"*You* make me happy," she replied, kissing him again.

He reached for her hands. Entwining his fingers with hers, he said, "And you make me happy, sweet Keelan. Wait—*Cailyn*."

She laughed. "They are so much alike, it doesn't matter." She sobered. It seemed wrong to feel so happy when her brother was in the hands of pirates. "I fear for Conal."

He pulled away enough to look into her eyes. "You don't know Brendan well, but I do. I sailed with him and his father from the time I was twelve years old. Brendan—" Landon paused, looking up as if he'd find inspiration for his word choice written on the bones of the hold. "Brendan is like a dog with an old stocking. He won't let go until he has complete possession." He squeezed her shoulders. "He'll find the *Seeker,* and we'll free Conal. I promise you as soon as our business is complete we will join him. We'll find both your brother and your cousin."

She wanted to believe him, she truly did; her mind wouldn't let go of visions of Conal being tortured by Gampo and his crew. "But, Gampo is a cruel man. What if he—"

Landon pulled her into the circle of his arms and gave her a comforting squeeze before releasing her slightly. She was startled to realize he was chuckling. How could he take such a situation so lightly?

"Why do you laugh? I'm concerned and terribly fearful for Conal, and Brendan as well," she said, both bewildered and annoyed. "How can you be so light-hearted?"

Landon bent down and kissed her cheek, then trailed his lips down her neck, raising the gooseflesh on her throat, shoulders, and arms. "Because, I've been around both Conal and Brendan long enough to tell you that I almost feel sorry for Gampo for raising their ire." He pulled away and traced his finger along her jawline. "I promise you, Keelan, we will find them."

A tight warmth radiated from her heart throughout her chest, and her eyes watered. Rather than try to express what she was feeling, she drew his head down and kissed him. He pulled her hips to him, his hardness urgent and hot against her belly. This time, it was her hands traveling down his ribs and over his muscular buttocks, and sliding into the back of his breeches.

"I'm slightly disappointed in your boat," she murmured.

He pulled away from her and lowered his brows in a mocking scowl. "The *Desire* is a *ship*, not a boat," he said sternly. "A *boat* has only two masts. A ship has three. The *Desire*, as you can well attest, has three masts. Therefore, she is a *ship*, not a boat." He tugged playfully at her hair before sweeping his arm around the hold. "And why are you disappointed? She's almost as big as the *Seeker*, although just a little shorter stem to stern."

"I have yet to be invited to the captain's cabin," she said, fighting hard to appear disappointed. "So, I must come to the conclusion that there is none, and I shall have to lash up my hammock with the rest of my mess mates."

"It will be my distinct pleasure," he said, eyes warm and knowing, "to give you a personal introduction to the captain's cabin." He lowered his head for another kiss.

Landon's aura would always consist of leather and the sea, of the wind and the earth, and he belonged to her and she to him. Wherever in the world Landon would go, she would be at his side.

He was her home.

He grasped her hand and then led her toward the hatch. Before leaving the quiet darkness of the hold, he paused and enveloped her in the warmth and love of his embrace. "I love you, wife."

She smiled. "And I love you back, husband."

Complete the trilogy with
If You Give a Hellion Your Heart

An accident robs Landon of his memory and turns his new wife Keelan into a stranger.

Worse, a series of catastrophic events has Landon accusing Keelan of conspiracy and betrayal.

Each explanation sounds more and more outlandish, and her hope for Landon to remember her love becomes more and more futile.

Can she persuade him to trust her before the bounty hunters close in?

Keelan's fight for Landon's love soon turns into a fight for his life.

If you love romance swirled with adventure and intrigue, you'll love reading about Landon and Keelan's road to their happily ever-after!

EXCERPT from
If You Give a Hellion Your Heart:

A long, lithe, orange cat darted past Keelan as she walked down the narrow passageway to the galley. She poked her head around the corner. Marcel wrestled a barrel toward a closet along with Yanda, a young brown-skinned girl. Now that they were safely away from port, the family of runaways had come out of hiding to help the crew.

"Mahdi! Where have you been, boy?" Marcel drove his hip in to the barrel, but it only moved an inch. "Come, help us prepare for the gale."

"Captain Hart had me hauling the ropes. What can I do here?"

The little girl paused to clutch her stomach. Marcel harrumphed and glared at her while he rocked the barrel forward in small steps, "Dozens of men to help with ze sails and no one helps old Marcel."

"Where is Elle?" Keelan asked Marcel. Yanda's mother, Elle, had been a cook for her last master, so it seemed practical to place her in the galley.

"She iz checking the cabinets in zee next room, making sure they are latched." He glanced up at Keelan and muttered, "Useless lubbers, both of zem."

When Elle stumbled in from the next cabin, arms pressed tightly against her belly, Keelan understood and took pity. The woman glistened with sweat. Her eyes were red and her face ashen.

Seasickness. It's hard to want to do anything but die when hit with that kind of nausea.

Marcel gestured to the other side of the barrel. "It iz heavy, but we must lock it in zere. You push, I pull, eh?"

She nodded and together they managed to wiggle the cask into the narrow pantry closet while Marcel spat a string of French curses at the stubbornness of the barrel, at Elle's lack of strength and Yanda, who vomited on the floor. After it was secured, he pointed to a bucket of sea water and a mop and the girl nodded with a mumbled, "Sorry, Monsieur."

They secured the pantry shelves to prevent items from pitching to the floor in rough seas. Marcel placed a tin of dried meat, biscuits and a couple rounds of cheese handy before he shut the door. He nonchalantly pressed a broken biscuit into Yanda's palm on his way out and popped the other half into his mouth.

From there they moved elsewhere on the orlop deck, tying down loose items or stowing them. Port holes were closed and locked, although seawater had already surged in. They trudged through an inch of water on the lower decks. The ship pitched and groaned. Keelan caught her breath and listened to the *Desire's* inhalations and exhalations. Would it stay together through the storm or break into pieces? She studied the beams. Like huge fingers clutching a vase, they held the squirming ship in their grasp. The vessel squealed and moaned her pain and distress.

Marcel, sensing Keelan's trepidation, pointed to the water which had seeped in. "Iz from the hause bucklers."

At her confused expression, he tried again. "Zee pressing of zee ship against the water when swells come, push water through zee house bucklers. The *Desire*, she iz strong and brave. And nimble as a cat. No reason to worry. We have sailed through worse."

As they finished, a large group of crewmen came down below and collapsed wearily at the tables propped between the guns on the gun deck. Marcel jerked his head toward the galley and they went to prepare the meal, which would be nothing more than a piece or two of dried beef, hard biscuits, grog and a chunk of cheese.

The lurch and groans of the ship had Keelan gripping edges of the tables as she staggered past. She'd been getting used to being on the water, and actually enjoyed it before today. She still moved like a landlubber and was anxious to develop her "sea legs." Lanterns swung in unison, casting quick shadows followed by fans of light. The *Desire* pitched sharply and Keelan stumbled. A burly arm shot out and grabbed her collar.

"Careful, boy," Gus said. "Best ye find a spot and stay there."

"How do you keep your footing when the ship bucks and tilts?" She was breathless from her effort to stay upright.

Gus sat back and scratched his salt and pepper beard, then gripped his tankard before it flew to the floor. "Seein' how yer father is a horsemaster, I'll put it this way..." He finished his grog. "When the horse jumps a hedge, do ye try to keep yer seat straight and still on the saddle?"

At last. Here was something with which Keelan was familiar, although she hadn't jumped a horse since she was twelve. She shook her head. "You'd fall off if you tried to keep your seat on the saddle. You have to stand in the stirrups and keep your legs soft to absorb the impact of the landing."

Gus cocked his head. "Ye Persians sure do use peculiar language, but, aye. So, ye does the same thing on the water. Mount the *Desire* as ye would a proud filly. Ye'll never tame her, so don't try. All ye can do is melt into her rhythm. Keep yer knees soft and let her rise up to ye. When she sighs and falls away, don't fight her and try to follow. Let her go. She'll come back to ye in her own time. Keep yer guts even with the horizon and ye won't gets seasick."

Keelan let go of the table and heeded his advice. Sure enough, it was similar to jumping her pony. She'd have to mention this method to poor Elle and Yanda. She grinned her thanks to Gus, then asked, "Where's the captain?"

"He has first watch," Gus replied, dipping his tankard into a bucket hanging from a rope secured to the ceiling. "Best fer ye to stay below, outta the way, though."

After serving the men their rations for the evening, she helped Marcel secure the galley before she went back to the cabin. The room tilted and shifted, causing her feet to slide and her stomach to slam into her ribs.

Keep my guts even with the horizon. Keep my guts even with the horizon.

Relaxing her legs, she allowed the *Desire* to take the lead in this rolling dance. A powerful wave hit the ship, and she was pleasantly surprised and happy with the way she rode it. Now that Gus had revealed the secret to handling the motion, it was much easier to move about. Although it would probably be even easier if she could see the horizon.

She slipped a couple biscuits in her pocket for Landon and left the galley to make her way to the ladder and up to the main deck. Was he alone at the helm? She'd forgotten to ask Gus. If so, perhaps he might like some company.

When she raised the hatch, a lash of stinging sea spray hit her full in the face. The main deck forward sloshed with water, and the entire ship rose and fell in a furious coupling with the sea. The waves crashed against the ship's sides and exploded into the air, spraying the decks.

For a second, she hesitated. Her old self might retreat below to stay dry, but the boy, Mahdi, would be more courageous, wouldn't he? She looked toward the helm. Her husband's form was blurry figure amidst the torrent. If Landon could brave the gale, so could she. Had she not once raced a horse through similar weather, trying to beat a terrible storm? This couldn't be any worse than that.

Keelan climbed out and took a step. The deck jolted, as if trying to fling her away from the safety of the hold. Everything was shiny and slick with seawater. Her feet flew away from her and the tilt of the ship sent her crashing to the boards. Gasping, wet and bruised, she pulled herself to her feet by grasping the lines attached to a belaying pin.

Terror pulsed through her limbs. This was a mistake. She shouldn't have come up on deck. She'd underestimated the power of the ship and the winds and the storm. Landon was only a hundred feet away, but he might as well have been in China. Through sheer will and self-preservation, she managed to gain her footing in time for the *Desire* to send her tumbling toward midships, her shriek of alarm flung into the sea by the wind.

Panic ripped through her chest. Unless she found some sort of solid purchase, she'd soon be flung like a piece of cloth into the furious ocean. Rolling across the glistening boards that locked together to form the bones, the sinew, and the skin of the *Desire,* she splayed her hands and legs in hopes of catching something, *anything*, as the brave vessel heaved against the rage of the ocean.

She tumbled against the side of the ship. Thank goodness there was a plethora of ropes secured to belaying pins, providing something to grasp while she struggled to her feet. The ship fell into another swell and just as she gained her footing, her feet flew away from her again, and she hit the deck hard, her breath knocked from her chest. Before she had time to inhale, the *Desire* saw fit to pour her into a space between two of the petite guns on the deck, instead of tossing her into the sea. She curled her cold, wet fingers around the thick ropes securing the gun and held on for all she was worth.

If she'd had the time, she might have screamed or sobbed in fear, but the tempest didn't permit a pause for such frivolous displays. It only continued to pound the ocean like a giant child throwing a tantrum, plunging the left fist into the water, then the right, then the left again.

Keelan peered through the rain back to the hatch leading into the hold, then the distance to the helm, and then to Landon. Retracing her steps back below was more treacherous than continuing her fight to the helm at this point. It took every ounce of strength and courage to release her grip from the ropes and drive forward, where two other sailors were clinging on to the wheel with Landon, straining to keep the ship from broaching into the sea.

The thrumming, creaking and whistling of the ropes, lines and spars cracked and whined in her ears. The wind and rain pelted her skin. She'd no idea the storm had become so viscous while she'd been below. In her defense, she'd no idea what to expect of it, but then again, she'd never been one to take heed of a storm warning, had she?

To say that the journey toward the helm was arduous would have been grossly understating the event. If she'd been any less stubborn, she'd never have made it. The bowsprit reared up skyward as if to impale the turbulent clouds, making Keelan's legs as heavy as stone. Then it swooped down to crash into the waves in a violent explosion of white, which had her teetering on her toes, light as a mouse. She finally made it past the main mast encircled with the barrels she and Daniel had secured earlier. Only a few paces to go, thank God.

Several smaller sails were still in service, their sheets flat and rigid in the wind. Shielding her eyes against the salt spray, she sought Landon. His feet were braced wide, and he was heaving his broad chest into the wheel. His dark wet curls whipped around his face, his jaw set. She pulled herself toward the companion ladder that led up to where he stood. Almost there.

"Keelan!"

His shout stopped her. There was a note of panic in his voice that made her pause. He waved his arm. "Move leeward! Starboard!"

Confused, she froze.

"To your right!"

A loud crack followed by a low rumble sounded behind her and she turned as the barrels around the main mast came loose. They began to roll away, toward the front of the ship. One hit the foremast and split open, spilling sand across the deck. The bowsprit once again crashed down into the waves.

A jolt of horror shook her limbs. Next, the front of the ship would rear back up and when it did, the barrels would reverse direction and roll toward the stern.

Toward her.

Dear God, help me.

She turned and ran. The pitch of the ship had her running up a steep, slippery slope. A half dozen strides away from her goal, the plume of water hit and shook the front part of the ship. For a second the rumble ceased.

But only for a second.

Panic nearly paralyzed her limbs. The barrels began to roll and bounce toward her. She turned toward Landon. He had leapt down the companion ladder toward her.

"Take to my arm!" He reached out to her as his boots hit the main deck. "Hold on!"

With that, he grabbed her and flung her toward the shelter between two canons secured on the right side of the ship as a barrel clipped the farthest gun, and launched into the air, whirling fiercely. Twisting his body, Landon put himself between Keelan and the flying barrel.

It hit them with the force of a raging bull, then crashed to the deck and broke into pieces.

Keelan gasped in pain and tried to take a breath. A heavy weight prevented any movement. She was face down on the deck. She craned her neck enough to see Landon's body covering hers. And he wasn't moving.

"Landon!" she cried his name. No movement, no sound. Nothing.

Another voice pierced the gale. She strained to raise her head until finally, Landon was lifted away from her. A sailor dashed up the companion ladder to take the helm along with two others. Gus tossed Landon over his shoulder and Ronan, Brendan's brother and her cousin, grabbed Keelan's wrist and pulled her to her feet.

Together, they battled the pitch and roll of the ship to the captain's cabin. Gus dropped Landon on his bed then turned to her, his eyes flashing. "What the blazes did ye think ye were doin' out on that deck? Yer a *lubber*. Ye ain't got any sailin' know-how. Ye just 'bout killed yerself and yer captain, ye witless scamp!"

Gus's fists were clenched, and he advanced upon Keelan like a raging ox. If she hadn't been braced against the cabin wall, she'd have collapsed right there in her boots. As it was, she was trembling so violently, her teeth clattered against each other.

Ronan stepped between Gus and Keelan. "Twas a greenie

mistake, sir." His eyes shifted between the two. Gus hadn't been told that Keelan was Landon's wife. They'd decided to wait until after they left Charleston.

In Gus's eyes, she was a young boy, a novice and a liability. Gus was as furious as the tempest outside. "Well, if it wasn't fer this gale, he'd get five lashes from the cat," he spat, shaking his fist.

Ronan cleared his throat and shifted on his feet. "Mahdi has some knowledge of healing. He can help the ship's sawbones treat the captain. It'll keep him outta the way."

Gus scowled, then shrugged before stomping out. "Go git the surgeon then, Ronnie. I'm on watch," he snapped before slamming the door.

Keelan leaned against the cabin wall and squeezed her eyes shut. What had she done? A choked sob escaped her throat, and she fell away from Ronan's grip and staggered to her husband's bedside. "Landon!"

His shirt was soaked and stuck to his chest like skin. She placed her ear over his heart and closed her eyes, listening.

Dear God, please let him be alive.

Was that a soft, distant heartbeat?

It was!

She examined him, checking for bruises, blood and feeling for broken bones. A small trickle of blood flowed from his ear.

"Let's pull him out of these wet clothes, Miss Keelan," Ronan whispered, touching her shoulder. "The doc will want to see all of him."

☙❧

A day later, steady rain still pummeled the ship, but the wind and rough seas had abated, somewhat. The sun tried to shove its way through the grey blanket, but the clouds refused it.

The ship's surgeon examined Landon's head, touching a large lump on his temple. "It hasn't changed since last night. A good sign. We'll just have to wait it out," he said, packing up the wooden carrier holding his surgeon's supplies. "That large bruise on his upper back and shoulder may be hiding a broken bone or rib, but it's the hit on the head to worry about."

"How long until he wakes?" Keelan asked, dreading the answer.

"Don't know." He shook his head, turning toward the door. "He may not."

Two days later, Landon still hadn't moved nor made another sound since he'd been placed on his bed; not when they'd removed his clothes, nor when Keelan poured whiskey on the small cut on his temple. Landon didn't even flinch. Putting her head on his chest, she checked yet again for his heartbeat.

Again, she folded her hands and made her appeal to God for Landon to gain consciousness soon. Her chest flooded with regret. If only she hadn't tried to traverse the deck in the storm. If only she'd stayed below and out of the way, Landon might not have been injured. Why hadn't she simply turned back?

For the thousandth time, she whispered, "Please Landon, my love, wake up." She pressed another kiss on his forehead.

This time, as if he'd heard her, Landon's eyelids twitched and he let out a low moan.

"Landon?" Keelan tried to keep her voice level and calm, but she couldn't contain the intertwined notes of relief and concern.

His eyes finally opened, and he slowly moved his startling blue gaze to her face. His expression changed from wariness to confusion. He lifted his head and winced.

She pressed his shoulders back down. "Go slowly, you're hurt."

"Where am I?" He rubbed his forehead.

"You're in your cabin aboard the *Desire*. You were hit on the head and have been unconscious for two days," she explained.

He attempted to sit up, then grimaced and sunk back to a reclining position. "What happened?"

Keelan bit her lip, then answered, "It was my fault. I shouldn't have come up on deck. We were hit by a rogue barrel during the gale. I didn't tie it down correctly. You were struck on the side of the head and back by one of them. Do you remember that?"

"There was a storm?" His hand was over his eyes, as if the light pained him.

He didn't remember the storm? She spoke in a low tone, "Yes. It's blown us quite a way off course, but Gus said we should arrive in Charleston in a day or two, depending on the wind and the current."

Landon glanced at her from under his hand. "What about Captain O'Brien and Captain Ahern? Did they weather the storm fairly? Have their ships been sighted?"

For a moment, Keelan wasn't sure how to answer. It was impossible for either to be sighted. Both ships were currently bound for Jamaica. Perhaps now wasn't the time to tell her husband his memory was off. She put her hand on his chest. "You're a bit disoriented. You were hit hard."

He stared at her hand, then brushed it away impatiently. Hurt by this, she sat back and regarded him. He was acting... differently.

Something was wrong.

His cool, aloof stare had her heart pounding in her chest and her stomach flipping in trepidation.

"Who are *you*?" he finally asked.

Continue the adventure with the next book:
If You Give a Hellion Your Heart!

MORE BOOKS BY CHLOE FLOWERS

WANT SWEET ROMANCE INSTEAD?

Read Chloe Flowers' *The Hearts of Adventure Sweet Romance* Series!

PIRATES **& P**ETTICOATS **N**OVELS

If You Give a Hellion Your Heart
Not 'til Death Will She Part
Pirates & Petticoats Book 3

Remember me...
His memory of her is gone.
Bounty hunters are closing in.
Her fight for his love soon turns
into a fight for his life.

*NOTE: This is the *sexy version* of the novel *The Heart of a Bride*, (Book 3 of The Hearts of Adventure Sweet Romance Series By Chloe Flowers).

An accident throws him back five years into his past turning his new wife into a complete stranger.

Worse, a series of catastrophic events has Landon accusing Keelan of conspiracy and betrayal. When each explanation sounds more and more outlandish, her hope for Landon to remember their love becomes more and more futile. Bounty hunters are closing in and a nefarious landowner has discovered Landon's secret identity. More than ever Keelan needs Landon on her side if she's going to save both their lives.

Can she persuade him to trust her? Will he remember his love for her before it's too late?

If You Give a Smuggler a Secret, If You Give a Rake a Reason and *If You Give a Hellion Your Heart* is a trilogy that follows Keelan Grey and Landon Hart on their adventure of discovery and a love of a lifetime. Two hearts have never battled harder to be together...

If you love romance swirled with adventure and intrigue, you'll love reading about Landon and Keelan's road to their happily ever after, because true love always finds a way.

If You Give a Pirate a Treasure
She'll Steal your Heart for Good Measure
Pirates & Petticoats Book 4

Her twin siblings have been kidnapped.

The ransom is a ship called The Seeker.
She's not a real pirate.
But their lives depend on
her playing the part.

*NOTE: This is the stand-alone, *sexy version* of the novel *The Heart of a Pirate*, (Book 4 of The Hearts of Adventure Sweet Romance Series By Chloe Flowers).

Captain Conal O'Brien's ship is overrun by the most unlikely band of pirates to sail the seas. When he discovers their true objective, he develops a scheme of his own. But these nutty brigands aren't who they seem to be, and if Conal's not careful, he's going to lose his heart as well as his ship to a lady pirate determined to possess both.

Stevie Sauvage is on a quest to find a hidden family treasure. When her eight-year-old twin siblings are kidnapped by the pirate, Captain Gampo, and the ransom demand is a merchant ship, she must find the courage to conquer her fears and fight for those she loves before time runs out for the twins.

If You Give a Pirate a Treasure is a high seas, historical, pirate romance filled with action and adventure, mystery and intrigue, and a quest for hidden treasure (with a few laughs along the way).

What readers have to say:

> *This storyline itself was well thought out and engaging. I have read a fair few "pirate romances," and I have to say that (this book) is up there with the best. FANTASTIC READ!!*
> *I thoroughly enjoyed (the book), and I look forward to reading more books from this author. Well done, Chloe Flowers!*
> *I Highly Recommend.*

- Amazon Review

❧

If You Give a Spy a Scheme
He'll Fight to be Redeemed
Pirates & Petticoats Book 5

He steals for the French crown.
She heals for the Catholic church.
He will heal her heart.
She will steal his.

*NOTE: This is the stand-alone, **sexy version** of the novel *The Heart of a Spy*, (Book 5 of The Hearts of Adventure Sweet Romance Series By Chloe Flowers).

"Dramatic, engrossing, suspenseful, exciting."

French Privateer and former pirate, Captain Drago Gamponetti is given one final mission from his employer, the king of France: reclaim religious relics from a New Orleans cathedral. Trouble begins when he's forced by a mysterious, veiled, novitiate nun to swear on the Bible to protect the very items he was instructed to steal.

Church healer, Eva Trudeau hides more than her face behind the veil. The convent has been her safe haven since she crawled, beaten and bloody, to its door nine years ago. When an old enemy re-surfaces and threatens to drag her back into the dark under-world from where she'd escaped, both she and her dark pirate captain stand to lose everything they've fought so hard to protect...including each other.

What readers have to say:

Set against the backdrop of the famous Battle of New Orleans, This story will have you turning pages into the wee hours of the night. If you love pirates, history, humor and a bit of romance you will love this newly released book by Chloe Flowers. The author has a way with historical fiction that enthralls and entertains.

ABOUT CHLOE

Chloe supports the National Breast Cancer Foundation.
Chloe Flowers constantly looking for the next adventure. Her pets have always been named after her favorite characters or action heroes: Indiana, Luke, Gimli, Thelma, Rocket, Forrest, Al Giordino, Severus, Mushu, Mérida, Gibbs, Jack...Dead Pool (he's a goldfish).

Chloe is an award-winning author and the recipient of the University of Akron, Wayne College *2018 Writer of the Year* Award. She writes small town contemporary women's fiction, and historical women's action and adventure romance novels about scoundrels, pirates, and spunky, independent heroines.

Chloe's biggest fault is the apparent inability to say "no" whether it's in response to a call for aid or a double-dog-dare to hike home through 30 acres of a snow-covered forest at midnight...during a full moon. It was early morning during said adventure when she came upon a group of sheriff's deputies searching for a lost girl. So, of course she offered to help (turns out, they were searching for her).

She is a member of the Romance Writers of America, Northeast Ohio Romance Writers where she served as president in

2020, and RWA Contemporary Romance Writers, The Beau Monde Romance Writers group, where she served as secretary 2017-2019.

She has given workshops and presentations on creating a critique group, how to provide effective critiques, story structure, marketing and self-publishing lessons to writers groups, library patrons and school children.

In 2014, she started her own small publishing company, Flowers & Fullerton. Currently, she's the publisher of record for authors Sheridan Jeane, Heather Knight, H.O. Knight as well as herself.

Chloe has a weakness for good red wine, Calvin & Hobbes comics, pie, dark chocolate and brown-eyed guys with beards, which is probably why she digs pirates, men in uniform and trea-sure hunters and writes about action and adventure and of course romance, which is the greatest adventure of all.

RECIPES

BANNOCKS

(Originally a Scottish bread) evolved to this recipe in the low country where corn meal was more plentiful than oats:

Boil 1 pint of milk and whisk in 1 pint of Indian Corn Meal. (Yep-use the same container to measure)
Beat well the yolks of 4 eggs with 1 pint of cold milk.
Add the 4 egg whites.
Add 1 tsp baking soda.
Add 1/2 tsp salt

Bake.

Yup. That's the recipe. I did some experimenting, and found that if you make 1/2 inch thick, round, scone-like patties, about the size of a dessert plate, and place on a cookie sheet and bake at 350 for about 12 minutes they turned out fine. Traditionally, you would grease a cast iron skillet and cook on the stovetop. 15 minutes for the first side, about 10-12 on the other side.

* If you want a more *traditional* Scottish Bannock, then you need a recipe that calls for oat flour or barley flour. I found a terrific one developed by chef Theresa Carle-Sanders. On her blog "Outlander's Kitchen," she presents historical and character-inspired recipes from the fictional world created by Diana Gabaldon, author of *The Outlander* series. It's *brilliant*. I found one similar to it on another recipe site and tweaked it a bit until I came up with the one below. I have made flaky southern biscuits for years, but I have to say, the oat flour keeps the bannock moist without falling apart. I like it better that a regular biscuit, plus they are good even when they're cold!

TRADITIONAL SCOTTISH BANNOCKS

Yield: 12-18

Preheat oven to 400° F.

2 Cups All-Purpose Flour
1 Cup Oat flour (or you can use old-fashioned or quick oats-just pulse them in a food processor or blender until fine)
2 Tsp Baking Powder
1 Tsp Baking Soda
1 tablespoon Sugar
½ tsp. Salt
½ cup of cold Butter, cut into small pieces
¾ Cup Cold Milk
½ Cup Greek Yogurt

Combine all dry ingredients in a large bowl and mix well. Cut cold butter pieces into dry ingredients and mix well. I like to use a pastry cutter.

Stir together milk and yogurt. Add to dry ingredients and stir with wooden spoon to make a sticky dough.

Turn onto a floured counter and sprinkle with more flour. Knead dough lightly 5 or 6 times, working in additional flour, so that dough is no longer sticky

Roll about ½" thick. Use a biscuit or a 2" square cutter. You can also use a floured butcher knife and cut squares with it. Don't forget to keep dusting it with flour before you cut. Depending on the size of the square, you should get at least 12-18.

I usually use parchment paper instead of greasing a cookie sheet, but either works. Bake until just golden around the corners, about 15 minutes. Cool on a wire rack for a few minutes before serving.

Serve warm with butter, honey, or jam. For a more savory version, add 1/2 cup of shredded cheddar cheese in with the dry ingredients and serve with meats or soups.